JUST A LITTLE RIVALRY

MERRY FARMER

JUST A LITTLE RIVALRY

Cover design by Erin Dameron-Hill (the miracle-worker)

ASIN: B093XW8KKJ

Paperback ISBN: 9798549968509

Click here for a complete list of other works by Merry Farmer.

If you'd like to be the first to learn about when the next books in the series come out and more, please sign up for my newsletter here: http://eepurl.com/RQ-KX

❀ Created with Vellum

CHAPTER 1

NEW YORK CITY – APRIL, 1891

*C*entral Park in New York was much the same as Hyde Park in London in the early morning. Both parks were oases of calm in an otherwise hectic world, refuges from the bustle of the city, and exactly the wrong place for John Dandie to be when his whole world was upside down. Central Park was all green and pretty in the morning light of late April, complete with well-ordered gardens and expertly-maintained paths, which made John feel like he stuck out like a sore thumb. He was neither pretty nor well-ordered at the moment, which went against everything he'd fought so hard to build for himself.

He thrust his hands into the pockets of his jacket as he paced his way across the park, hat pulled low to hide his troubled expression. In London—and in Liverpool for a time—his life was all about solving problems and helping his clients out of sticky situations. He was the steady one, the man people came to for help when they were in trouble. He was a solicitor by profession, but in practice, he did so much more than that for the men of the Brotherhood.

In New York, he was at the beck and call of Blake Williamson, the Duke of Selby, and Blake's beau, Niall Cristofori as he assisted them in the seemingly endless search for Blake's son. Blake's soon-to-be former wife had absconded with the boy months ago, stealing him away to America, where her parents lived. After months of searching and digging, bargaining, and finally chasing, John could feel that the end was near. He could feel little Alan Williamson within his reach. If only he didn't also feel at sixes and sevens over his own life.

He stopped his walk near the corner of Fifth Avenue and Sixty-First Street, staring up at the fashionable apartment building where they'd determined Blake's wife, Annamarie, had been hiding herself for the last few weeks. John let out a sigh. They were so close—so close they could taste it. He had no idea how to take the final step to return young Alan to his father, where he belonged, but he was confident a course of action would come to him.

And then what?

He let out a breath and turned away from the building, wandering deeper into the park for a moment. Annamarie wasn't going to run off at nine in the morning and ruin all of the hard work he, Blake, and Niall—and an entire list of others who were waiting anxiously in London to hear news that Alan was back in his father's arms—had done in the past few months. If he knew anything about high society ladies, Annamarie was probably fast asleep and would be for a few more hours. She would probably rise after noon, even though she hadn't been out the night before—which John knew, seeing as they'd been watching the building around the clock—bully her maid into bringing her breakfast and some sort of society gossip rag, then she would spend the day staring at herself in a mirror or going through her wardrobe while some nursemaid took care of Alan.

John huffed a laugh as he took a turn around the end of the park, hands in his pockets again, merely because he didn't know what else to do with them. Annamarie's wasn't actually a bad life, for a vain and selfish peacock. He'd known plenty of men who enjoyed a good lie-in and a lazy day in his time. Brandon, his partner when he's been living in Liverpool, would have stayed in bed all day on Sundays, if John had let him. Preferably with John in bed too.

John smirked as he strode toward a bench facing Annamarie's building and sat. He hadn't thought about Brandon in ages. The two of them had shared years of their lives together, but it had simply fizzled out a year ago, and both of them had gone their separate ways without a second thought. It had been peaceable and strange. He'd liked Brandon well enough. The sex had been satisfying, if not particularly adventurous. Brandon was gorgeous and intelligent and discreet, everything a man in his position could have wanted, but even now, John couldn't summon so much as a shrug over the way their relationship had ended.

He leaned back on the bench, crossing his arms and frowning at Annamarie's building, a restlessness burning in his soul as he watched. Brandon had meant everything and nothing to him. David had meant more. He'd met David at university, the two of them had fallen in love and become partners in every sense of the word. They'd moved to London from York and started the offices of Dandie & Wirth together. They'd lived discreetly together for five years. Again, David was handsome and intelligent, his presentation was masculine, which John liked, and sex had always been satisfying. But again, things had just fizzled between the two of them, and they'd each moved on. David was a thousand times happier now, with Lionel Mercer, than the two of them ever were together.

So what was wrong with him? Why did every amorous relationship that had been important in his life simply dissolve, without rancor or anxiety? And why had he only ever been satisfied instead of overwhelmed with lust and excitement?

There was something wrong with him. That was the only answer he could think of. If he'd never felt the deep, carnal fireworks of desire fulfilled or an orgasm so explosive that it left him drained and dizzy, then that was his fault. There had been men since Brandon, since he'd returned to London—willing partners he'd met at The Cock and the Bear and taken home for the night for their mutual pleasure—but none that had intrigued him so much he would want to—

He stopped his thoughts with an irritated huff. What kind of a fool sat around Central Park at nine in the morning on a Tuesday, contemplating his previous sexual partners and finding himself wanting? He was in New York to work. He had been employed by Blake to find and return his son. His full attention should be on the apartment building in front of him and figuring out a way to catch Annamarie out and convince her to return Alan. He should appeal to New York's law enforcement agencies, and he would have much sooner, except for Blake's fear that if the New York Police caught wind that he was an invert, they would take Annamarie's side instead of his. That was why John had come along in the first place. He was Blake's solicitor. He should be able to do something.

John rubbed a hand over his face. He was so far out of his normal bounds of operation that it was embarrassing. Chasing soon-to-be former duchesses halfway around the world to retrieve a stolen son was not what a solicitor did. He could handle the legal paperwork ensuring Blake and Annamarie's divorce once they had Alan back, but before that?

He shook his head as though he'd been having the

conversation with someone else instead of merely in his own head. He didn't have a wealth of experience when it came to missing persons and retrieving a stolen child. That was why he'd invited Detective Arthur Gleason along on the mission.

As soon as John thought the man's name, a jolt of electricity shivered through him. The mere thought of the short, shrewd, wily detective did things to him that he would rather not think about. There was something about Gleason, something dangerous and alluring. The man was an arrogant arse who thought far too highly of himself. He'd been working for the wrong people at the beginning of the search for Alan, causing more trouble for the rest of them than he was worth. Only when he realized he'd been on the wrong side had he changed his tune and started working with John instead of against him.

Although John could still remember that night, in Brompton Cemetery, when Gleason had been literally, bodily against him. Gleason had trapped him against a wall, kissed him, groped him, and left his head spinning. In all the years John had been with David or with Brandon, no one had ever made him feel so dizzy just from a kiss. He could still feel the way Gleason had held him completely in thrall, helpless and panting for more, even though it wounded his dignity and went against everything he held dear. For Christ's sake, even now, just thinking about it, his cock twitched and tried to stand at attention. It was embarrassing that something essen-

JUST A LITTLE RIVALRY

tially humiliating could send him into a spiral of lust that—

"You're thinking about me, I can tell."

John nearly jumped out of his skin and twisted to see Gleason leaning against a tree only a few yards away, as if he'd been there all along. And yes, the cocky bastard looked exactly as though he could see right into John's thoughts. A grin pulled at the corner of the man's fascinating mouth, and his shrewd, sparkling eyes were narrowed just enough to be suggestive. Gleason had a way of looking at him that made John feel like he was on the menu. It was irritating, it was disconcerting, and it was fiery hot.

"Gleason. What do you want?" John pretended nonchalance, staring straight forward at Annamarie's building again.

"Mmm," Gleason hummed as he sauntered over to the bench. "What do I want?" John could feel the man approaching, even though he refused to turn and look at him. "I want you on your knees, for one," he said once he was close enough to speak in a seductive murmur that none of the passersby in the park might overhear. "For another, I want you bound in black, silk rope, fastened to my bed with your legs spread and your arse on display for my pleasure." He leaned his arms on the back of the bench, bringing his lips to within inches of John's ear. "I want you screaming my name as you come and begging for mercy as I fuck you."

Deep shivers of temptation roiled their way through

John, making him sweat and writhe and go as hard as iron. Yes, yes, yes.

"No!" He flinched away from Gleason, looking over his shoulder at the man with a grimace of disgust. "I have no interest whatsoever in your sordid little games, Gleason, and I'll thank you to stop bothering me with your salacious sense of humor."

Gleason chuckled and came around the bench to take a seat with John. "What makes you think I'm joking?" he asked, lounging comfortably on the opposite end.

John scowled at him. "You must be. No man of my acquaintance is that depraved."

Gleason continued to laugh and grin at John as though he were a simpleton. "You need a wider circle of acquaintance, then," he said. "Or, more likely, there are people in your circle who are just as depraved, you simply don't know about it."

John continued to scowl, sneaking a look at Gleason before concentrating on the apartment building again. Gleason was probably right about that bit. What people got up to in the privacy of their own homes was likely every bit as outlandish and erotic as the illicit stories that were passed around in private circles.

Again, he wondered if his mediocre feelings about past relationships were his fault because he'd never been particularly adventurous. Gleason, on the other hand, was one of those erotic stories personified, and it unnerved John.

"What are you doing out here anyhow?" he asked

Gleason in a peevish voice.

"Watching the watcher," Gleason replied. He demonstrated by resting his elbow on the back of the bench and leaning his head almost coquettishly against it. His eyes took on a decidedly dreamy look—one that was entirely for show, since Gleason was absolutely not the sort of man to go all dreamy over a potential beau.

John made a scoffing noise and shook his head. "You'd better watch what you're doing," he said. "Anti-sodomy laws in America might not be what they are in London, but I doubt the authorities here take kindly to open flirtation of that sort in Central Park."

"Am I flirting with you?" Gleason asked, his sensual gaze proving that he absolutely was.

John sent him a flat, sideways look.

"Is it flirtation if a man simply looks upon another, dreaming of all the ways he's like to see him tied up and at his mercy?" Gleason went on.

"Will you please stop?" John hissed.

"No," Gleason said, his smile turning even more wolfish. "My mind is too busy." John glanced to him in confusion, then immediately regretted it when Gleason said, "It's been a long time since I've had need of the *shibari* skills I learned during my time in Japan, but lately I've had the urge to refresh those skills."

"*Shibari?*" John knew he shouldn't ask. He'd seen intriguing bars with shackles and lengths of black rope when he'd visited Gleason's London flat to invite him on this journey—visited the flat without Gleason's permis-

9

sion and before he'd returned home. Whatever *shibari* meant, he was certain it had something to do with all those things he didn't want to know about—things that sent his insides into a torrent of shivers every time he thought of them.

"I learned quite a bit in Japan, you know," he said, the coquettish look back on his face. "I'd be more than happy to share all of that with you."

"I'm surprised they let you remain in the country after your naval commission expired," John grumbled, staring at Annamarie's building again—mostly to prevent himself from giving in to the temptation of looking at Gleason and feeling things that he knew were wrong.

"I had strong ties to the country," Gleason said, then laughed at what he must have thought was a joke.

He was silent after that, though. A little too silent. John peeked at him, expecting to find the bastard staring unnervingly at him. To his surprise, Gleason seemed lost in his thoughts, perhaps his memories. His smile had faded. It was as if the joke he'd made had led his thoughts down a path that ended in a wistful, almost pained look.

"Do you miss it?" John asked, letting go of some of his resentment for the man out of genuine curiosity.

Gleason took a long time to drag himself out of his thoughts with a slow inhale. "No," he answered with what felt like uncharacteristic honestly. "I do not miss it. My time in Japan made me who I am, and I wouldn't trade it for the world, but I have no wish whatsoever to go back."

John had the distinct feeling that Gleason wasn't simply talking about a physical return to Japan. Something about his experiences there had left an indelible mark, but one Gleason didn't want to revisit.

He was about to say something to that effect when Gleason suddenly snapped straight and stared at the apartment building. His actions made John tense as well, and he turned to see whatever Gleason had seen. A beat later, he caught his breath. Ian Archibald, Annamarie's lover, hurried up to the building and ducked inside.

"Archibald," John hissed. "That little rat. Now Annamarie will never come out."

"The two of them could hole up indefinitely in there with Lord Stanley," Gleason said, referring to little Alan Williamson by his lofty title.

"How are we supposed to confront the blasted woman and force her to return Blake's son if she refuses to come out of her hiding place and we keep being barred from entering?" John hissed his frustration aloud.

"It's Lord Selby's fault for wanting this entire endeavor handled discreetly," Gleason said, inching closer to John, but remaining on the alert as they watched the building. "The man is clearly within his rights to get his son back. He's a bloody duke, for God's sake. He could waltz in there and demand Lord Stanley be returned at once."

"In America?" John asked dubiously. "When Annamarie's father is one of the wealthiest industrialists in the city? That man has more power here than any British

11

duke ever could. Not to mention Blake's fears of the New York authorities learning he's an invert."

Gleason made a scoffing sound. "Lord Selby is far too worried about what other people think. No one truly cares about our sort." He inched closer to John, leaning in so that he could speak without being overheard, which seemed deeply ironic to John. "Certainly, there are a few cases that have reached the newspapers, a few men who have been exposed for frequenting boy prostitutes, but the majority of us are so far beneath anyone's notice as to be laughable. Every family has that bachelor uncle who shares a flat with his old school chum."

"Yes, and none of them are dukes who have already earned a notorious reputation to the point where they have to live in secret," John argued. "I cannot blame Blake for his reticence to make a fuss. You didn't see the way he was treated at that ball last autumn."

"Actually, if you will remember, I did," Gleason said, pulling his eyes away from the building to stare at John. "And if you ask me, Lord Selby is doing himself and his station a great dishonor by not simply demanding that the world treat him as he deserves. The man is a duke! He dictates the rules, not the other way around."

"Blake is a sensitive soul who is only now being freed from a prison of his father's making. Is it any wonder that he would rather acquiesce to those who seek to judge him, or that he would choose politeness over confrontation? Not every man is a bull in a China shop who browbeats people into giving him his way," John argued, putting his whole self into it. If he were honest, he liked arguing with Gleason. He liked the sparks and the banter. It fired his blood and made him want.... No, he refused to think about the things it made him want. "Is it such a crime for Blake to want this whole thing handled quietly?" he asked instead.

"If the mighty Duke of Selby had been willing to exert his power and influence from the start, we wouldn't be in this mess," Gleason argued. "We would be—"

He stopped suddenly, reaching out to grab John's arm and sitting straighter. John flinched as Gleason's touch sent a sizzle through him. The damnable man was like a magnet, and John was as helpless as iron filings that jumped to do his bidding every time the two of them were in proximity.

That thought lasted only a heartbeat, though. As soon as he turned his head to see what had Gleason so excited, he spotted Ian Archibald and Annamarie stepping out of the apartment building, dressed to go out.

"Bloody hell, they left the building," John said in disbelief, jumping up.

Gleason was already on his feet and tapped John's arm excitedly a few times, as though the moment they'd been waiting for was finally upon them. And maybe it was. Annamarie had finally exposed herself, she was in a relatively vulnerable position, and this time, come hell or high water, John was not going to let the blasted woman get away.

CHAPTER 2

*J*ohn Dandie was an absolute treat in every way imaginable. Arthur had felt it from the moment the two of them met. He'd been physically attracted to the handsome and serious solicitor at first sight. Who wouldn't be? The man was tall with broad shoulders, thick, blond hair, and captivating green eyes. He was fit and muscular, and within minutes of meeting him, Arthur was already planning how he would tie ropes around the man to restrict him and turn him into his own personal work of art.

Those thoughts were at the forefront of his mind as he and John jogged across the park, dodging a few pedestrians who got in their way as they chased after Lady Selby and Ian Archibald. He hung back a few feet so that he could watch the move and strain of John's muscles as he ran, thanking the weather gods for the warm snap they were experiencing that had prompted John to go without a long, concealing coat for the day. Arthur only wished the bottom of John's jacket didn't completely cover his bum, because from his experience of that bum so far, it was a sight to behold.

"Don't fall behind," John snapped over his shoulder at Arthur. "I'll have your hide if they get away."

"No, John, I'll have your hide," Arthur murmured as they dashed out to the sidewalk, following Lady Selby and Archibald with their eyes, even though the pair was far ahead of them. "I'll have your hide and a lot more of you besides."

John sent him a momentarily confused look, but kept running.

That hint of confusion was like catnip for Arthur. The more he came to know about John on this mission to America, the more Arthur couldn't wait until they were in a position to play. John didn't know what he wanted. He likely thought he did, but the confusion that the man wore whenever Arthur pushed things over whatever imaginary lines of propriety John had drawn around himself was delicious. John had no idea how ripe he was for the picking or how ready he was to explore. Arthur had seen that sort of readiness in other men, but it had never allured him the way it did with John.

"Hurry, hurry," John urged him as they reached the street corner and prepared to cross. "If they hail a cab, we'll never catch up with them."

"If they were going to hail a cab, they would have done so already," Arthur argued in return, waiting as anxiously as John was for the busy traffic crisscrossing Fifty-Ninth Street to break. Lady Selby and Archibald had crossed on the other side of Fifth Avenue without as many carriages and carts to impede their progress, and if he and John weren't careful, they truly would get away.

John sent him a look as though he were right about the cab, but he didn't like it. Of course, John wouldn't like it whenever he was right. At the moment, the delicious man's entire identity was determined by being the man in charge, the one who had all the answers and could fix things for his friends. If Arthur had his way, he'd soon turn those tables on John and give him the moments of release he could see John craved.

As delightful as they were to contemplate, Arthur had to let those thoughts go. There wasn't time to indulge in fantasy when Lady Selby was in danger of getting away yet again. At last, there was a break in the traffic, and he and John dashed across the street, earning strange looks and a few shouts from the New Yorkers who had gathered at the street corner with them.

"At least they're heading straight down Fifth," John said as the two of them picked up their pace, ducking and dodging around a sea of people who stood in their way.

"It's too early for lunch and definitely too early for the theater," Arthur thought aloud for John's benefit. "They must be going shopping."

"What shops are in the area?" John asked.

Arthur didn't have the foggiest idea. The only cities he knew well were London and Tokyo, though if he were given a map and a guidebook and few weeks to study them and wander, he was convinced he could know any city like the back of his hand. He'd always been clever that way, and those skills had come in handy in his years as a private detective. He'd been too busy studying John since they'd arrived in New York, however, to learn the city the way he should have.

The biggest impediment between him and John and Lady Selby and Archibald was the other pedestrians going about their business on the crowded, New York streets. The city was teeming with life and movement. Every three steps, someone else would step in their way.

"Move to the street," John suggested, tugging on Arthur's sleeve. "We'll catch them faster."

"And we'll be plowed over by a carriage or step in horse shit for our troubles," Arthur countered him. He had to clap a hand to his hat as he nearly collided with a newspaper boy hawking his wares on the next street corner. "We'll do better if we just charge through."

John sent him a sideways look and nodded. Arthur had to hand it to the man. When he wasn't nearly coming out of his skin with latent lust or trying to argue with him in order to avoid that lust, John made an excellent investigative partner. In spite of everything else, when it came to investigations and working for clients, the two of them thought alike. All Arthur needed to do was study John's face to know which way he was going to move, what he was thinking, and what he thought their chances for success were. As soon as they dashed across Fifty-

Seventh Street and came within yards of Lady Selby and Archibald as Archibald stepped forward to hold the door of a haberdasher's shop for her, Arthur could see by the spark that filled John's eyes that he knew they'd caught the couple.

"Stay right where you are," John called out to them as he and Arthur leapt into the shop behind Lady Selby and Archibald. A jolt of lust shot through Arthur. John was the perfect knight in shining armor when he was full of confidence, the way he was now. He was the personification of strength and beauty. Hell, when he was like that Arthur might have even been willing to let the man top him. "Don't move another inch, Archibald!" John said, his voice booming.

Lady Selby screeched at the sight of John and leapt to hide behind Archibald—as if John were armed and Archibald would make a good shield. "Go away, go away, go away!" she squealed, hiding her head against Archibald's shoulder.

A murmur immediately went through the front room of the haberdasher's shop. The pair of women who were there perusing the ready-made hats for sale gasped and rushed out to the street, as though it were a hold-up and not simply Lady Selby getting her just deserts at last.

"How dare you accost Lady Selby this way?" Archibald demanded as Arthur moved to stand by John's side.

Arthur did a quick sweep of the small but elegant store. There was only one way for Lady Selby and

Archibald to leave, and they would have to go through him and John to get there. There was a door to a back room behind the counter, but Lady Selby wasn't the sort to be caught dead in any room where people worked, even to use that room as an escape route. Finally, after months of more trouble than the spoiled chit was worth, they had her well and truly cornered.

"I will make this easy on you, Lady Selby," John said, fully in his knight in shining armor persona. Arthur had to focus not to drool over the way the man squared his shoulders, tilted his head up, and looked as though he could call lightning down from the sky. "Tell us where we can find Lord Stanley and you will be free to go about your business."

"I am not handing my son over to the likes of you," Lady Selby said with a sniff, straightening, but keeping Archibald's body between her and John.

Arthur wanted to shake his head at the woman. She was the worst duchess he'd ever come across. Among the legions of American heiresses who had been marrying their way into the British aristocracy of late, she was the least suited for the position. The way she deported herself was a disgrace, and the way she'd handled her split with Lord Selby was abominable. As far as Arthur was concerned, the lady got what she deserved and then some. But it would do no good to communicate that to her until Lord Stanley was returned.

"My lady, you know that this charade has gone on for too long," John said, taking a step toward the wicked pair.

19

Arthur's mouth twitched over the fact that John had failed to address Lady Selby as a duchess should be addressed, and that Lady Selby hadn't noticed. No, the woman was not duchess quality at all. "Lord Selby is here to demand his son back, and it would behoove you to concede to his demands and turn the child back over to his father."

"To that disgrace of a man?" Archibald said, speaking for the first time. From what Arthur knew of the idiot, opening his mouth would only make the situation worse for Lady Selby. "No child should be entrusted to the care of a man like him."

Arthur knew of about thirty little girls in Darlington Gardens under the care of Stephen Siddel and Max Hillsboro who would disagree.

"Oh, what does Blake want the little demon for anyhow?" Lady Selby stepped out from behind Archibald's back with a sigh. "The brat is more trouble than he's worth."

Arthur had never been the sort who doted on children, but even he was offended by Lady Selby's flippant tone. "That demon is your son, madam," he chastised her. "Do you not have even the slightest concern for him or for his welfare?"

Lady Selby sighed, and her shoulders drooped. "Of course, I do," she huffed. "I gave birth to him, after all. But no one ever told me how difficult it is to have a child without a reliable nanny to mind them."

Arthur wanted to shake his head. Some women

simply shouldn't be entrusted with children. "If you care so little for the boy, why not simply give him back to his father?" he asked.

John glanced to him approvingly, which made Arthur gloat inside far more than it should have. He was the one determined to have the upper hand on the man, after all, not the other way around.

"I would gladly give Alan back to Blake," Lady Selby sighed, pressing her fingertips to her forehead, as though the whole thing were just a headache for her.

"Then why have you not done so?" John asked, his tone clipped. "Why lead us on this mad chase across the ocean, wasting time and causing expenses for people who have far better things to do?"

"Don't answer that question, darling," Archibald snapped, his face splotching.

That chastisement was as good as an answer, as far as Arthur was concerned. He could have guessed the plot was mostly Archibald's doing.

"At this point, I do not know," Lady Selby answered with a shrug.

"Then why not just give him back and end your troubles?" John asked. Arthur was tempted to grin at the smooth way he'd switched from authoritative and demanding to calm and sympathetic to match Lady Selby's mood.

"To be quite honest," Lady Selby said, now sounding exhausted on top of put out, "my mother wanted to have him. For some unknown reason, she likes the boy."

"Then you must tell your mother to cut her visit short and return Lord Stanley to his father," Arthur said, taking up the demanding, authoritative role while John continued to play the sympathetic one.

For a moment, John peeked at him, as if he understood the game Arthur wanted to play. His expression remained nearly neutral, but his eyes flashed with the knowledge of how they could play off of one another.

"Come now, Det. Gleason," John said. "Lady Selby has been through enough already. There's no need to harangue her further."

Arthur loved this new game. He put on an air of impatience, huffed, and threw out an arm at Lady Selby. "The woman is clearly unworthy of motherhood. She has no right to keep a child from her father. She is a negligent parent and a harpy to boot."

"How dare you?" Lady Selby gasped, placing an offended hand on her breast.

"Be reasonable, Gleason." John maneuvered to stand closer to Lady Selby, taking over from Archibald as her champion. "She's done the best she can in a role that does not come naturally to her."

"That is true," Lady Selby said, tilting her chin up.

"She has loved her son as best she can," John went on.

"I have," Lady Selby agreed.

"I do not believe it." Arthur crossed his arms and glared at the woman, exaggerating his role so that John could emphasize his. "What sort of a mother goes out without her child, leaving him unattended in an apartment in a city such as this?"

"He is not unattended," Lady Selby protested. "And he is not in the city. My mother has him at our family home in Peconic."

Arthur caught the spark of triumph in John's eyes. Damn, but the man was handsome when he got what he wanted. Arthur would have to make certain to give him everything he desired and more in the future.

"Annamarie!" Archibald barked, turning to her in horror. "You weren't supposed to say anything about your parents. You've given the whole thing away."

"I have not," Annamarie insisted, then added in a less certain voice, "Have I?"

"Ask for money at the very least," Archibald schooled her, visibly frustrated. "You cannot simply tell them everything they need to know. Ask for a divorce."

"Lord Selby has been attempting to divorce you for months now," John said. "As his solicitor, I have been trying to serve you with papers to sign so that you are free, but every time we come close, you fail to complete them."

"I thought I had already," Annamarie said, her brow knit in confusion. She shook her head. "Never mind. Give me something to sign and I will sign it."

"Ask for money," Archibald hissed, again tipping his hand and possibly revealing why Annamarie had yet to sign.

John ignored him. "I will approach Lord Selby about the matter at once."

He glanced to Arthur. Arthur couldn't think of anything else they needed from Lady Selby or Archibald. The couple no longer had Lord Stanley with them, but they had revealed where the boy was. Even without telling them a specific address, they could find the Long Island home of a man as wealthy and influential as Lady Selby's father, Mr. Cannon.

"Good day, Lady Selby." John sketched a lovely bow for the duchess, ignored Archibald entirely, then turned to leave the shop.

Arthur nodded to Archibald rather than Lady Selby, continuing the roles they'd played to get the information they needed. He also winked at the two women who had come out of the back room of the shop—likely the owner and a female apprentice—to watch the drama unfolding on their premises. The lucky women would probably end up as the talk of the town, once news of the confrontation reached the streets. Arthur was glad for them and for the business they would do.

"That went better than expected," he told John once they met up on the street in front of the shop. "Well done for playing the angel to my devil."

"Something tells me it won't be the last time," John murmured.

That simple statement sent a dozen different kinds of lust and adoration through Arthur. "Certainly not," he said as they headed back up Fifth Avenue toward the park. The hotel where they were all staying was on Fifty-Ninth Street, and Blake and Niall would likely be up and about by now. "In fact, I relish the opportunity to play devil to your angel as much as possible in the future," he went on.

John sent him a wary, sideways look. "Don't you start with me again, Gleason."

"Come now, isn't it time you started calling me Arthur?" Arthur teased him. "Seeing as it is only a matter of time before I have you sweaty and panting beneath me."

John's eyes flared in alarm, and he darted a look around the crowded street as they walked. "Keep your voice down, man," he hissed. "Anyone can hear you."

"The safest place to have an intimate conversation is in a crowd," Arthur told him. "No one is interested in listening when there are so many things to listen to."

"That is absurd," John grumbled as they crossed the street and headed along to the hotel.

"It's not," Arthur laughed. "It's the truth. Just as it's the truth for me to say that this devilish mind of mine has been absorbed in all the ways I could use a good man like you."

He turned to Arthur with a look of angry horror, but Arthur winked at him in return. That had John's face flushing bright pink, which only spurred Arthur on.

"Come on, now," he said, enjoying every moment of the torment he was inflicting. "You've known for months

25

now how this is going to end, and you want it as much as I do."

"I do not," John protested.

"Your trousers tell a different story."

John glanced anxiously down his front, taking Arthur's bait. He wasn't bulging or obvious in any way, but Arthur was willing to bet that after being teased and baited that way, he would be soon.

"You are a disgrace to your profession, sir," John snapped at him.

Arthur laughed out loud as they approached the door to the hotel. "Why am I a disgrace for pointing out the obvious?"

"Because it is unseemly," John snapped, lowering his voice as they entered the lobby.

"Oh, be honest," Arthur teased. "You like unseemly. You're desperate to be unseemly. You've spent your whole life being a paragon of virtue, and now you just want to let loose and give yourself up."

John sent him a scathing look as he veered toward the hotel's restaurant. "I have no idea what you are talking about," he grumbled.

"Yes, you do," Arthur laughed in return. And the time was drawing near when he would be ready for Arthur to show him.

*a*s much as it pained John to admit it, he and Gleason made an excellent team. It was the reason he'd invited Gleason along on the trip to New York. There was so much more that a detective could do, so much more that Gleason knew about finding missing persons and tracking people down, that a solicitor like himself just didn't know. And now John's instincts had been proven accurate. They'd located Annamarie, convinced her to hand Alan over, and learned the exact location where Alan was being held. That was why John had wanted Gleason with him.

That was the reason. Not all of the other things.

Certainly not.

John tried his best to ignore the salacious things Gleason had said to him as the two of them strode into the hotel's dining room, where he'd spotted Blake and Niall having coffee with Blake's valet, Xavier Lawrence, and Xavier's intimate friend, Alexander Plushenko. John hated the way that Gleason could get under his skin so easily by speaking the unspeakable aloud. The man had some gall to suggest that John would want anything other than a professional relationship with him. He certainly wasn't interested in any of the wicked, lascivious, intriguing, titillating—

John gave up his train of thought with a shake of his head as they approached Blake's table. Underneath his insistence that Gleason offended him, he knew what his true feelings on the matter were, but the last thing he wanted to do when they were so close to getting Alan back was to give in to any of them.

He acknowledged Blake and Niall and the others with a weak smile and a nod, and Gleason did the same.

"Aren't one or both of you supposed to be perched in Central Park, watching Annamarie's building for any signs of movement?" Niall asked, getting up to make more room at the table for them and pulling over a chair from the table beside them.

"There's no need anymore," John said. "We've just come from confronting Annamarie."

Blake's eyes went wide with alarm and expectation, and he started to rise from the table. "So where is my son?"

John held out a hand to settle him, gesturing for him to take his seat again. "He's with his grandparents in a place called Peconic, which, as I understand, is on Long Island."

"How did he end up with his grandparents on Long Island when we saw him in Central Park just a few days ago?" Niall asked, glancing to Plushenko. He was the one who had actually seen and spoke with Alan, after all.

John shrugged. "I've no idea, but that's where he is."

"Anything could have happened," Gleason added. "The grandparents could have taken him out a back door. They could have moved him before we confirmed which building Lady Selby lives in. There could be any number of explanations."

"What else did Annamarie say?" Blake asked, visibly agitated. Niall rested a calming hand on his arm, in spite of the fact that they were in a public restaurant. John found the touch endearing rather than dangerous, and he glanced to Gleason briefly as if to say that was how it was done, not Gleason's sledgehammer method of connection.

"She said that she is perfectly willing to hand Alan over as long as your divorce is finalized," John said.

Blake blew out a breath and scrubbed his hands over his face. "We've been trying to get her to finalize the entire mess for months now."

"Something tells me your lady wife isn't particularly good with the details of things," Gleason said. "And that Archibald has been insisting she hold off so that they can demand more money from you."

John frowned at him, not liking the cheeky way Gleason spoke to the duke. Then again, Gleason didn't seem to think much of titles and protocol.

Gleason must have caught his disapproving look, because even though his expression remained focused and stern, he reached a hand to John's leg under the table, curling his fingers against John's thigh far too near to his groin. It took all of John's powers of concentration not to jerk or cry out.

"It's clear what we need to do, then," Blake said, full of excitement and heedless of the interplay between John and Gleason. "We need to go to Peconic and get Alan back from Mr. and Mrs. Cannon."

"Precisely," John said. "I can go to the train station and see if there is a line that would take us there as soon as possible."

"I'll pack up our things and check out of the hotel," Niall said, standing.

"Wait." Lawrence lifted a hand to stop the sudden burst of movement. Everyone glanced to him. He looked dismayed for a moment before saying, "Please forgive me for overstepping my place, sir," he said to Blake, "but you promised to help release my friend, Jasper Werther, from jail today."

Blake and Niall slowly resumed their seats.

"I did," Blake said, blowing out a breath. He glanced regretfully at Lawrence and went on with, "I'm sorry, Xavier, but Alan is my priority."

"Will one day truly make a difference?" Niall asked him in a soft voice. Blake glanced to him, and the silent communication that passed between the two was as sweet as the bowl of sugar on the restaurant table. "Alan is with Mr. and Mrs. Cannon," Niall went on. "I've never really liked them, but, unlike Annamarie, they are good, stable people. I think Alan is safe."

"My fear is that he is too safe," Blake said. "My fear is that Cannon will decide he wants to keep his grandson."

"I understand that." Niall took Blake's hand in both of his. "But Cannon has other grandchildren. His son's son is the important one, the one he would expect to take over the business someday. Alan doesn't have the same expectations from him. Mr. Werther, on the other hand, will likely need a duke with ready money to spring him from jail."

Blake sighed. "You're right." He glanced past Niall to Lawrence. "I'm sorry, Xavier. I made a promise to help your friend, and so we'll do that."

"Thank you, sir," Lawrence smiled.

As there was nothing else to do and he had no intention of being left alone to stew in his uncomfortable thoughts, John decided to go along with Blake and Niall, Lawrence and Plushenko, to free Mr. Werther. The jails of New York City might not have been a tourist attraction to everyone, but John was curious about how the law worked in America, especially laws pertaining to sodomy, which was what Mr. Werther was being held for. But because John went, Gleason had to come as well. So much for using the interlude as an escape from his emotions.

"I wonder what it would take for the two of us to be arrested for indecency in New York," Gleason murmured

31

in John's ear, leaning a little too close to him, as they stood waiting for Mr. Werther's paperwork to be processed after Blake paid the man's bail. "I wonder if American police would have the nerve to arrest foreigners for fiddling with each other in public."

John crossed his arms and huffed a breath through his nose. "First of all, it's not called gross indecency in America. I think it's something having to do with morality or disturbing the peace."

Gleason hummed as if tasting a chocolate. "I love the idea of disturbing the peace."

John sent him a flat, sideways look. "You would."

The grin Gleason sent him in return was so cheeky and tempting that John had to force himself to stare straight ahead again to calm his heart from thumping against his ribs.

"Second of all," he went on, "foreign citizenship is never a deterrent for police action."

"Balderdash," Gleason laughed. "It's always more complicated to arrest someone of a foreign nationality, especially for that sort of crime. Can't you just imagine the fuss that might happen if a New York police officer arrested an Englishman for indecency, and said Englishman kicked up a fuss, claiming that it was simply his British mannerisms and how dare the brute accuse him of a crime when he was only being refined?"

John stared at Gleason again, his lips pressed tightly shut. Gleason had a point. From what John had heard and seen around New York in the past two weeks, the

Uranian set in America was mad for all things English and affected what they assumed were British mannerisms as part of their play. Perhaps that was their way of coming up with an excuse for their affected behavior when they got into trouble, or perhaps it was because of the reputation certain circles of the British upper classes had.

John would think about it more some other time. At the moment, he and Gleason pushed away from the wall where they'd been standing as the officer Blake and Lawrence had been speaking to gestured for them to come around to a door off to one side of the waiting room. Niall and Plushenko stood from where they'd been sitting in a small sea of other men—and a few women—waiting to do their business with the police, and the six of them converged at the door.

It opened a minute later as a policemen led the inimitable figure of Jasper Werther out to them.

"Well, isn't this a welcome party fit to soothe a troubled man's heart," Werther said with a wide smile for them all.

"Jasper." Lawrence stepped forward and took his friend's hand, shaking it vigorously. John had the impression the young man wanted to embrace Werther, but given the circumstances, that would have been out of the question.

"I take it you are responsible for this fairy taking flight?" Werther asked Blake as openly as if they were discussing plans for supper.

John nearly choked.

"I like him," Gleason said with a broad grin.

John frowned at him as their group headed quickly to the exit.

"I am responsible," Blake said, darting a look around as if to make certain no one was listening to them that shouldn't have been. John didn't blame him. Gleason could be as cavalier as he wanted about exposure, but Blake had suffered for it too many times before.

"Then you must allow me to thank you in the best way I know how," Werther said once they reached the street. When Blake stared questioningly at him, Werther went on with, "By inviting you all to a night of merriment and revelry at The Slippery Slope."

Again, John nearly choked.

"The club was raided but a week ago," Lawrence said. "Is it already open again?"

"Of course, dear boy," Werther said with a broad smile and a smooth shrug of his shoulder. "We have to remain open in order to pay the rent. I'm certain things are considerably more subdued at the moment, but our patrons will still come for supper and a show at the very least. And that is what I am offering to you."

Blake exchanged a look with Niall, and as he did, John risked glancing at Gleason. The formalities and technicalities of paying Werther's bail and getting him free had taken the better part of the day. The sun was already close to setting, and since they'd all skipped lunch while waiting in interminable lines, John was up for anything that involved food.

"We accept your invitation," Blake said, reaching out to shake Werther's hand. "Just tell us where to go."

They ended up taking two cabs from the police station down to The Bowery. John hadn't visited that colorful neighborhood yet during their trip, and he felt like a green tourist as he glanced around at the sights and sounds, scents and colors of the neighborhood. He'd been confused about how a club that had so recently been raided could open up again so quickly, but as he took in the sights of other clubs on Bleeker Street, spotted more than a few women, men, and some whose gender he couldn't determine who were clearly prostitutes looking for customers, he began to understand.

There was something seedy about the world of clubs and sin they'd walked into, but something exciting and invigorating as well. The Slippery Slope was almost tame in comparison to the things going on up and down Bleeker Street. It was only half full at such an early hour of the evening, and as Werther had predicted, most of its patrons were sitting at tables, enjoying a meal. The fact that those patrons consisted of men with painted faces and effeminate clothing in some cases—some even wearing dresses—and that they sat freely fawning over tougher, working-class men, betrayed the true nature of the club. That and the brightly colored decorations and festive music being played by a small band on the stage at the front of the room. It was a world John had never seen before.

John's observations were cut short as Gleason

clapped a hand on his shoulder, then left his arm there, draped almost suggestively. "If you could only see the look on your face right now," Gleason laughed.

John's face heated, and he shrugged Gleason's arm away. "Show a little decency, man," he whispered sharply. "We're in public."

Gleason continued to laugh. "Yes, and what kind of public do you see around you?" He boldly slid an arm around John's waist and leaned into him.

John's eyes went wide at the intimacy of the gesture, until he made a second sweep of the room with his eyes. There were couples in far more intimate positions all throughout the room. He even caught a slender young man with a painted face sitting on the lap of a muscled sailor, feeding him his dinner with one hand and playing his fingers through the man's hair with the other.

"There are no rules at The Slippery Slope," Werther told him, laughing as openly as Gleason was over John's shock. He gestured them all to follow him deeper into the club, pulling out a few chairs at an empty table in the middle of the room for them. "The clubs are one of the few places where we are free to be ourselves in pseudo-public."

"Not unlike the Chameleon Club in London," Niall said with a bright smile, holding out a chair for Blake, then kissing him soundly on the mouth once Blake had taken his seat.

"This is nothing like the Chameleon Club," John said, breaking away from Gleason long enough to sit and pull his chair into the table. "The Chameleon Club has strict rules about propriety and behavior."

"How very British," Gleason said in a wry tone, taking the seat next to John's and scooting his chair so close that their legs touched.

John stared at him with widened eyes. "What are you doing, man?" he demanded.

"Lining up my pudding so that it's ready as soon as I finish my meal," Gleason answered without hesitation, then boldly reached between John's legs to fondle him.

John let himself react, but only so far as flinching and feeling his face heat like a furnace. His mind was in turmoil and his senses ran riot. Part of him rejoiced and panted for more, but another part of him was near panic as everything he knew and had governed his life by was thrown into question. It made it nearly impossible for him to pay attention to the conversation around the table, or to properly greet and remember the patrons and employees of the club who came over to introduce themselves and thank Blake for rescuing Werther.

John was grateful when their supper was served, as it gave him something else to think about.

"Here, have another of these," Gleason said, leaning into him again and refilling his half-finished wine glass from one of several bottles that had been left on the table.

"I do *not* need more wine," John protested, his head already spinning with sound and color and activity as more and more patrons entered the club and as the band started playing dance tunes.

"I think you need a great deal more wine," Gleason laughed, filling John's cup, then handing it to him. "I want to see how much alcohol it takes for you to loosen up that stiff upper lip of yours."

"I am not going to turn into some sort of whirling dervish, no matter how much alcohol you ply me with," he told Gleason with a frown, taking a drink.

"Let me be the judge of that," Gleason said, a sparkle in his eyes as he downed about half of the glass in front of him. "I have been dreaming of the day you let go of all your pride and propriety for months now."

"I just bet you have," John grumbled, sending him a sideways look and taking another modest drink.

The truth was that he couldn't remember the last time he'd really let himself go and have a good time. He liked his beer when he visited The Cock and Bear, and while he wasn't quite a connoisseur of wine, he enjoyed it. He always seemed to find a reason not to overindulge, though. He was always working, or he usually had important clients to meet. It had never seemed right for him to be anything other than perfectly in control at all times.

"Come on, you can do better than that," Gleason egged him on once John's glass was half empty. "One glass isn't nearly enough for you to feel free enough for a dance."

"It's been more than one glass, and I will not be dancing this evening," John insisted with a growl. He hesitated, then rushed to prove his point by downing the rest of his glass in one, long swig.

He knew it was a bad idea the moment he set the glass back on the table. Gleason filled it up again, then grinned at John in challenge. John's head was already swimming a little, but he couldn't say no when Gleason was being so bloody smug. He drank a bit more of the wine, then was taken completely by surprise as a firm hand clapped on his shoulder.

"You look like you're ready for a turn around the room," a man who was as tall as John, but who wore an elegant gown accented with feathers and beads, addressed him.

The man's deep voice was contrasted by the perfectly-executed cosmetics he wore. John was so stunned by the suddenness of the man's appearance—or perhaps he should refer to him as a woman—that he could do nothing but blink.

"My, but you're a tasty dish, aren't you?" the woman said, biting her lip. "Come and dance with me."

"Go on, John," Gleason told him, laughing, his blue eyes dancing. "You know you want to."

John didn't know what he wanted. All he knew was that he was no longer in London, or in anything that resembled the life he was used to. He let the glittering woman drag him out of his seat, then over to the open section of the floor, where couples of every description were dancing something that might have been a polka, but didn't seem to follow any rules of steps, or even timing. Werther had been right—The Slippery Slope didn't seem to have any rules at all. That point was proven further when his dance partner tugged him close, but positioned him to dance the woman's part.

It was all completely mad. John's head spun from alcohol, noise, and pure novelty as his partner whipped him around the floor. She was flirtatious beyond anything John would have expected, and her hand moved firmly down to his arse as they danced. It was such a new thing that John didn't ask her to move her hand for fear he would offend her.

When that dance ended, John was immediately snatched up by one of the muscled men who he was certain were sailors. That was an entirely different experience, as that man used all of his muscle to lead while pressing his cheek against John's and his lips to John's chin. As they made their way through the dance, John spotted Gleason dancing not that far away from him. Gleason widened his eyes in utter shock over the way John was being handled, and with good reason. John was over six feet, for Christ's sake, and not even remotely effeminate, but his sailor partner was handling him as though he were a delicate miss. Gleason laughed openly at the alarm in John's eyes, then turned his attention to the handsome young man he was dancing with.

A shot of jealousy jolted John out of his alarm when Gleason leaned close to the man to whisper something. It burned through him so ferociously and so quickly that John missed a step in the dance, causing his burly partner to step on his toe.

"Sorry, love," the sailor apologized as John hopped on

one foot. "Can I get you another drink? Maybe a bit of a slap and tickle in one of the back rooms? I just got paid."

John's eyes snapped wide. "I'm terribly sorry, sir. There seems to have been some sort of misunderstanding. Please excuse me."

The sailor looked momentarily disappointed as John limped his way over to the shadowy side of the room, where various chairs and benches rested against the wall, and sat heavily on a stool. He wasn't certain he liked the mad world of the club. He wasn't certain he disliked it either. Blake and Niall were clearly having a delightful time as they polkaed their way around the dance floor, falling all over each other with laughter. That made John smile. Good for them. The two of them deserved a bit of fun and merriment after all they'd been through. Lawrence and Plushenko were having a grand time as well, although their enjoyment of the club consisted of Lawrence sitting astride Plushenko's lap in an even darker corner of the club, their mouths seemingly fused together as their hands roved each other's bodies.

"I think they had the right idea, don't you?" Gleason asked, plopping onto the stool beside John's and catching him watching the two men kissing.

"I beg your pardon?" John asked, blinking as he turned to Gleason.

Gleason grinned suggestively at him, then surged forward, pinning John to the wall, and slanting his open mouth over John's.

CHAPTER 4

*T*he trouble with attempting to intoxicate the object of one's affection—or at least lust—was that it often meant one ended up hopelessly drunk himself. That was a sacrifice Arthur had been willing to make as he'd poured more and more wine for John. And a drunk John was a sight to behold, even if the man wasn't *very* drunk. Arthur watched him with glee as he'd danced with the queen who was an inch taller than him, then with the sailor who was twice as big around as John. The whole time, John was completely out of his depth, and it was beautiful. John needed to be out of his depth more often, and he would be, if Arthur had his way.

He'd loved that green-eyed look of jealousy in John's eyes when he'd accepted an invitation to dance with a lovely, gamine young man. Under any other circumstance, Arthur would gladly have taken the young man home and enjoyed a night of testing the lad's limits. It was something of a shock to him that he wasn't really interested now. Ever since John had stepped into his life, Arthur had only wanted one thing.

Which was why it was so sweet when he managed to get a tiny part of that one thing once he had John pressed up against the wall of the club.

"I didn't say you could kiss me," John panted once Arthur gave him a chance to breathe.

"I don't need your permission," Arthur growled, leaning back into him. That wasn't true, of course. He'd never forced a man, and he wasn't about to start now. It was clear to him that John wanted to have his feathers ruffled a little, which just so happened to be exactly what Arthur was best at.

He slanted his mouth over John's, sliding his hands up John's chest and pinning him to the wall as he did. John groaned and shifted against him, not exactly trying to break free, but restless all the same. Arthur parted his lips, tasting him deeply and playing his tongue against John's. The man still tasted of wine, which was entirely fitting, considering how dizzy he made Arthur. John started out the kiss too stunned to do more than let Arthur in, but when Arthur refused to relent in his pursuit of everything he wanted, John responded with enthusiasm, kissing him back.

It was perfect, everything Arthur had waited for since the night at Brompton Cemetery. John did nothing to stop him when he worked open the buttons of his coat and waistcoat so that he could feel the heat of John's body more fully. He wasn't about to undress John entirely or move beyond kissing him. They were in public after all, and being watched wasn't on the long, long list of unusual sexual behavior that excited Arthur. He did want to feel the reactions of John's body as closely as possible as they kissed, though.

"We shouldn't do this," John panted as Arthur let him breathe. They adjusted their positions so that Arthur's back was more to the wall. "This is a crowded club. There are people everywhere."

"I don't think they mind, love," Arthur said, gripping John's shirt and tugging him close.

John groaned and rested his arms against the wall on either side of Arthur, returning his mouth to where it belonged, flush against Arthur's. Alcohol was definitely in play as John slipped his tongue into Arthur's mouth, humming with hazy pleasure as he bruised Arthur's lips with his kiss. Arthur told himself he would enjoy John's abandon for a little while longer, then he would take responsibility and make certain John got home safe and unmolested.

That was what he told himself, but it proved harder and harder to actually do as John unbuttoned his jacket and reached his hand down toward the waistband of Arthur's trousers. The move was so unexpected, not to mention everything Arthur wanted, that Arthur's mind started to scatter, and he rethought his plans. It wouldn't be so terribly wrong if he let the alcohol loosen John's inhibitions to the point where they both got what they wanted, would it? He could just let them slide into bad behavior and apologize in the morning when—

Arthur's thoughts were instantly cut short as he caught sight of an Asian gentlemen walking past, several yards deeper into the club. All of Arthur's carnal and morally-ambiguous thoughts went cold, and he pushed against John, slipping out from under him. He took a half step forward, scanning the room for the man he was certain he'd just seen—a man he hadn't seen for nearly ten years.

"Is something wrong?" John slurred, standing straighter. "Have I done something?"

"No, no, love." Arthur turned back to him, taking John's hand and patting it, which was a ridiculously infantilizing gesture, all things considered. He glanced out over the noisy crowd in the club, desperate to find the man and confirm whether or not he'd actually seen Hiroshi.

"Dammit, I didn't mean to let myself get so carried away," John cursed, sounding a bit more sober than Arthur imagined he was. "I hold you responsible for this fix, Gleason."

"Yes, yes, it's all my fault," Arthur said, distracted. "I shouldn't have made you drink so much." He patted John's hand again, then stepped away from him, searching even more frantically.

John kept hold of his hand, preventing Arthur from getting away from him entirely. "It's more than that and you know it, damn you," John said. "You're what I find so intoxicating. You're the man I cannot get out of my thoughts, waking or sleeping. The last thing on earth I want is to fall into your sway, but I cannot help it. There is something about you that turns my head to mush, and other parts of me to the opposite of mush."

Arthur dragged his eyes away from the dancing, writhing crowd and glanced to John. He'd waited to hear those words, or something like them, for months, and they had to be spoken now? Now, when a single glimpse of a face from his past suddenly brought back everything he'd worked so hard to run away from for years?

"I have to go," he said, turning away from John and shaking out of his hand. Where had Hiroshi slipped off to? He couldn't have left the club so swiftly.

"That's it?" John demanded, following as Arthur started to weave his way through the crowd of revelers. "I just confessed something that has had me tied in knots for months, and you have to go?"

At any other time, Arthur would have made a ribald joke about John tied in knots. But his thoughts were too scattered as he continued to push through the crowd, searching in every nook and shadowy space. Hiroshi was there, he was certain of it. It was as if he could feel the man, feel the decade-old resentment and the war between them. He could feel Shinobu in the space between them as well, feel his ghost, which turned Arthur's soul inside out.

"What is going on?" John asked. His voice felt

distant, even though he was only a few steps behind Arthur. "What are you looking for?"

The question felt rhetorical. Arthur didn't answer. He made it to the center of the room, along the edge of the dance floor where the tables started, and then he saw Hiroshi. His old rival was half hidden by shadows, leaning intimately toward a man in a business suit who appeared completely out of place in the colorful environment of The Slippery Slope. That man looked uncomfortable as well, but whatever Hiroshi was saying to him held most of his attention.

Arthur started toward them, John following and saying something that he couldn't distinguish. He was forced to glance away momentarily to avoid a pair of dancers, then to absently refuse a request to dance made by a painted patron of the club. When he glanced up again, Hiroshi was looking right at him.

It was as though the years and the miles dropped away. Hiroshi wore the same expression the last time the two of them had met, standing over Shinobu's fresh grave. The fury was still there, the grief was there was well. Hiroshi had aged, but very little of any importance had changed in the man's hard face. Arthur could tell Hiroshi was having the same sort of thoughts about him, the same eruption of memories that threatened to spill like lava between them, burning anything that got in their path.

"Excuse me, sweetheart."

Arthur blinked as a queen nearly stepped on him as she lost control of her dancing and reeled drunkenly toward the tables. Arthur wasn't quite quick enough to get out of her way and was bumped to the side. He lost his balance, and John had to leap to catch him. John wasn't particularly steady on his feet either, which sent both of them tipping into one of the tables. Arthur was only just able to catch himself before he and John spilled to the floor.

"Sorry," Arthur mumbled, righting himself and John as well.

"Bit too much of the good stuff?" a man at the table asked him with a broad smile.

Arthur didn't reply. He glanced back over to the shadows where he'd seen Hiroshi, but the man was gone. That sent a wave of panic and anger through him. How dare the man up and disappear a second time. The bastard still had things to answer for.

"Gleason. Gleason. Arthur!"

John's shout shook Arthur out of his overly emotional thoughts, causing him to whip around and stare hard at the man. John stared back at him with wide, confused eyes.

"What is the matter?" John asked. "You look as if you've seen a ghost."

"That's because I have seen one," he said, turning back to the corner where Hiroshi had been. "And I have to find him before he gets away from me again."

"Find who?" John asked, following after him as Arthur resumed his dash across the room, dodging around dancing couples and tables. "Arthur, please tell me what has you so spooked. I've never seen you like this, and it's worrying me."

"Save your concern for someone who needs it," Arthur snapped, his heart pounding against his ribs.

He was startled a moment later as John grabbed his arm in a powerful grip and yanked him to stop and face him. "That was uncalled for," John shouted. It was more than just a shout to be heard over the din of the club. "All I want is to help you. Not five minutes ago, you were kissing me as though attempting to fuse our mouths into one. I will not have you shut me out of what is obviously a moment of crisis for you now."

Memories of the past and the last man who had given two fucks about what happened to Arthur blended with the feelings he had for John in the present. He couldn't go through it again. Losing Shinobu had nearly destroyed him. What had he been thinking to let himself grow so close to another man the way he had with John?

He shook that potent thought away as soon as it smashed into his brain. Now was not the time for him to contemplate the true nature of his attachment to John Dandie.

"I saw a man," he said. "A man from my past. Hiroshi."

"Is he Japanese?" John asked in his serious, solicitor's voice, wearing the frown that usually made Arthur's cock hard.

"Yes, of course he is," Arthur snapped. "He was here just a moment ago. I cannot let him get away."

"Then we'll find him," John said, striding ahead and pushing a path through the crowd.

Arthur wasn't certain if the feeling squeezing his chest was gratitude or resentment, or something worse that he didn't want to think about. He followed John for a few steps, then strode ahead of him as they reached the side of the room where Hiroshi and the businessman had been. They were nowhere to be seen now, but that didn't stop Arthur from searching.

"What does this Hiroshi look like?" John asked, attempting to take charge as they searched the wall along the entire length of the room. "How tall? What was he wearing?"

Arthur sent a sweeping glance around the room. "You'll be able to tell him apart from everyone else here this evening because he's bloody Japanese," he said peevishly, sending John a flat look.

"I'm trying to help you, man," John growled at him. "Stop trying to push me away while I do it."

Arthur shook his head and moved on, knowing he wasn't being fair. His heart and mind were in too much turmoil as every feeling that had driven him away from what could have been a lifelong home in Japan assailed him. The plans he and Shinobu had made had been beautiful. The house they had invested in together was lovely and simple. They'd been happy, in love, and then all of that had been blasted to pieces.

And now, the tiny taste of that past, the briefest hint that he'd be able to tie up the last loose end of that chapter of his life, had disappeared almost the moment he'd spotted it. He gave up with a sigh as he and John reached the club's front door and rubbed his hands over his face. Hiroshi was gone. Yet again, the bastard had gotten away without being held accountable for his actions. Arthur didn't even know what those actions were this time.

"He's gone," Arthur spoke aloud, condensing so many thoughts and emotions into the two words that it was almost laughable. Hiroshi was gone, Shinobu was gone, and the man he'd once been was long gone.

"Who is this Hiroshi person?" John asked, slightly out of breath, face pink from wine and exertion, eyes only a bit glassy. "Is he someone from the time you spent in Japan?"

Arthur stared flatly at him, even though something deep within him screamed at him to stop putting up walls and let John in already. The man might actually be able to help him. "Well done," he said instead, thick with sarcasm. "You're a clever boy, aren't you?"

John glowered at him, grabbed his arm, and marched him out of the club and into the street. The noise was much less apparent on the street, but Arthur's ears rang from being inside for so long. He would almost have preferred noise so loud he couldn't think to the furious silence of the way John looked at him.

"I've known you for months now, Arthur," John said. "I've known you to be cheeky, irascible, difficult, and stubborn. I have never, in all that time, seen the sort of look that came over you when you spotted this Hiroshi fellow. Yes, I know he must be someone from your past. I was merely asking the question as a way to prompt you to speak about him. I've never known you to be so downright surly in all the time we've been acquainted, and all of that taken together tells me that you are in some sort of deep distress and that something is amiss."

Arthur opened his mouth to tell John off again, but thought better of it. Instead, he kicked the pavement, turned as if he would storm off, rocked to the side but didn't go anywhere, and finally clenched his jaw as he stared back at John again.

"I thought we were friends," John said, his voice a fraction calmer. "I thought you wanted to be more than that."

Again, Arthur had to resist the urge to bark at John that two people didn't have to be friends to fuck. That would have betrayed his true feelings about John, though, and undone months of work he'd done to bring the man to where he wanted him.

"Hiroshi is an extremely sensitive part of my past," he said instead. "He was a rival, of sorts, during the time I lived in Japan."

"A rival?" John arched one eyebrow, a hint of humor tugging at his mouth. "Like you and I?"

"Nothing like it," Arthur snapped, irritated that John would suggest it, utterly rejecting the idea that there had ever been anything sexual between him and Hiroshi. The truth couldn't have been further from that.

John's hint of humor disappeared. "What is Hiroshi doing in New York, then?"

"I don't have the slightest idea," Arthur sighed, pushing a hand through his hair. He didn't realize his hand was shaking until he felt it against his scalp.

"The man has obviously upset you," John said in a softer voice. It was a little too cloying for Arthur's liking. "Arthur, you know you can tell me anything, don't you?" he asked.

"Oh, so it's Arthur now?" Arthur asked, letting his bitterness get the better of him. "Are we using Christian names now?"

John scowled at him. "Fine. Be a prick." He turned to walk back into the club.

Arthur winced and cursed at himself, then dashed after him. He caught John just inside the door of the club. "I'm sorry," he said, uncertain whether he was doing the right thing in opening himself up to John or whether he was putting everything he held dear about himself in jeopardy. "Yes, I'm a prick. You know this about me. You've always known this about me."

John turned to him, letting out a breath and sending him a weak smile.

Arthur went on. "There are things about my past that you don't know, things that overwhelmed me. Ten years on, they are still prickly and brittle. I'm not ready to discuss them, not even with you."

John hesitated for a moment, then said, "I suppose, coming from you, that's a compliment?"

"It's the closest you're going to get," Arthur said, softening into something close to a smile. "If you're after a man who will be your sunshine and set up a lovely little flat in Darlington Gardens with you, then I am not your man. I have broken bits strewn all over my life, and they will hurt you if you don't tread lightly."

He thought his words would put John off, but instead, John looked as though Arthur had just handed him a wounded puppy that needed minding.

"Stop that," Arthur growled at him. "That is precisely what I mean."

"I did not say or do anything," John argued.

"I can see it in your eyes," he said, his anger growing. "You are already making me into something I'm not. Please stop."

"Arthur, I just want to be your friend," John insisted.

It was a lie, whether John knew it or not, but before Arthur could call him out for it, a young man with a powdered face and shaved eyebrows rushed up to him and handed him a folded scrap of paper.

"What is this?" Arthur asked the man as he turned to dive back into the crowd.

"He said you'd know when you read it," the lad called over his shoulder as he dashed off.

Arthur opened the note, and his blood seemed to freeze in his veins.

"What does it say?" John asked, scooting to Arthur's side and looking over his shoulder at the note.

Arthur made no move to hide it from him. He

wouldn't have been able to read it anyhow unless he somehow understood Japanese. It had been years since Arthur had read it himself, but he remembered the characters, remembered the words, and remembered Hiroshi's handwriting as though it were his own. The message in his hand was simple: "*It is not over.*"

CHAPTER 5

*H*iroshi. John would have given anything to know who the man was and what had happened between him and Arthur years ago. Whatever it was, it clearly still weighed on Arthur's mind. John had never seen the man react so strongly to a single person or search so frantically as he did while scanning the club. He wished he'd caught so much as a glimpse of Hiroshi so that he could begin to assess what sort of a man he was, and perhaps even guess what the conflict between him and Arthur had been.

But Hiroshi was clearly gone by the time Arthur received his note, and minutes later, Arthur had made some vague excuse and left the club himself. Left John as well. Left him feeling confused, strangely bereft, and a little too tipsy for his comfort. John had spent the rest of the evening either sulking in a corner or with Blake and Niall, refusing every offer to dance or to step into the back rooms that apparently existed at the club until his friends were ready to go home.

Now there he was, the next morning, packing up his things and leaving the hotel room he'd lived in for the past two weeks, his thoughts still fixed on Arthur. He should have asked more questions about the man's past. All he really knew was that Arthur had served in the Royal Navy in Japan, and that he'd stayed there after leaving the navy. John had never asked how long he'd stayed, and he'd never asked why he'd stayed, or why he'd eventually returned to England. Part of John had assumed it was because of a lover, but was that lover Hiroshi? He doubted it.

"Feeling the effects of last night?" Blake asked him as John handed his room key back to the hotel's front desk and paid his bill.

John turned to him, his thoughts still distracting enough that it did, indeed, feel like the morning after overindulgence. "Not really," he said truthfully. "I find that I suddenly have a great deal on my mind."

"I trust that great deal is strategy about how to retrieve my son from his maternal grandparents," Blake said with a teasing smile.

John sucked in a sudden breath, feeling suddenly horrible. "Forgive me, but it was something else. You're perfectly correct, though. I should be focused on returning Alan to you."

Blake clapped a hand on his shoulder. "You are allowed to have other thoughts besides my son's welfare," he said. "You've worked tirelessly for months on this case. You gave up the caseload you have in London to come all the way here to New York. That goes above and beyond the call of duty."

"I had only just begun to establish my new office in London," John argued. "So it's not as though I have a vast list of clients in desperate need of my services yet. Besides, Cameron is far more competent than he believes himself to be, and I asked David and Lionel to help him out if anything becomes too overwhelming."

"Still," Blake said, "you're a good solicitor, a good friend, and a good man."

As Blake spoke those words, Arthur appeared around the corner from the stairs, traveling bag in hand. He must have heard Blake's comment about John being a good man, because his mouth stretched into a smile that had John's blood pumping faster.

"John is a very good man," he said as he approached. "Very good men are a favorite of mine."

He put too much of a purr in his voice, narrowed his eyes a little too much in his attempt to blatantly flirt. And with the concierge behind the front desk standing only yards away—albeit helping another customer. Arthur had no sense of propriety at all, no respect for the opinions of the masses, even if none of their group shared those opinions.

Or perhaps that wasn't it. Instead of letting his feathers ruffle, scowling, and telling Arthur off, John studied him intently. It wasn't as though he now believed

Arthur's salacious bent was an act. Arthur was wicked and randy and full of himself. But after the events of the night before, John was beginning to see Arthur's behavior in a different light. The man was hiding from something, hiding behind brash statements and a too-forward mien.

As desperately as he wanted to come up with a witty reply to Arthur's statement, his mind went blank. The best he could manage was, "At least one of us is a good man."

That feeble reply was close to embarrassing in its inadequacy, and its inability to test his newly-emerging theory that Arthur could dole it out, but he couldn't take it. John was grateful beyond measure when the conversation was prevented from going anywhere by the arrival of Niall, Lawrence, and Plushenko.

"My room is empty and tidy," Niall said with just a hint of a grin that left John wondering what he'd needed to clean up to avoid suspicion that Blake had been rooming with him. "Xavier here will maintain yours while we're in Long Island." He turned to hand his key over at the desk and pay the bill.

"Thank you, Xavier." Blake smiled at his valet, then turned to Plushenko. "I trust things are progressing with your efforts to gain custody of your sister?"

Plushenko sighed. "As well as could be expected. My father has no use for a little girl, but as you can imagine, my mother is quite attached." He paused. "Well, attached enough that she's asking for money in exchange for Anya."

"You know that I will give you anything you need, within reason," Blake told the young man.

"For which I am deeply grateful, your grace." Plushenko bowed to him. "I am also grateful for the assistance of the lawyer you've hired to assist with things. I'm confident that by the time you have your son back, my sister will be with me, and the two of them can be playmates on the voyage home. If you don't mind my saying so, your grace." He nodded his head again.

"I think Alan would love to have a friend on the voyage home," Blake said.

It was all sweet and hopeful. Both men simply assumed that they would have the children they cared about in their arms soon. John didn't doubt that they could, but instinct told him that these things were never simple and that they still had a long way to go.

He caught Arthur staring off into the distance as they all turned to head out of the hotel and down to Grand Central Station. The man's expression was almost bereft, as if his thoughts were painful. John's mouth twitched into a grin in spite of himself—not because he wanted Arthur to feel bad about anything, but because at last, he felt as though he was getting a glimpse behind the armor Arthur wore, armor John hadn't even realized he was wearing until the night before.

The mood in their group was light and hopeful as the cab they'd hired took them to the station, and as they waited to board their train to Long Island. John studied Arthur the entire time, speculating to himself about who

Hiroshi was and why the man had affected Arthur so much. He wasn't a former lover, John decided. Perhaps a former business partner? Had Arthur attempted to start a business in Japan that had gone wrong? Japan had only recently opened up to foreigners, so perhaps Hiroshi had caused Arthur to be expelled for some reason. Or perhaps they were rivals for whatever lover Arthur had had while in Japan. It could have been anything.

"If you keep staring at me like that, I'm going to assume it's because you want to escort me to the loo and drop to your knees for me," Arthur said without looking directly at John as they waited near a small café, watching the arrivals and departures board for news of their train.

Instead of flinching, John grinned. "Do you know, I've learned that whenever you make rude suggestions to me, it's because I've skated too close to discovering something about you which you do not wish me to know."

Arthur dragged his gaze away from whatever he was ostensibly looking at and stared hard at John. "Is that what you think?" he asked with a half-grin, standing straighter.

He couldn't maintain eye contact, which was all the confirmation John needed that his assessment was right. He shifted closer to Arthur, leaning against the railing behind them. "You know," he tilted his head to Arthur, emphasizing the difference in their height, "you could just save yourself the trouble and confide in me about what's bothering you."

Arthur laughed and tried to school his expression into careless derision. Tried, but failed. John was beginning to see through him. "What makes you think anything is bothering me?"

"Everything that happened last night?" John suggested.

Arthur stared right at him. "You mean the way I had my tongue halfway down your throat while you sighed and jerked your cock at me?"

John swallowed his initial instinct to be offended, grinning right back at Arthur instead. "Taking advantage of a man when he was in his cups," he said, then tutted. "No, I was referring to the chase in search of a certain Hiroshi. You never did tell me who the man is and what he is to you."

"What he is, is not your concern," Arthur grumbled, looking straight forward again.

John's smile grew. Finally. For the first time in their acquaintance, he finally felt as though he had the upper hand with Arthur. It was an amazing feeling, one that filled him with excitement and fired his imagination.

"I am only concerned for your happiness and wellbeing," he said instead of following his instincts to take Arthur up on his offer to go to the loo with him. "You're my friend, Arthur. You're more than that. You're upset, so I'm concerned."

Only once the words were out of his mouth did John feel the full impact of them in his chest. Good Lord, when had he come to actually care about Arthur Gleason? Not as a business rival, not as an object of fascination, but as a man, a special man.

Arthur turned to him with a look of impatience. "Fuck off," he said, pushing away from the railing. "I don't need your pity. I don't need anyone's pity."

He marched off without looking back, leaving John's mouth hanging open. It was not even close to the reaction he would have expected from offering his friendship and caring. Rather than being offended at being told off, John felt more anxious on Arthur's behalf than ever. Something was desperately wrong, and it galled him that Arthur was so prickly about it.

Their train arrived, and they took their seats. Arthur ended up seated right next to John, but he could have been in a different car, on a different train, the way he ignored him.

"What is our plan for when we reach Cannon's house?" Niall asked, twisting from the seat in front of John's and Arthur's to consult with them. Blake turned as well. "Do we simply knock on the front door and demand Alan back?"

"I wouldn't even bother to knock if I had my way," Blake said with a frown. "This villainy in keeping me apart from my son has gone on too long."

"I think it would be best if we handled the whole exchange as politely as possible," John said.

Arthur huffed a laugh. "Just like a good Englishman. Let's handle everything politely."

Niall and Blake looked surprised at Arthur's surly

answer. John knew better. "Do you have a better suggestion?" he asked, forcing himself to remain calm and not
rise to Arthur's bait.

Arthur stared at him. "I'm inclined to agree with
Lord Selby." He turned to Blake. "Demand your son back
in no uncertain terms."

"The less contentious we make the situation, the
more likely I believe Mr. Cannon is to agree to let the boy
go," John said.

"Do what you wish, then," Arthur said, turning to
glance out the window as Long Island rushed by outside.

Niall and Blake exchanged a look as though they
believed something important had happened at the club
the night before, but they weren't certain what. Niall
then cleared his throat and said, "I think the gentle but
firm approach is probably best. As soon as we're safely
ensconced in our hotel, we should go directly to
Cannon's summer house and make our intentions
known."

"Agreed," Blake said, bursting into a relieved smile.
"Finally," he went on. "I am finally about to get Alan
back. We'll have to telegraph the girls at Stephen and
Max's place as soon as we have him."

"Oh, of course," Niall said.

John still wasn't certain it would be that easy.
Nothing was easy at the moment. He crossed his arms
and peeked at Arthur out of the corner of his eyes as
Niall and Blake faced forward again. Arthur was meant
to be there to help—and he had been a huge help in the

JUST A LITTLE RIVALRY

case so far—but he was also behaving like a complete prick at the moment.

Arthur's withdrawn attitude continued when they reached the seaside town of Peconic and headed to their hotel. John had asked around before they'd left and located a small inn just half a mile down the beach from Douglas Cannon's summer home. It was charming and picturesque with a lovely view of the Long Island Sound from its back porch. It was the sort of place John would have chosen for a relaxing holiday, if he ever had time for such a thing in his life.

But as he'd predicted, things did not go smoothly from the start.

"I'm terribly sorry," the concierge at the desk told the four of them as they attempted to check in, "but we're nearly fully booked, due to the Spring Festival this weekend."

"Do you have any rooms at all?" Blake asked, standing and addressing the man as the duke he was. John was always amused when Blake decided to exert the influence of his title, especially on Americans. "My friends and I have most particular business here."

The concierge scrunched his face and studied the ledger in front of him. "I suppose I could make two rooms available. It would mean shifting around a few other bookings." He glanced up at Blake. "It might be able to be done, your grace, if you don't mind sharing."

John's brow inched up. He was impressed that the young concierge addressed Blake correctly, and he nearly laughed when Blake sighed, turned to Niall, and said, "Do you think you could demean yourself enough to share a hotel room with me?"

Niall frowned, then sighed dramatically. "If that's what needs to be done, I suppose I can suffer through it."

Even Arthur had a hard time not grinning at the farce. That settled John's anxiety on the man's behalf a little, but that anxiety flared all over again when the concierge said, "I suppose that means the two of you will be sharing as well?"

John's grin vanished.

"If we must," Arthur said with a smirk, taking the offered key from the young man.

They gathered up their things and headed off to the various parts of the inn where their rooms were located. Blake and Niall's room was on the second floor, looking out over the sound, which John supposed was the concierge's way of making up for not having separate rooms for a duke and his friend. The room John and Arthur would be sharing was a tiny thing on the third floor, facing the unimpressive garden and the road that had taken them to the inn. More than that, as soon as they opened the door into the chilly room, they discovered it only had one bed.

"There you go, Dandie," Arthur said, marching into the room and plunking his traveling bag down on the small table that sat under a tiny window. "You're finally getting everything you've wanted."

"How so?" John asked cautiously. He shut the door,

knowing that everything Arthur was about to say would be utterly inappropriate, then took his suitcase to the bureau.

"One bed." Arthur nodded to the bed. "You'll be completely at my mercy. And what a lovely brass bedstead that is too. Perfect for tying you to."

"I beg your pardon?" John asked, playing along for the moment. At least, that was what he told himself. And his heart was racing from climbing the stairs, not from Arthur's suggestions.

"I'll have to tie you to the bed so that you don't fall off," Arthur said, his usual salacious glint back in his eyes. Seeing that was an immense relief to John. "Of course," Arthur went on, sidling over to John, "there would be even less of a chance of falling off if I tied you to the bed spreadeagle. Or perhaps with your wrists and ankles fastened together and pulled tight to the corners of that lovely bedstead. I dare say you wouldn't be able to move at all then."

John swallowed as his mind conjured up the image Arthur was painting. In a position like that, his important bits would be completely vulnerable. Arthur could have him in any way he wanted.

He cleared his throat and marched quickly away to the window. "The room is a bit stuffy," he croaked, nearly smacking his toe into the table under the window. "Perhaps a bit of air would do."

As he cracked open the window to let air into the already chilly room, Arthur chuckled behind him. "You are fun to play with," he said. John could feel him watching. "Or perhaps I should say that you will be fun to play with."

The intention of those words sent a sort of excitement that John had never known down his spine. He was supposed to be getting the upper hand on Arthur, not the other way around. He had to help the man, now that he had all sorts of newly-discovered feelings for him. It shouldn't feel like it had before, when Arthur goaded him and he became flustered. They were on track for a more mature relationship, like he'd had with David or with Brandon. There was no place in that sort of a relationship for ribald teasing and lascivious suggestions...was there?

"We'd better head back downstairs to meet Blake and Niall so that we can go straight to Cannon's house," he said, voice hoarse, crossing the room to the door without looking at Arthur.

Arthur remained silent, but John caught the man's devilish grin in the room's mirror.

Blake and Niall were already back downstairs and ready to complete their mission when John and Arthur reached the lobby. An air of excitement followed them as they left the inn and walked along the road to the grand and elaborate mansion. Douglas Cannon was one of New York City's premier businessmen and industrialists. He'd made an extensive fortune in steel, then had doubled it through shrewd business partnerships and investment in New York City real estate. From what John had discovered about the man in his research prior to embarking on their mission, Cannon's wealth continued to grow as he formed corporations and partnerships with other industrialists who had done well, but not quite as well as he had. He was exactly the sort of man who would have been proud of his daughter becoming a duchess to add yet another feather in his cap.

At the same time, from what John had learned and from what Blake had to say about the man, he wasn't the sort to be sentimental about an English grandson. By the time they reached the front door of the vast, seaside mansion, John had talked himself into thinking that there was an even chance he would drop Alan back into Blake's arms and move on with things before they'd finished tea. Which also meant there was an equal chance the man would use his vast resources to fight to keep Alan permanently.

Blake rang the doorbell, and they all stood back, waiting. The tension in the air was like that before a storm. John found himself holding his breath as the handle turned and the door began to open.

The storm broke over them as a handsome, middle-aged Japanese man in a butler's livery opened the door and asked, "Can I help—"

The moment the butler's and Arthur's eyes met, John knew that he'd finally come face to face with Hiroshi.

CHAPTER 6

*A*rthur had never been one for surprises. He'd never had a good surprise in his life. Every shock and unexpected turn in his life had been a bad one. Standing on Cannon's front doorstep, suddenly face to face with Hiroshi in daylight, realizing his nemesis was Cannon's butler, was something he wasn't prepared for.

Lord Selby and Cristofori had no idea, but John figured everything out in an instant, damn him.

"We're here to see Mr. Cannon," Blake announced, standing tall and proud and looking every bit like a duke.

Hiroshi's eyes were locked with Arthur's, though Arthur did an admirable job of hiding his feelings behind a banal expression, if he did say so himself. All the same, he could feel his temperature rise and his chest constrict, and judging by the fire in Hiroshi's eyes, the feeling was mutual.

Hiroshi cleared his throat and masked his expression

to the point where he looked like some sort of statue of himself as he faced Lord Selby. "Mr. Cannon is enjoying a holiday with his family, and he is not available to see guests," he said, almost without an accent.

Arthur's mouth twitched. Hiroshi must have worked hard in the last ten years to be able to speak nearly unaccented English. The last time they'd seen each other, in Tokyo, Hiroshi could barely manage enough English to deal with the customers who frequented his brothel. Now, he sounded like a scholar of the language.

"Mr. Cannon will see us," Lord Selby insisted, raising his voice. "Tell him that Lord Selby has come to retrieve his son. We'll see if he's home to guests then."

The slightest hint of understanding sparked in Hiroshi's eyes before he bowed formally, then took a step back, gesturing for Lord Selby and the rest of them to enter the house. As they did, and as Arthur stepped past him, Hiroshi glanced up and met Arthur's eyes with pure venom.

A moment later, as the four of them lined up in what seemed like an elegantly-decorated foyer, Hiroshi was back to being the definition of an excellent butler as he stood with his back straight and his expression neutral. "Please wait here while I inquire as to whether Mr. Cannon is available to speak to you." There was a touch more of an accent in his words, which made Arthur think he was unnerved. No one who didn't know the man well would have noticed from Hiroshi's regal bearing as he walked sedately down the hall and turned a corner.

"That's him," John said, whipping to face Arthur as soon as Hiroshi was gone. "That's Hiroshi."

"That's who?" Cristofori asked. Both he and Lord Selby looked utterly confused.

"An old friend of Arthur's," John said. "We spotted him at The Slippery Slope last night."

Both Cristofori and Lord Selby blinked in surprise.

"He is not a friend," Arthur growled, glaring at John. "And I will thank you to keep silent on this matter, as I do not wish it discussed."

John opened his mouth as if to argue the point—which was absurd, since the whole thing was none of his business anyhow—but was cut short as a tall, greying man who bore a slight resemblance to Lady Selby marched around the corner.

Instantly, they were all on alert.

"Lord Selby," Mr. Cannon said with a deep frown as he approached. "I have not invited you to my house."

"I do not require an invitation when the life and happiness of my son and heir is at stake, sir," Lord Selby replied with an anxious ferocity that went above and beyond anything Arthur had seen from the man in all the time he'd known him. Then again, with the end of his long and painful journey in sight, Arthur didn't blame the man for being beside himself, not one bit.

Cannon seemed to understand, even though he continued to scowl. "This whole business has been a debacle on all sides," he said, as stiff and formal as if he'd been born a duke himself. "My daughter was wrong to take your son from you, but you, sir, were very much in the wrong to importune her the way you did." He glanced viciously at Cristofori, as if he knew everything and then some.

Come to think of it, the man likely did know everything. From what Arthur understood, Lord Selby had first met Cannon and his daughter while he was at university in York. Cristofori had been at university with him. He'd never asked for the full story, but since both men seemed to recognize each other, Arthur was certain they'd met before.

"I require my son to be returned to me immediately, sir," Lord Selby went on. Arthur could see him trying to contain his fury, but failing completely do so.

"And why should I displace the boy from a stable home, in which he has been given the finest care, in order to hand him over to a man with a perverted lifestyle?" Cannon demanded in return.

Arthur burned with fury on Lord Selby's behalf. "Lord Stanley has not been in a stable environment, nor has he been cared for by your daughter since the moment she wrenched him from the father and sisters who actually care for him," he blurted, unable to stop himself.

Cannon stared at him in offense. "And who are you?" he snapped.

"Detective Arthur Gleason. I have been tracking your daughter's movements on behalf of Lord Selby and assisting Lord Selby's solicitor, John Dandie, in his efforts to retrieve the boy. I have more information on the activities and proclivities of your daughter than you would ever care to know about, and if we are holding a contest of moral uprightness, I can assure you, sir, your daughter would lose."

The foyer sizzled with tension as Arthur finished, gasping for breath. Arthur quickly became aware that Hiroshi was glaring as though he would murder him on the spot. It was a familiar expression for the man to wear when looking at him. What surprised Arthur even more was the look of assessment Cannon wore as he, too, studied Arthur.

A blink later, and it was as though Cannon had dismissed Arthur entirely. He faced Lord Selby again and said, "Why does a man like you have so much as a hint of a care for a child?"

Lord Selby gaped at him. "Alan is mine, my heir, my heart and soul. I love him with my whole being, and he has been kept away from me for far too long." He took a step toward Cannon. "It does not matter where my love lies in other directions. I am a father, first and foremost. You know as well as I do that I was forced into marrying your daughter by my father. I would have let her marry Archibald right from the start, if forces were not working against us. Forces that you were a part of, might I remind you."

Cannon snorted derisively. "Archibald," he grumbled as if he didn't think much of the man.

"You are a father too, sir," Blake went on. "You know what it is to love a child more than yourself." Arthur wasn't certain a man like Cannon actually did know that, but Lord Selby was caught up in the passion of his argument. "Alan has been the sole focus of my every waking and sleeping thought since Annamarie absconded with him. I stand here before you today at the end of a long and bitter chase. I have crossed an ocean to retrieve my son. I have hired a detective and a solicitor, importuned every one of my friends, and destroyed my reputation in England just to have him back in my arms. Do you stand before me today, telling me you will deny me the piece of my heart that is missing?"

The foyer fell silent again. Lord Selby's speech had been so moving that even Hiroshi had been startled by it. Arthur peeked at him, but his simmering resentment of the man was too strong to feel any sort of compassion.

At last, after what felt like an eternity, Cannon blew out a breath and rubbed a hand over his face. "Alan is down on the beach with his grandmother, my wife, at the moment. Come with me and I will take you there. We can discuss arrangements for his return immediately."

Lord Selby let out a small sound, as if he'd stifled a sob before embarrassing himself. He reached for Cristofori's hand, squeezing it. Arthur was certain the two of them would have kissed and embraced if they'd felt free to do so.

They all started down the hall, following Cannon. Hiroshi watched for a moment, his expression betraying indignation before he called out, "Sir!" When Cannon turned to face him with a quizzical look, Hiroshi hesitated. Arthur was certain he wanted to hurl every sort of accusation at him and have Cannon agree to throw him out on the street. Hiroshi must have realized he couldn't possibly make such a request, though. "Do you intend for these men to join you for luncheon?"

The corner of Arthur's mouth twitched up. All these years later, and Hiroshi was still capable of a clever save when he needed one. Intelligence had never been the bastard's problem. Hiroshi was too smart for his own good. Smart enough to hide his nefarious brothel from the authorities, but also smart enough to land himself in trouble for overthinking things. Arthur could tell that was what he was doing now, could tell he'd only made the suggestion so that Cannon could deny it and make the four of them feel unwelcome.

Instead, Cannon sighed and rubbed a hand across his chin. "I'll have to consult with Mrs. Cannon about it. We already have Mr. Stone to deal with."

"Very good, sir," Hiroshi said with a bow before turning and walking away. He sent a threatening glance to Arthur as he went.

Arthur smirked as he followed Cannon, Lord Selby, and Niall down a small hallway and through what appeared to be a ballroom—though it was broken up into several sitting areas and a music corner with a piano at the moment—and out to a porch that stretched along the entire back side of the mansion. John fell into step by Arthur's side.

Arthur expected him to start in with questions about

Hiroshi immediately, but instead he asked, "Who do you suppose Mr. Stone is?"

"I don't know," Arthur replied, feeling as though he were missing an opportunity to marshal his defenses where John was concerned by not snapping a sharp reply. "A guest, I suppose. A friend of the family or a relative visiting for the Spring Festival?"

John hummed in consideration, but blessedly said nothing else as they descended the stairs from the porch, walked along a short boardwalk, then made their way down to a narrow stretch of beach. Arthur could see their hotel in the distance along the beach to the east. He also spotted an older woman dressed in lace with a small boy in a sailor's suit toward the west.

"Alan!" Lord Selby called out the moment he saw the boy and broke into a run. "Alan!"

The boy jerked his head up from whatever he was drawing in the sand with a stick. Even across the distance, Arthur could see the pure, ecstatic joy in the boy's expression as he saw his father for the first time in months. "Papa!" he squealed, instantly breaking into a run. The woman tried to grab at him to keep him from going, but she missed.

It was the sweetest reunion Arthur had ever witnessed. Lord Selby and his son raced toward each other, heedless of the sand and driftwood and other detritus on the beach. Lord Selby shouted wordlessly, throwing open his arms, then crying out as the boy catapulted himself into those arms. The two of them wept and squeezed each other as Lord Selby fell to his knees. Both father and son were shaking with emotion, and buried their heads against each other's necks one moment, only to pull back so that Lord Selby could kiss his son's cheeks before embracing him again.

Arthur was struck hard by a memory he'd nearly forgotten. He hadn't seen Shinobu for weeks. Their future together was still uncertain. Hiroshi had promised to rain hell down on them if they so much as thought of seeing each other again, but neither of them had been willing to play by the rules anymore. They'd made arrangements to run away together, and when they'd finally spotted each other across the flowered distance of the imperial park, just like Lord Selby and his son, they'd run to each other and kissed and embraced as though neither of them had been able to breathe during the entire time they'd been apart.

Arthur sucked in a sudden breath, stopping just short of letting it out on a moan of grief. The memories were too potent, and he had to turn away from Lord Selby and his son. With a fist raised to his mouth, he walked swiftly away, back toward the boardwalk and the house.

"Arthur, what is the matter?" John asked behind him.

Of course, the prying bastard would follow him.

"Nothing," he snapped, his voice hoarse. "Leave me alone."

John did nothing of the sort. Arthur hadn't really expected him to. When they reached the manicured lawn between the sand dunes and the mansion's back porch, Arthur turned to glare at him, hoping that would be enough to turn the man away.

"I didn't realize you had become so sentimental about Blake being reunited with his son," John said in a tone that implied he knew full well that wasn't what had upset him.

Arthur stared daggers at him for a moment, then turned to march off down the length of the lawn, even though he had no idea where he was going. He'd run to the other side of the globe to get away from the pain that losing Shinobu had caused, and it had done no good. That pain was something he'd never escape from.

"Dammit, man," John shouted at him as they reached the edge of the lawn, where it became sandy dunes again. "You're obviously in distress about something. If I had to guess, I would say it is about your past, and I would venture to guess that this Hiroshi person is involved. It's obviously eating you alive, so just tell me. Were you and this Hiroshi lovers?"

Arthur barked a humorless laugh at the very idea. "Far from it."

John took a step closer to him, looking unsurprised by the answer. "Then tell me about it. You're obviously in pain, and it pains me to see you suffer so."

"Good men are so sentimental," Arthur said, his voice hoarse, shaking his head.

"Yes, we are," John said, stepping closer still. "And if you didn't enjoy that somehow, you wouldn't be half as interested in me as you are. Deny it all you want, but I fascinate you for some reason, even though we are like night and day to each other. You joke about all the ways you plan to fuck me, but if you cannot lower yourself to be honest with me, that will never happen."

Arthur's brow inched up. John was delicious when he was in a temper. He was also right.

Arthur sighed and rubbed his hands over his face. "You're right. I have always been fascinated by good men. I've been drawn to them like a moth to the flame. I was drawn to Shinobu that way."

John blinked, taking a half step back. "Was he your lover?"

Arthur nodded. It felt like pulling off a barely-healed scab to admit even that much. "At first, he was just a pretty whore I liked to visit when I was on shore leave," he said, feeling ashamed as he confessed. Chances were that John wouldn't understand at all. "Hiroshi owned a brothel that catered to a very specific clientele. Even back then, I had...particular tastes. Shinobu was a perfect angel, body and soul. Nothing I wanted was too much for him. The more I hurt him, the more he adored me, and I him."

John flinched in confusion. Of course, he would.

Arthur shook his head. "It was all mutual, so don't give me that look. Pain and pleasure make perfect bedfellows, but not everyone is inclined to understand it. Shinobu understood me, though, and I him. We were in love before I could stop it."

"And I take it Hiroshi didn't approve?" John said, his voice shaky.

Arthur grinned, or perhaps sneered—the expressions weren't that far apart—and shook his head. "Shinobu was more than just an asset to Hiroshi."

"An...asset?" John asked.

"Hiroshi owned the brothel," Arthur explained. "He fancied Shinobu, but those feelings weren't mutual. I offered to pay whatever Hiroshi wanted to take Shinobu out of that life and keep him for myself. I threatened to go to the authorities, but the authorities were on Hiroshi's payroll. When we'd exhausted every other option, we ran away together." The rest of the story froze in Arthur's throat.

After too long a silence, John asked exactly what Arthur knew he would ask. "Where is Shinobu now?"

"Dead," Arthur answered. He turned away from John as grief squeezed around him. It was entirely unfair. Ten years should be more than enough to overcome the grief of losing a lover. He and Shinobu had been so young at the time anyhow. Given more time, they could easily have fallen out of love or realized their cultural expectations did not match. They could have grown apart naturally, or they could have had an explosive fight and ended up hating each other. But they'd never been given that chance. Their story had ended before it had truly begun.

"I'm sorry, Arthur," John murmured, stepping up behind him and resting a hand on his shoulder. "I'm so sorry that you lost someone you loved."

Arthur let himself feel the heat of John's hand and the warmth of his affection for only a few seconds before shrugging him off. "I don't need your pity," he said, sniffling away the tears that threatened to unman him and pushing away from John.

"It's not pity, it's caring," John insisted, following as Arthur stormed back to the center of the lawn. He was still trying to be considerate, but Arthur could hear frustration in his voice. "Arthur, please."

Their melancholy little scene was forced to an end as they met Lord Selby with his son in his arms, Cristofori, and Mr. and Mrs. Cannon walking up from the beach to the porch.

"Please don't take him from me," Mrs. Cannon pleaded, weeping openly. "I love him so. He is so precious to me. Please don't take him away from me so soon."

A moan of reflected grief gripped Arthur's throat before he could swallow it. John stepped up behind him and rested a hand on the small of his back for a moment as the others passed in front of them, climbing up to the porch. Then Arthur shook John away again and followed.

"Roberta, please stop," Mr. Cannon grumbled.

"We've had so little time together," Mrs. Cannon continued to plead. "I just want to be with him a little while longer. The festival is this weekend, and we were so looking forward to it."

"Can we go to the festival, Papa?" Lord Stanley asked, his arms still clasped tightly around Lord Selby's neck. "Grandmama says there will be cake and toffee and balloons and animals in cages."

Lord Selby glanced forlornly at Cristofori. "Don't you want to return to London to see Greta and Jessie?"

"Can't Greta and Jessie come to the festival?" Lord Stanley asked.

"No, my boy," Lord Selby laughed. "They are a long way away. We will need to take a ship across the sea to reach them."

"Not another ship," Lord Stanley sighed.

Lord Selby laughed louder. "I promise, you will like the ship you take home."

"Please don't take him from me yet," Mrs. Cannon continued to weep.

"You realize," John said with a wince, stepping away from Arthur—which was a blessed relief from the intense emotions the man made Arthur feel, "that the ship we have tentatively booked passage on to take us home does not depart for another fortnight."

Arthur had thought it outrageously optimistic that John had already arranged for a return voyage so soon after their arrival, but it seemed that his optimism was founded after all.

"Two weeks?" Lord Selby asked, his expression pinched with conflict. He glanced to Mrs. Cannon, clutching his son tighter. "I suppose it wouldn't hurt to let you continue to visit with Alan until we are needed back in New York."

"Oh, thank you, Lord Selby," Mrs. Cannon wept, as

though Lord Selby had overtly agreed to let Lord Stanley stay instead of just implied it. "You must come for supper, then. Tonight. Tonight, we are hosting a small party. You and your friends must attend."

Lord Selby looked uncertain, but one glance at his son and he said, "Very well, Mrs. Cannon. We will accept your invitation."

"In that case, we'd better go prepare," Arthur said, starting off immediately for the inn by peeling away from the others, descending the stairs to the boardwalk, and heading to the beach again to walk back to the inn that way.

It was a rude way to make an exit, but in his current state of mind, it had been absolutely necessary. After vomiting the story of his painful and somewhat sordid past to the one man who had even come close to matching the love he'd had for Shinobu, Arthur felt raw and scraped. He needed those few moments to himself, needed to lick his wounds and fight to forget the past again. Because he knew that as soon as he was face to face with John, the bastard would just drag it all out of him again and leave him hurting worse than before.

hen he'd been at university, sneaking around with David and attempting to conduct a love affair without either of them being exposed as sodomites, John had felt grievously wronged by the world. He'd been convinced that his life was utterly unfair, but also that he was daring and wicked, and far more interesting than most of the other men that puttered around the university, resigned to their fates of marrying, producing heirs, and never setting foot outside of the boundaries life had established for men.

From the moment he'd met Arthur Gleason, however, John had begun to understand that his life was charmed, his path had been easy, and his choices were as dull and unimaginative as any of his university chums.

"And what is it that you do?" Cannon's guest, Mr. Walter Stone, asked as the two of them sat beside each other at the long, elaborately-decorated table in Cannon's formal dining room that night.

"I am a solicitor," John answered with a polite smile. Those words had never seemed so completely and utterly boring before.

Stone frowned. "You'll have to educate me, Mr. Dandie. What is the difference between an English solicitor and an American lawyer?"

"Nationality?" John suggested.

A middle-aged woman seated across the table from John laughed as though he were droll. John wanted to stab himself with his fork. It was a safe joke, an easy joke. Just as the law was a safe and easy profession. Everything about his life was safe, easy, and painfully dull, and he was only just realizing it.

"A solicitor handles the day-to-day legal affairs of his clients," he explained to Stone with a smile. "Wills, business contracts, any sort of non-criminal legal trouble that arises." Which, in all honesty, was the bulk of his business.

"I see," Stone smiled. "But no trials? No courtroom escapades and dashing speeches made in front of magistrates with powdered wigs?"

Clearly, Stone had only a vague understanding of the British legal system. "You are thinking of a barrister, sir," he said. "They are the ones who argue at trials."

"But not you?" Stone asked.

"I'm afraid not."

John gave the man his best apologetic smile and was

completely unsurprised when Stone turned to converse with Niall on his other side.

The entire exchange took the wind out of John's sails. He stared down at his plate, at the perfectly-cooked roast, the surprisingly delicious vegetables, and the plain, white potatoes that he suspected had been overcooked and under-seasoned. He was the potatoes. Yes, he had spent his entire life helping people. He had dedicated his time and his energy to serving others. But his life was as bland as mushy potatoes.

He looked up, stealing a glance down the table to where Arthur sat conversing with an older woman who had come for supper. John's heart still ached over the agony in Arthur's eyes as he'd told the story of his Japanese lover, Shinobu, that morning. His face heated as he remembered some of the other confessions Arthur had made as well. John's initial reaction to Arthur's statement that he had hurt Shinobu for pleasure and that they had both enjoyed it had been revulsion. Then confusion. Then curiosity. He wasn't a complete rube. He had heard of such sexual practices before. He was a fool for not connecting the clues in his mind earlier, particularly after seeing Arthur's flat.

But that was precisely the point. He was dull, unimaginative, and unadventurous. Arthur might have been as smooth as a still pond on the surface, but he was a roiling tumult of emotion and experience underneath that surface. The emotions he'd displayed that morning had taken John aback, but only because the last time he had felt something so deeply was...he couldn't even remember.

No wonder he and David had parted company when things simply wilted between them. No wonder Brandon had shaken his hand and thanked him for being such a good man when they'd parted ways. He was good and competent and thoughtful, and he was as bloodless as a corpse.

But not Arthur.

"Mr. Dandie, are you quite alright?"

The question came from Cannon, seated at the head of the table, just two seats away from John. Conversation at the table ceased, and everyone glanced John's way. Including Arthur. Arthur was too slow to hide his initial burst of intensity as their eyes met, but as soon as John glanced to Cannon, then quickly back at Arthur, Arthur had returned to conversing with the woman beside him.

"I am quite well, thank you, sir," John said to Cannon. "I was merely struck by an odd thought is all."

"Would you care to share?" Cannon asked.

John cleared his throat and peeked back at Arthur. The man was still talking to his seat partner, but everything about him screamed awareness. "Mr. Stone and I were discussing the difference between British solicitors and American lawyers," John said. "I was suddenly struck by how insufferably dull we all are."

That earned him a laugh from nearly everyone at the table. It also earned him a long, curious stare from Arthur. John risked sending a look Arthur's way that turned unforgivably maudlin before he could stop himself, then focused on his plate once more.

Conversation continued, but John was surprised a moment later—surprised enough to jump—as Hiroshi leaned in beside him with an open bottle of wine and asked, "Would you like more, sir?"

The question shot straight to John's heart, nearly making him groan aloud. Yes, he wanted more. He wanted more than a stable life of work, sleep, and being a good man. He wanted to feel his heart pound the way it did when he was with Arthur. He wanted to be terrified, to feel as though he were taking risks, like he did every time he entered a verbal sparring match with Arthur. He wanted to work with the man, as they'd been doing for the past several months, feeding off of the lust for life and the unconventional enthusiasm and salacious humor that Arthur had. He didn't simply want to be John Dandie, solicitor and good man, anymore.

"No, thank you," he told Hiroshi, moving his half-full wine glass away from his plate. "I think I've had enough."

"Very good, sir." Hiroshi bowed and stepped back, but John could feel the man's gaze continuing to bore into him. John could only guess that Hiroshi was wondering who John was and what his association to Arthur could be.

John was wondering those things himself.

"Is that true?" Stone asked, glancing across the table to Blake, startling John out of his thoughts once again.

John felt a step behind in the conversation, but pretended to be interested in whatever Blake would say.

"Yes," Blake answered, "I am, indeed, a duke. The Duke of Selby, to be precise."

Stone nodded and hummed. "So does that mean you are related to Queen Victoria?"

"No, sir." Blake's expression was neutral, but his eyes danced with humor. "There are a few royal dukes who are relations, but regular dukes are merely descendants of medieval lords who controlled vast landholdings or who performed great services to the monarch."

"Oh, I see." Stone frowned, as though trying to make sense of it. "So if you're such a grand person, why is there some sort of scuffle over custody of your son?"

Again, all conversation at the table froze, and all eyes snapped to either Stone or Blake. Cannon went red in the face, and Mrs. Cannon looked as though she might weep with embarrassment.

John felt compelled to handle the situation. "Unfortunately, Lord Selby and his wife, Mr. and Mrs. Cannon's daughter, have decided to end their marriage. As you may be aware, quite a few American heiresses have been marrying into the British aristocracy of late, but those matches have not always worked out. It was deemed in the best interest of all involved to dissolve the marriage for various reasons. Young Lord Stanley has been here visiting his grandparents before proceedings are finalized."

Cannon looked as though he wanted to give John a

medal for his kind, if not entirely accurate, description of the situation.

Stone stared at John with even deeper confusion. "Who is Lord Stanley?"

"Lord Selby's son," John said.

"He's a lord too?" Stone blinked.

John was beginning to wonder who the devil Stone was and how a man of such dull intellect had been invited not only to dine at the Cannon's house, but to stay with them. Of course, he'd been made aware of the answer to that question earlier. Stone was the son of a miner who had risen up not only to own the mine where his father worked, but to purchase and consolidate several mines throughout Pennsylvania and West Virginia. But as John was learning, just because a man had a head for business and the ambition to rise above his place didn't mean he had grace and finesse.

But Stone was interesting. He'd grabbed life with both hands and made so much more of it than he'd started with. He put John to shame.

"Lord Selby's son is the Marquess of Stanley. The marquessate is a subsidiary title held by the Williamson family," he explained.

Stone looked more confused than ever. "But he's just a child."

"Age is no impediment to title," John said, his back beginning to itch with impatience. God, but the aristocracy had so many mad rules and regulations of order. No wonder he was such a dullard himself. He was surrounded by hollow protocol, whereas Arthur had ventured out and lived a life of color.

He glanced down the table only to find Arthur grinning outright as he pushed food around his plate. At least the man was laughing instead of tearing his heart out with memories of his past, even if he was laughing at John.

John cleared his throat. "Lord Selby's given name is Blake Williamson. The Williamson family dates back to the twelve-hundreds. Their primary title is Duke of Selby, but their subsidiary titles include the Marquess of Stanley, the Earl of Leyburn, and I believe there may be a viscountcy as well. Seeing as Lord Stanley is Lord Selby's heir, he takes the uppermost title as a courtesy."

"So if he had other sons, would the other titles get doled out to them?" Stone asked. "Or does he keep them all in the bank along with the family jewels." He laughed out loud at his joke.

"Since Selby is a duke, if he were to have younger sons, they would be referred to as 'Lord whatever their Christian name was Williamson', but they would not be entitled to a title of their own. Were Lord Selby a marquess or earl, or anything less than a duke, his younger sons would be referred to simply as 'Mr.'."

"That isn't fair at all," Stone said with his mouth full of supper. "What's the use of having all those titles if everyone doesn't get one?"

As grating as the conversation was, John rather

agreed with Stone. "Fortunately, there will be no other sons."

"And why not?" Stone shrugged. "The man is a duke, and he's reasonably attractive. What's to stop him from remarrying and popping out a whole new crop of gentlemen?"

"Perhaps we should adjourn to our after-supper activities," Cannon said, rising from the table with a wary look for Stone. "Roberta, would you care to take the women into your sitting room for tea?"

"Yes, darling," Mrs. Cannon said.

The ladies headed out in one direction and the men in the other. John couldn't edge away from Stone fast enough, but that didn't seem to matter, as Stone seemed intent on speaking with Blake directly.

"I'm putting that entire conversation in a future play," Niall chuckled as he and John walked together across the hall to a billiards room. "Comedy like that can only write itself."

"You must forgive my friend, Mr. Stone," Cannon said, joining them. "I am in the process of deciding whether I wish to go into business with him. He's a prominent mine owner, and my steel operation would benefit from the alliance, but as you can see...." He let the rest of his sentence drop and nodded across the room to where Stone had just draped an arm around Blake's shoulders with shocking informality.

The men settled into the room as Hiroshi poured strong drinks for them and a footman—if they were called footmen in America—lit cigars for the gentlemen who wanted to indulge. Arthur was conspicuously absent. John searched for him, as though he would have been able to hide in the relatively small room. He wondered if Arthur had left entirely or if he was avoiding Hiroshi and planned to wait until the man left the room.

John had no intention of waiting. He excused himself from the others and stepped back into the hall, back-tracking in the direction of the dining room, but figuring it was more likely that Arthur had retreated to the porch that looked out over the sound.

"Mr. Dandie, may I please have a word with you?"

John nearly jumped out of his skin as Hiroshi stopped him a few steps away from the dining room. Pulse pounding, John turned to the man, schooling his expression to neutrality so as not to give away how much he knew about Hiroshi. "Certainly," he said, completely affable.

Hiroshi nodded and gestured toward the end of the long hallway. John walked with him until they were all the way at the far end, beside a window that looked out to the cool, April night.

"Sir, I must warn you about the man you have found yourself associated with, Mr. Gleason," Hiroshi began.

It took everything John had not to gape in surprise. "Oh?" he asked, playing the role of disinterested Englishman well.

Hiroshi stood tall, hands clasped behind his back, and

said, "I regret to inform you that the man you find your-self associated with is a criminal and a pervert."

John had no idea how to react to that, so he merely tilted his head to the side, frowned slightly, and asked, "How so?"

"He is a perversion of nature, sir," Hiroshi said.

John thought as quickly as he could, wondering how much he could risk in this conversation. "I believe we all saw each other at The Slippery Slope the other night."

Hiroshi shook his head. "That is not what I mean. I refer to Gleason's...tastes. He is a sordid and villainous man. Not the sort you want to associate yourself with. I could tell you things." He paused and glanced back over his shoulder to the doorway to the billiard room, as if afraid they might be overheard across that long distance. "I advise you, sir, as someone who knows the evil Gleason is capable of, to eschew his company at once. You will only come to harm if you do not."

John was utterly baffled by the man's advice, if it could even be called advice. It felt more to him as though Hiroshi were attempting to undermine Arthur as part of whatever feud the two had once had. Hiroshi couldn't possibly think that John was imbecilic enough to take the word of a man he'd barely met over that of a man he'd been working closely with for months, a man he had large and conflicted feelings for.

Then again, Hiroshi had no idea how closely associated he and Arthur already were. For all the man knew, they'd only just met at The Slippery Slope. And something about the aura Hiroshi radiated was emotional and desperate enough that he might attempt to leap before he looked if he thought doing so might injure Arthur.

"I thank you for your wise counsel," John said with a serious nod, pretending he took the advice seriously. "Now would you be so kind as to point me in the direction of the loo?"

"I wish only to serve, sir," Hiroshi said with another bow, then gestured to a small water-closet near where they stood.

It was close enough that John was obliged to enter it. He waited until Hiroshi had enough time to go about his business, figured that as long as he was in a handy water-closet, he might as well use it, then stepped back out into the hall. He wasn't inclined to rejoin the men in the billiard room, so instead he went off in search of a door that would take him out to the porch, where he was still certain Arthur must have gone.

That search took him several more minutes, but once he was out on the porch, he discovered he was wrong about Arthur being there after all. He found Arthur all the same, in a way, when he heard Arthur's raised voice through a window at the far end of the porch from where he'd left the house.

"...over and done a decade ago," Arthur shouted. John was able to make out the words as he reached the window to the small parlor—or perhaps it was a staging room for the servants' activity—at the corner of the house. "I have put it behind me, and you should as well."

"I will never put it behind me," Hiroshi's voice roared back at Arthur, sending John's brow shooting up to his hairline. "I will never allow a man with no honor to rest as long as it is within my power."

"My honor is not yours to bestow or to take away," Arthur argued, lowering his voice a bit, perhaps aware of how loud he'd become. "Shinobu chose me."

"Shinobu was led astray by a fool of an Englishman," Hiroshi said. "He was mine. He belonged to me. You stole what was mine."

"He was a man," Arthur insisted. "A man cannot be owned by another man, no matter what rules you thought you could make in your seedy little world."

"He signed a contract."

"When he was too young to understand what it meant." Arthur raised his voice again.

John hung back from the window, loath to be seen at that moment, but from where he stood, he was able to see the red-faced fury that seemed to consume Hiroshi.

"You stole from me. You took what was mine," Hiroshi said. "I vowed revenge once, and I make that vow to you again now."

"Revenge," Arthur scoffed, shaking his head. "You are not living in some samurai novel, Hiroshi. You are a pimp who somehow, miraculously, managed to obtain a position as a butler to a wealthy man, worlds away from where you started. Stop pretending that you are the hero of your own story, let the past go, and appreciate the luck of what you have now."

John was rather impressed with Arthur's words, but Hiroshi made a disgusted sound and turned to march out of the room. As soon as he did, Arthur jerked toward the window, visibly seething with anger, and shoved a hand through his hair.

That was when he spotted John standing in the shadows.

His eyes went wide as he moved to the window and threw it open. "What in the devil are you doing standing there?" he demanded.

"Wondering if you plan to take your own advice," John shot back.

Arthur scowled at him in confusion. "I beg your pardon?"

"The advice you just gave Hiroshi about letting go of the past and appreciating the luck of what you have now," John said.

Arthur muttered something peevish and unintelligible. He glanced over his shoulder, then back at the window, and swore as he opened the window all the way and climbed onto the porch. "You've no right to listen in on private conversations that do not concern you," he said, marching toward the steps and storming down to the boardwalk.

John followed him. "I have every right when said conversation is shouted so loud it could wake the dead. And when it involves a threat to someone I hold dear."

Arthur stumbled as they reached the sand and started

down the beach in the direction of the inn. "You're a fool if you hold me dear."

"I'm a fool for a great many more reasons than that," John insisted.

"Then let me assist you in your journey not to be a fool anymore," Arthur called over his shoulder as they strode swiftly down the beach, the gentle lap of the tide whispering across the sand. "Stay out of my business."

John shook his head. "Hiroshi threatened you. He does not seem like the sort to make hollow threats."

"He cannot touch me now," Arthur growled. "There is nothing he can do to me that would hurt more than the things that have already hurt me."

"I would not like to see him try to prove you wrong," John insisted. When Arthur didn't reply, John went on with, "He said you stole Shinobu from him."

Arthur stopped abruptly, whipping to face John, ferocity and pain in his eyes that John could see clearly in the moonlight. "I didn't just steal the boy," he said, pain lacing his voice, "I killed him."

CHAPTER 8

The moment the confession was out of his mouth, Arthur wanted to shout every obscenity he'd ever known and take it back. The shock that filled John's eyes was bad enough, but the realization that he cared what John thought of him, that he valued John's opinion and wanted the man to continue to be fascinated by him, stung even more.

He growled and peeled away from John, storming down the beach with an even more desperate sense of panic and the need to flee the situation he'd created for himself.

No, he hadn't created it. The situation had roared into being ten years ago amidst first love and youthful folly. It was just his damn luck now that he couldn't do a thing to get away from the pain that flew at him from all sides.

"Arthur, stop!" John called after him, jogging to catch up. "Please."

"Why?" Arthur snapped as John reached his side and matched his steps. "So you can tell me it isn't as bad as I imagine it to be? So that you can say there must be some mistake? So that you can be a good, nice man and make everything better?"

"No, dammit," John shouted. "Stop and explain to me. There's obviously more of a story than you're letting on."

Arthur laughed humorlessly and picked up his pace. He would never be able to move fast enough or run far enough to get away from the hurt and the guilt.

"Arthur." John grabbed his arm and forced Arthur to stand still. "You're driving yourself mad with this, and it has to stop."

Arthur sucked in a breath, intending to use it to tell John off, but he held it instead. No good would come of revealing more of himself than he already had. He knew that he was already too much for a man like John to take, and the more he let his heart slip out to his sleeve, the more inclined John would be to leave him entirely.

That thought startled him. He wanted John to leave him alone, didn't he? He wanted to keep John, and everyone else, at arm's distance, preventing them, or himself, from being hurt. That was what his life had been since returning from Japan. He was the man who found people so that he didn't have to go in search of himself.

He shook his head over that thought and pulled away

from John, striding down the beach at a deliberate, if less furious, pace. "You wouldn't understand, John," he said, knowing that John would follow him, no matter what he did. "You haven't lived the sort of life I've lived."

"No, I have not," John agreed. "I've lived a safe and sheltered life. I've never gone hungry. I've always had a home and friends. I was able to attend university and become a solicitor. I have never once had to challenge myself or feel anything deeper than mild annoyance when a case hasn't gone my way."

Arthur glanced at him and frowned. "You make it out as though those are bad things when most men I know would give anything to have that sort of a life."

John huffed ironically. "I would have agreed with them, until recently."

Arthur wanted to ask what had happened recently, but he knew. He knew, and it left him feeling unsettled and awkward. "Enjoy your good life," he said in a quiet voice. "Not everyone gets one."

They walked for a few more yards, growing ever closer to the inn, before John said, "You're talking about Shinobu, aren't you?"

Arthur couldn't even bring himself to nod. Hearing Shinobu's name on John's lips was like train tracks being crossed at the wrong time with two, powerful locomotives careening toward one another. He'd done so well at separating his past from his present, until now.

"I know you didn't murder him," John said in a steady, measured voice. It was so like him that Arthur nearly laughed. "If you had, you'd be in a prison in Japan right now."

"How do you know I didn't simply get away with it?" he asked.

John sent him a wry sideways grin. The man was gorgeous in the moonlight with his expression so filled with concern and confusion. "You're good, Arthur, but you're not that good."

"Few people have ever used that word when describing me," Arthur laughed.

John didn't call him out for being flippant, or for attempting to change the subject. He just continued to stare at him, patiently waiting for an answer, like the rock he was.

Finally, as they reached the beach in front of the inn, Arthur rubbed his hands over his face, took a deep breath, and said, "I did not murder Shinobu, but I killed him all the same."

He waited for John to have some sort of reaction, to grimace or frown, or even to demand an explanation. The implacable bastard just stood there, arms crossed against the chill in the night air, waiting.

Arthur drew in a long breath, his body beginning to shake as the words rolled around in his mind, preparing themselves to be spoken. When he couldn't stand the buzz they'd created in his brain and his heart for another moment, he blew out the breath and said, "Shinobu killed himself, but it was entirely my fault."

He dragged his eyes up to meet John's, waiting for judgment to rain down.

John blinked. "I'm so sorry. Why do you feel as though it was your fault?"

His voice was too soft, too compassionate, too John. It felt like stinging nettles against Arthur's soul. He turned and marched on to the inn, avoiding the question while old, resurrected emotions that had overruled his thoughts on the subject for so long rattled through him. John followed, of course, and the two of them made their way across the inn's porch, nodding to a lone guest who stood, braving the night air while he had a cigarette, before they stepped inside.

Of course, they couldn't speak about the subject as long as they were in the common areas of the inn, or even in the hallway leading to the room that Arthur now wished to God they weren't sharing, as much of a lark as it had seemed before. He dragged his feet, walking as slowly as he could get away with, until John finally lost his patience and marched ahead, unlocking their door and gesturing for him to move inside.

As soon as the door was shut and locked behind him, John said, "There. You've had more than enough time to figure out your answer. Now, tell me why you think you are responsible for your former lover taking his own life."

Arthur walked as far away from John as he could in the small room before turning toward him. It took another few seconds to raise his eyes to meet John's. "I put him in an impossible position. I insisted he leave

Hiroshi's house, that he come away with me. I said I would bring him back to England with me so that we could live together in peace for the rest of our lives."

John's brow creased in confusion. "That cannot be what caused him to take such extreme actions."

Arthur shook his head, feeling as though his insides were on fire. He prevaricated more by removing his jacket and taking it to the wardrobe, then dragging himself to the bed and sitting on the edge.

"You heard my argument with Hiroshi?" he asked, glancing up at John. It was an even greater distance with him sitting on the bed and John being so much taller than him already.

"Some of it," John nodded.

"Hiroshi is not wrong when he says he owned Shinobu," Arthur confessed. "I still do not entirely understand the system his brothel operated under, but his whores did take an oath to serve him. It wasn't legal, though, only a matter of honor."

"He accused you of having no honor," John said.

Arthur huffed a humorless laugh. "What sort of honor is it to keep a young man like Shinobu in prostitution? It would never be allowed in England. I doubt it was really allowed in Japan. But the entire point of an underworld is that it is outside of the influence of the law."

"So you more or less rescued this lad from a life of prostitution, Hiroshi viewed that as stealing his property, and Shinobu killed himself because of it?" John shook his head in confusion.

Arthur sighed and scrubbed his face. He'd revealed so much, he might as well reveal it all. "The British consulate in Japan refused to grant Shinobu the clearance he needed to return with me to England. I was nearly out of money, and it was made clear to me that I would not be able to find employment or keep the small house I'd purchased in Tokyo. I swore to Shinobu that I would work something out the moment I got home, that I would appeal to whomever I needed to in London to allow him to come to me. I insisted I would hire a solicitor to handle the matter." He gestured to John with an ironic smirk. "Shinobu believed I was abandoning him."

"But you weren't." John surprised Arthur by dropping to his knees in front of him as he sat on the bed. "You didn't abandon him. You did everything you could for him."

Arthur's chest squeezed with a dozen, conflicting emotions. How long had he waited to have the tall, handsome, strong man on his knees for him? Even now, with the compassion in his eyes and the pain Arthur was in, the sight stirred something primal within Arthur.

He shook his head. "I didn't do everything I could. I didn't hide him from Hiroshi when he finally discovered where we were staying. Shinobu was more than just an asset to Hiroshi. I wouldn't go so far as to say he loved Shinobu, but he felt Shinobu was special. When I knew that he was close to discovering us, knew I wouldn't be able to bring Shinobu home to England, instead of warning Shinobu and finding another place for us to go, I did nothing. I figured it would be better for Shinobu to be back under Hiroshi's care than to live on the streets."

"And that led to...his decision?" John asked.

Arthur nodded. "I'd gone out, only for a brief errand. Hiroshi arrived at the house. Instead of letting him in, as Hiroshi demanded, Shinobu slit his own wrists and bled to death. The worst part is that Hiroshi was the one who found him, not me. I wasn't even there to hold him as he died."

His breath caught on his last words, and it took everything he had not to let the tears that stung him flow. He glanced away from John, unwilling to see the pity he knew would be there. He didn't deserve pity; he deserved the misery he felt.

"Oh, Arthur," John sighed, leaning closer to him.

Arthur felt John's warm hands clasp the sides of his head, but the last thing he expected was for John to turn him to face him, then to claim a kiss that took his breath away. It took him utterly by surprise, leaving him breathless and aching.

Whatever John's original intention, the kiss quickly turned feverish. Arthur didn't have it in him to resist as John molded their mouths together, sliding his tongue against Arthur's, and raking his bottom lip with his teeth. It was pure and sweet, but their kiss was also alive with fire and energy. Arthur couldn't stop himself from sliding his hands along John's shoulders as he leaned down to kiss him harder, sighing as he did. At the same time, it was almost laughable. He was the one aroused by the suffering of his lover, and yet it was the pain of his story that had prompted John to kiss him. It was all completely mad.

It turned madder still in an instant. John pushed himself to his feet, but instead of standing, he surged across Arthur, shoving him to his back on the bed and covering him. The change in position and the burst of arousal that shot through Arthur left him disoriented. Lust took over from sense, though, and when John fumbled through the buttons of his jacket and waistcoat, Arthur responded in kind on instinct.

Everything spiraled into chaos from there. John continued to kiss him, and they both groaned with need into each other's mouths. Arthur wasn't entirely certain how they both ended up without their shirts, but he'd waited so long to slide his hands across John's firm chest, to feel the tickle of his chest hair against his palms, and to play his fingers across John's nipples that he didn't care. He wanted more than that and pried his mouth away from John's to taste his neck and his shoulder, biting gently when what he truly wanted was to bite hard.

"I've wanted this for so long," John murmured, sliding his hands down Arthur's stomach to undo the fastenings of his trousers.

Alarm bells started to sound in Arthur's head. He was alive with arousal and groaned when John became distracted halfway through undoing his trousers to stroke

his hard cock over the fabric that constricted it. Part of
Arthur wanted to return the favor, to slip his hand
beneath John's waistband to stroke his cock and tug his
balls, perhaps hard enough to make John wince in beautiful pain, but it was all wrong. It was too delicious, too
perfect. John was making him feel too much too fast.
Arthur wasn't used to being on his back, to being the once
receiving the attention. He certainly wasn't prepared to
have John shower him with what Arthur was certain the
man believed was love.

"No," he gasped, pushing John away. A brief panic
filled him as he realized how much bigger than him John
was and how John had leverage and gravity working in
his favor to hold him down. "No," he said, louder,
pushing harder. "Get off me."

John stumbled back, lust-drunk and bleary. His
trousers were tented, and his beautiful body was
flushed with need. If Arthur had been a lesser man, he
would have changed his mind at the temptation that
stood before him and dragged John back for more. It
was too powerful, though. He couldn't breathe, couldn't
feel himself think. He wasn't ready to be turned inside
out and made into something John would actually
want.

"Arthur?" John's brow knit in confusion as he fought
to catch his breath.

Arthur didn't look at him as he rolled to the side and
off the bed. He reached for his shirt, waistcoat, and
jacket, thankful that John hadn't removed his shoes or

undone his trousers entirely, and moved to the far corner of the room to dress as quickly as he could.

"I can't," he said over his shoulder, hurrying with his clothes. "I can't do it." He hated himself for the way his words came out as a wail.

"I...I don't understand," John said, shifting anxiously from side to side and pushing a hand through his hair. "I thought you wanted me."

Arthur winced, heart feeling as though it would tear itself to shreds in his chest. "I don't want your pity," he said, forcing himself to sound angry instead of hurt. "There's nothing arousing or flattering about a pity fuck."

"That wasn't what—"

"I don't want you like this," Arthur cut him off, spinning to face him. "I don't want you to make me feel good and nice and desired."

John's mouth worked wordlessly, and he blinked rapidly in confusion, as if he were a machine that Arthur had broken. Along with the confusion in John's eyes was a painful amount of hurt. The man truly had wanted him. He had wanted to help.

"This is not what I want," Arthur repeated, unable to stand still, his grief and misery and guilt were so torturous. "None of this was what I wanted."

He didn't want to be responsible for a good man's death back then, and he didn't want to be responsible for another good man's disappointment now.

"I can't stay here," he said, shooting past John to the door.

"Wait, no, you can stay, I'll go," John said.

Arthur glared at him, furious that John was trying to be so magnanimous, so caring.

"I just want you to be happy," John insisted. "I want to help you find some peace."

Arthur barked a laugh. "Impossible," he said, his voice hoarse.

He threw open the door and dashed out into the hall, praying John knew what was best for him and wouldn't follow.

By the time he made it down to the porch, then on to the beach, he groaned in misery, heartbroken that John hadn't followed him after all. It didn't make a lick of sense, but then, nothing in his life had made sense since Shinobu's death. Nothing had given him peace or taken away the gnawing pain of knowing he'd failed a man he loved at the very moment when failure was not an option. It didn't matter how strong or noble John was, he would never be able to free him from the pain he'd caused himself.

CHAPTER 9

*J*ohn waited for Arthur to come back. He moved to retrieve his shirt, but instead of putting it on, he just held it as he sat on the edge of the bed, staring at the door. Arthur would come back—he was certain of it. They'd shared something deep and profound. Arthur had opened his heart and shared the story of the most horrifying event he'd ever lived through. One didn't simply run away and never come back after revealing one's soul like that.

As soon as the thought struck John, he sighed, let his shoulders droop, and tossed his shirt on the bureau across from the bed. What sort of a high-handed fool was he for wedging himself into the most important thing that had ever happened to Arthur, an event that had happened ages before they'd met? Except that he'd seen first-hand how deep Arthur's emotional turmoil had been and couldn't shake the feeling the man was reaching out to him somehow. He'd felt it in the way Arthur had kissed him, with so much passion that he hadn't been certain he'd be able to match it. No, he knew he couldn't match it. He couldn't match Arthur's fire, and because of that, he was deeply worried that fire would burn both of them to cinders, or burn out before he could grasp it.

With a deep exhale, John flopped to his back on the bed, arms spread for a moment, before rubbing his face with both hands. Even now, his heart raced for Arthur, and not just with the concern of friendship. He'd been exactly where he wanted to be, kneeling in front of the man and kissing him until he couldn't think of anything else. He'd loved the feel of Arthur's body under his hands and the taste of his skin. But more than that, he'd loved the way he'd been able to feed off of Arthur's fire, doing things he never would have dreamed of doing before. The intensity of Arthur's emotions had made him as hard as iron, even though those emotions had been pain and misery.

"What is wrong with me?" John sighed up to the ceiling. Love was supposed to be sweet and comforting. It was supposed to be a soft place to land, not a raging battle and a walk across hot coals.

Arthur didn't come back immediately, so John got up and undressed, washing for the night, brushing his teeth, donning his nightshirt, and doing every banal, domestic task he would have done if he'd been at home. Arthur still didn't return when he climbed into bed with a book he'd selected from the small library at the inn and flipped through its pages. Arthur *still* hadn't returned by the time he realized how fussy and missish it was of him to be in bed with a book before ten at night. He tossed the book aside, settled deeper into the bed with his hands behind his head, staring at the door and wondering whether he should remove his nightshirt so that he would be naked when Arthur did finally return.

With that question in his mind, he fell asleep, head still turned toward the door. When he awoke, it was already light out, and sounds of the inn's other guests moving about indicated to him it was morning. As sleep dragged itself away from him, John jerked up from where he'd curled onto his side and glanced around the room. The bed beside him had been slept in, and Arthur was seated in the chair next to the window, fully dressed and groomed, drinking coffee and reading the book John had discarded the night before.

"Good morning, sleepyhead," Arthur said in his sly, teasing voice, as though nothing at all were wrong and no confessions had been made the night before. He glanced across at John after he finished speaking, his usual spark of wickedness in his eyes.

John dragged himself to sit with his back against the headboard and wiped the sleep from his eyes. "What time is it?" he mumbled.

"Just past eight," Arthur said, setting the book aside carelessly and taking a long sip of coffee. "You were done in last night and slept like a babe, even when I tried to molest you into waking up."

John glanced quickly down at himself under the covers. Other than his usual morning tumescence, he didn't feel as though he'd been molested. He rather wished he did. But, of course, Arthur was merely toying with him as a means of separating himself from the emotions and confessions of the night before.

John let out a breath. "How are you this morning?" he asked, full of affection and concern.

Arthur's teasing grin dropped, and he rolled his eyes as he stood. "Don't start that up again," he warned. "I have nothing more to say on the subject." He crossed to the bureau and fiddled with their combined toiletries with one hand while drinking his coffee with the other.

John frowned slightly, aggravated that Arthur was hiding from his pain, and even worse, hiding it from him. He threw aside the bedcovers and stood. "Arthur, we weren't finished talking about things last night," he said carefully.

Arthur stared at him, offended. "Yes, we were," he insisted.

John clenched his jaw in frustration and pushed a hand through his hair, which he was certain stuck out at odd angles. "We weren't finished with other things either," he said in a quiet voice, doing his best to glance coyly at Arthur.

He was terrible at seduction, though, which he realized when Arthur snorted and said, "We were done with your version of it, at any rate."

John's initial reaction was to feel hurt by the

comment. He blinked and considered it, and a few seconds later, he wasn't certain if Arthur had intended his words as an insult or not. He wasn't certain whether Arthur was upset or whether he thought less of him now, or whether the opposite was true and Arthur felt more, but was trying to hide it. He wasn't certain of anything.

"Thank you for sharing your past with me," he said, crossing to the wardrobe and taking out clean clothes for the day. "It meant a great deal to me."

"I'm sure it did." Arthur walked away when John stepped near to him, heading back to the window and glancing out. "Now you have all the excuses you need to move past your sordid fascination with me and to resume your upright life."

John frowned at him over his shoulder as he slipped on a pair of drawers under his nightshirt. "It's too late," he said. When Arthur turned to him in question—his expression lighting with interest for a moment as John removed his nightshirt—he went on with, "I have learned that you grow prickles and say rude things as a way to ward people off when they get too close to your heart. I won't be chased off by insults I know you don't mean, so you can give up trying."

"How can you be so certain I don't mean what I say?" Arthur glowered.

John finished pulling up his trousers, fastened them, then crossed the room in a few, long strides so that he could take Arthur's face in his hands. Arthur was too stunned by the movement to resist as John slanted his mouth over his and kissed him searingly. He responded before his defensive instincts could fight back, sinking into John and returning the kiss for a moment. When John felt the first stirrings of resistance tighten Arthur's body, he ended the kiss and stepped back, returning to the side of the bed where his clothes were laid out.

"That's how I know," he said with a sly grin.

"You're a bastard, John Dandie," Arthur growled, finishing the coffee that he somehow hadn't spilled while John was kissing him, setting the cup aside, then wiping the back of his hand over his mouth, as though he could wipe away John's kiss. "I don't want your pity. You're a fool if you think our interest in each other is anything other than carnal. I want to fuck you, I always have, and you want to be fucked. Stop pretending this thing between us is anything more than that."

John smirked at him as he pulled his clean shirt over his head and did up the buttons. Arthur's actions and his words contradicted themselves, which filled John with a sense of satisfaction and calm. He could fight and protest all he wanted, but there was more than just lust between the two of them, especially now.

"It's alright, Arthur," he said, tucking in his shirt, then lifting his suspenders over his shoulders. He crossed back to Arthur, resting a hand on the side of the man's surly face. "I understand you so much better now. I can see your pain for what it is, and I want nothing more than to alleviate it. I do not judge you for your past or for your present. I merely wish to help you heal from all of your wounds."

John was rather proud of himself for the care and sentiment of his speech. Arthur, on the other hand, screwed up his face and sneered at him in disgust.

"What sort of self-serving tripe was that?" he barked with a grimace. "I'm a grown man who has lived a life that would make you blanche. Don't go dressing me up in girlish sentiment and making me out to be some hapless victim of a sensational novel that needs a strong, handsome hero to come rescue me from a tower."

He made a sound as though he'd eaten something sour, then marched past John and straight out the door into the hallway.

All of the feelings of hope and contentment John had felt while making the speech fell flat. He dropped his arms and stared at the door for a moment, then crossed to don his waistcoat and jacket. On reflection, perhaps he had been a bit too condescending. But dammit, he just wanted Arthur to see that he cared, that the man was safe with him, that he could be trusted with feelings and pain. Arthur was being a stubborn prick.

He brushed his hair quickly, selected and tied a necktie, put on his shoes, cursing the tiny details of appearance for taking so long, then headed out of the room and downstairs in search of Arthur. He found him, along with Blake and Niall, smiling as though nothing were out of the ordinary. Arthur didn't so much as blink when John joined the small group.

"Ah, there you are, John," Blake greeted him with a smile that was so much happier than John had seen from him in months. "We were about to come fetch you so that we could all head over to the Cannon mansion together."

John's brow lifted in surprise. "Isn't it a bit early for a call?" he asked.

"Not when I am calling on my son," Blake said, beaming with pride. "We intend to take him for a walk along the beach this morning so that he can get to know Niall a bit better. The girls consider Niall a second father now, of course, but Alan needs to become better acquainted with him."

Niall sent Blake as open a look of affection as he could in the public space of the inn. John smiled, but he had his doubts about whether the two of them would be allowed to simply walk off with Alan in order to spend time together. It wasn't his decision to make. He glanced instinctively to Arthur to see what the man thought, but Arthur was staring out the window as if something had caught his attention.

"I think it would be a good idea for you and Gleason to come with us," Niall added. "I don't think Cannon would try anything underhanded at this point, but it would be wise for Blake to have his solicitor on hand all the same."

"Agreed," John said. He didn't have anything else to do. If they'd been in the city, he could have found any number of entertainments, but Peconic was not exactly a hub of tourist activity.

"Shall we walk up the beach to reach Cannon's?" Blake asked.

They all agreed, and headed out of the inn toward the beach and along the sand to the Cannon mansion. Blake and Niall fell into step together, and John could practically see how desperately they wanted to hold hands and enjoy the final, happy chapter of their tumultuous last few months. Out of respect, John held back, giving them space, but that also meant he was able to have his own space with Arthur.

"Where did you go last night?" he asked as the breeze off the sound ruffled their hair and sea birds circled above, crying out to each other.

Arthur scowled at him. "Are you my nanny now as well as my tormentor?"

John ignored him. "You were deeply upset. I assume you merely needed time to think things through. A beach at night seems like the perfect place to do that."

"I'm not a character—" Arthur stopped in the middle of his protest, shaking his head and shoving his hands into his pockets. He was silent for a few minutes before huffing, "I hate all this maudlin concern for me. I hate that you feel you have a right to intrude on the sacred space of my past."

John's brow inched up, and he turned to stare at Arthur. "What's this? An honest statement from the terrible and salacious Detective Arthur Gleason?"

"Fuck off," Arthur grumbled, hunching his shoulders a bit.

John smiled as though Arthur had whispered terms of endearment. "You can rail at me all you'd like and insist that you don't like me and that you hate the fact that I genuinely care about you, but I don't believe it."

Arthur whipped to him as though he could come back with a sharp retort, but instead, he stayed silent for several minutes. He only broke his silence as they reached the small boardwalk leading to the Cannon's back porch to say, "I despise concern and condescension of any kind."

"It's not condescension," John said, keeping his voice down, as Mr. and Mrs. Cannon, Alan, Stone, and two maids were already present on the porch. "But I do care about you, Arthur. Excessively."

Arthur only had time to grimace before their group mounted the stairs to join the others on the porch. Cannon looked surprised to see them, but Mrs. Cannon blanched outright and attempted to waylay Alan as he broke away from where they sat having tea on a white, wicker sofa to run to his father.

"Papa!" Alan cried out in joy, flinging himself into Blake's arms.

"My darling boy, how are you this morning?" Blake lifted him and squeezed him tight.

"I am well. Grandmama said we would fly kites this morning, since there's wind, and Lucy will help." When Alan turned back to the group of women, one of the maids curtsied, her eyes wide, as though curtsying to a duke was a grand treat.

"I was hoping we could go for a walk on our own," Blake said, glancing from Alan to Niall to Cannon.

Mrs. Cannon pushed herself up from her sofa and scurried over to rest a hand on Alan's back. "I...I don't think that's a good idea. Dear Alan has become so used to his new home here. That is, he has become used to visiting us. Perhaps it's best not to confuse the boy just now."

"I want to go with Papa," Alan told her.

John winced at the whole, uncomfortable confrontation, though he was impressed with the restraint Blake showed, all things considered.

"You know I am grateful for the care and attention you have shown my son while he has been staying with you, Mrs. Cannon," he said, "but he is still my son, and we have been apart for too long."

"But he is my grandson," Mrs. Cannon argued. "And I have not seen him for most of his life. There are so many things I wish to do with him before you take the boy away from me forever." She suddenly raised a hand to her face, as if to stifle a sob.

"It does not have to be forever, ma'am," Blake said, trying to smile at her. "You are more than welcome to come visit our family in London, and I would be open to all of us, the girls included, coming to visit at some time in the future."

"I wish to spend all the time I can with dear Alan, though," Mrs. Cannon argued. "If you take him away from me all day for these last few days—"

"Dash it, Roberta," Cannon interrupted, startling John, who had become deeply invested in watching the sentimental drama unfolding in front of him. "This sort of behavior is unbecoming." Cannon walked away from Stone, with whom he had been having some sort of a discussion at the other end of the porch. "There is a simple solution to this entire mess. Invite Lord Selby to stay with us for the remainder of his time here. That way, you can both lavish all of your attention on the boy."

Mrs. Cannon's expression flashed from surprise to delight. "Why, yes, that would be a cheerful solution. Please do stay with us, Lord Selby."

"I...." Blake glanced to Niall, who was doing an admirable job of hiding his feelings on the matter. "I would only be amenable to staying here if my friends were also allowed to stay."

The corner of John's mouth twitched, but he managed to keep himself from grinning at Blake's clever tactic. If all three of them were invited to stay, that would lessen the possibility of suspicion over Blake and Niall's relationship. Not that Cannon didn't already know. Blake had hinted as much to him before. John couldn't tell from her demeanor whether Mrs. Cannon knew.

Mrs. Cannon answered without hesitation. "Yes, of course. This is such a large house, and it's so much merrier when it is filled. I would be happy to host you as well, Mr. Cristofori, Mr. Dandie, Mr. Gleason."

"Thank you, ma'am." John bowed to her with a smile, then peeked at Arthur.

Strangely, Arthur didn't look at all pleased with the arrangement, but he still expressed his thanks. It only took a moment—and the arrival of Hiroshi on the porch—for John to realize what his reticence was.

Stranger still, Cannon seemed suddenly on alert when Hiroshi stepped into sight. He scanned the length of the porch quickly, then said, "Mr. Dandie, Det. Gleason, might I have a word with you?"

John exchanged a look with Arthur that wasn't latent with emotion and lust, for a change. "Certainly, sir." He checked with Blake, who nodded, then he and Arthur moved to the far end of the porch with Cannon.

It was the same end of the porch where he and Stone had been speaking earlier, but Stone was gone. As they reached that corner, Cannon gestured for Hiroshi to join them. Arthur's expression instantly went stony. John carefully positioned himself as a buffer between him and Hiroshi.

"Can I be of assistance, sir?" Hiroshi asked when the four of them were clustered together.

Cannon nodded, but instead of addressing Hiroshi directly, he said, "As you may have gleaned from supper last night, I have a few reservations about Mr. Stone."

"What sort of reservations?" John asked, immediately sensing his skills as a solicitor were being called upon.

"I believe it was mentioned that I am considering going into business with the man, perhaps merging our companies," Cannon said. "But as you saw, Stone is not precisely...." He paused as if searching for a proper way to phrase it. "I am uncertain whether it would be a safe investment," he went on at last. "I cannot tell if the man actually has a head for business or if the mines he owned fell into his lap by sheer luck. Further, I have been unable to ascertain whether he is a man of his word who deals fairly with his colleagues or if he is a liar and a cheat."

"I see," John said with a serious nod. "And I take it you would like our help in the matter?"

Cannon nodded. "If your duke friend hadn't insisted all four of you stay here with us for the next week or so, I would have. You are a solicitor," he looked at John. "You are a detective," he turned his gaze to Arthur. "I feel as though I could use your skills to determine whether Stone is a good investment or not. Will you do it? Will you accept the hospitality of a free vacation in exchange for wheedling the information I want out of Mr. Stone?"

Before either John or Arthur could answer, Hiroshi interrupted with, "Sir, I believe this is the sort of task you would usually entrust to me." John could see the bitterness behind his words as clear as day.

"Usually it would be," Cannon said with a shrug. "But as long as we have a real detective here, why not have all of you work together?"

Hiroshi and Arthur stared daggers at each other for a moment before both men had the good sense to hide their reactions.

"As you wish, sir." Hiroshi bowed graciously, but a blind man could have seen how much he resented being told he had to work together with Arthur.

"I shall do my best for you, Mr. Cannon," Arthur said, his voice strained, as he nodded to Cannon.

"Good." Cannon clapped his hands together. "That's settled then. I think my wife has already sent her maid in to prepare rooms for you all. Since we're not anywhere close to having a full house, I'll make certain you all have the best rooms, the ones that face the sound."

"Thank you, sir," John said. "That is most generous."

"I'd better get back to my wife now," Cannon went on, "before she vexes Lord Selby to death. She wants to keep the boy, of course, but I can assure you that I won't let her. Selby is a pervert. I would never have let my daughter marry him if I'd known. My wife doesn't know anything about it, of course. She's too innocent and wouldn't understand that the boy is probably tainted. That disease is inherited, after all." He sniffed. "I don't want her so much as touching the man or that playwright. The sooner Selby and his...friend leave, the sooner we can all get back to our usual lives."

In a paradox Cannon couldn't possibly understand, he thumped John's back before nodding, smiling, and striding back down the porch to rejoin the party there. John sent a look of wary amusement Arthur's way, but Arthur was too busy glaring at Hiroshi to catch it.

"So we're working together now, are we?" Arthur asked Hiroshi.

Hiroshi's jaw was clenched so hard John thought it might snap. He said nothing at all before turning and striding back into the house. Arthur's anger as he watched the man go was palpable, and when he sensed John watching him, that anger turned on him.

"And just what do you think you're looking at?" he snapped before turning and marching away himself.

John let out a breath and squeezed his eyes shut for a moment. He was uncertain whether Cannon had just done them all a favor or whether he'd thrust them into some new circle of hell.

CHAPTER 10

*I*t boggled Arthur's mind how quickly everything in his life had spun out of control. Working with Hiroshi, whatever the task was—and Cannon's request was something he could accomplish in his sleep—was tantamount to being asked to cut off his arm and prepare it as a nice roast for supper. It was only a small consolation that Hiroshi was obviously just as furious about their pairing as he was. But Arthur had a job to do, and his pride dictated that he would do it, come hell or high water. He had never let down a client before, and now that he saw Cannon as his latest client, he would be damned if he let anything get in the way of doing his job with perfection.

"It looks as though we'll all be relocating here," John said, sounding entirely too pleased with himself, as they rejoined Lord Selby, Cristofori, and the others. "Thank you so much for your hospitality, Mrs. Cannon."

"Yes, thank you," Arthur added. John wasn't the only one who could display proper manners when handed a boon. "We will endeavor to be the perfect houseguests."

"Thank you, Mr. Gleason, Mr. Dandie," Mrs. Cannon said, attempting to smile, but she was too busy staring anxiously at Lord Selby and his son as they finished their tea.

Cristofori sent John a look as though making note of what they would have to deal with for the next few days. "I suppose we should head back to the inn to pack our things," he said.

"That's what I was thinking," John said, glancing to Arthur.

Arthur felt everything in that look. He felt the compassion John was so intent on showing him. He felt the affection that part of him wanted to return and the rest of him screamed to reject. He also felt the sheer practicality of doing all the things they'd been asked to do as efficiently as possible. Arthur had watched John's expression as Cannon had commissioned them to investigate Stone. There had been more relief in John's face than Arthur suspected John was aware of. No matter what else irritated or unsettled him about John, the man was devoted to his work and the people he served. It was one thing they had in common. One thing.

"I'll just go get a start on packing my things," he said, nodding to Mrs. Cannon to make his goodbyes. He deliberately didn't look at John before striding to the porch stairs and making his way back to the beach.

"I'll accompany you," John said, hurrying to follow him. Because, of course, he would.

"I'll be along in a moment," Cristofori called after them. Arthur just barely heard him add, "If you give me your room key, I can pack your things with you so that you can spend more time with your son."

Arthur smirked at that as John caught up to him on the beach. "Mrs. Cannon is in for a shock if she ever discovers Lord Selby and Cristofori are devoted to each other." He spoke without waiting to see if John was in a mood for conversation or not. John was always in a mood for conversation. He needed it the same way a plant needed water to keep growing.

"Just as Cannon is in for a shock if he ever learns the truth about the rest of us," John added with a chuckle.

Arthur allowed himself to share that humor for a moment. A moment of letting his guard down couldn't hurt. "Men like Cannon have always amused me. They're the sort who don't even bother to moralize about our sort because they assume there are so few of us and that the ones who do exist are blatantly effeminate. If he knew the truth about our numbers and our presentation, he wouldn't know what to do with himself."

"True," John laughed. "And I consider myself lucky, in a way, that I'm the sort that no one generally discerns the truth about." He glanced sideways at Arthur. "You are too."

Arthur frowned. "Is that supposed to mean something I should be offended by?"

"Not at all," John said with a shrug. "It is a statement of fact."

Arthur narrowed his eyes slightly, intrinsically feeling as though John were about to use that statement as a jumping off point for an entirely different conversation that he didn't want to have. John was glaringly obvious in the way he let his thoughts shine through his eyes.

Sure enough, after a minute's pause, as they continued down the chilly beach, John said, "It is also a statement of fact that you are not the sort of man I would typically find myself attracted to, and yet I find you as irresistible as a moth does a flame."

Arthur nearly missed a step. "That *is* an insult," he said with a scowl.

"I beg your pardon?" It was John's turn to stumble in confusion.

Arthur snorted and shook his head. "That statement is akin to Mr. Darcy telling Elizabeth that he likes her in spite of his misgivings."

For some reason, John's face lit with delight. "Are you saying that you have read Jane Austen?"

Arthur scowled. Everything he did or said in order to push John away only seemed to draw the man in more, dammit. Perhaps he truly was like a moth drawn to a flame. Flames generally had a tendency to destroy the moths.

"I have read a great many things," he growled. "One tends to read on a naval ship between hours of duty, and generally there is not much choice as to reading material."

"I see," John said with a nod and a poorly concealed smile.

That seemed to be the end of the conversation, for which Arthur was grateful. He was uncomfortable talking with John now in a way that he hadn't been until all of his confessions were made. He no longer felt as though he had the upper hand, no longer felt like they were playing a game of cat and mouse. Cat and mouse he understood. Friendship was a whole different beast. Love was so far out of the question that it caused his spine to prickle and his skin to break out in hives at the very thought. If he were smart, he would invent some errand he needed to run, peel away from John, and spend some time alone so that he could get his bearings again.

Those thoughts in mind, he contradicted everything he thought that he wanted by opening a new conversation with John.

"Investigating Stone should be child's play," he said.

"I do believe I agree with you on that score," John said with a nod. "Cannon merely wishes to know if the man is honest and if he'd make a good business partner."

"We should be able to determine that with a few, quick conversations. Stone seems like the sort who would spill all of his thoughts to a stranger," Arthur said.

Of all the morsels John could have picked out of Arthur's statements, the bastard had to raise an eyebrow and ask, "We?"

Arthur scowled at him. "In case your memory is so deficient that you have immediately forgotten, Cannon commissioned three of us for this case."

Blast him, but John's eyes danced with mirth that made him nearly irresistible. His shapely mouth twitched into a smile, and Arthur instantly imagined all of the other things that mouth could do. He truly had gone deranged if his thoughts headed in that direction at a time when he felt at his weakest.

"We work well together," John said, more than a hint of suggestion in his eyes.

Arthur's nerves went taut. What game was the man playing, being businesslike one moment, far too sympathetic the next, and seductive one second later? Arthur needed time to breathe, space to sort himself out. He hated being so far on the back foot.

"Many men do," he said with a frown.

John threw him off again by saying, "But not you and Hiroshi?"

Arthur scowled at him. "Do not start that game again, John. I am well aware of the strain I will be under, being forced to work with a former rival and a sworn enemy. You may not use this as an excuse to dredge up my past once more and tell me how deeply you pity me for my pain."

John blinked and drew back. "That was not my intention at all," he said, clearly trying not to be offended.

Arthur laughed and shook his head. "You relish the opportunity to pity me," he said, keeping his voice down, as they were approaching the inn and more of its guests were idling away on the back porch than had been the evening before. "If you can pity me, that means you don't have to feel intimidated by me."

"I am not intimidated by you," John said, glancing furtively around as they headed from the beach to the inn. "You use intimidation as a weapon to keep anyone from growing close enough to you to see the man underneath the monster."

Arthur laughed again, drawing a few startled looks from guests as they passed into the inn. There wasn't as much confidence behind his laugh as he wanted there to be, though. He had the unsettling feeling as though John had picked the lock on a box in which he'd been hiding away secrets and now he was gazing at things Arthur wanted to keep to himself.

They traveled the rest of the way up to their room in silence, but Arthur knew full well that wouldn't be the end of it.

"You can talk to me about the discomfort of being made to work with your enemy, you know," John said, back to his good man voice, as soon as they were alone in the room.

The maid hadn't been yet, which suited Arthur just fine. He was more comfortable with the space being slightly mussed and the bed wrinkled instead of having everything as perfect and pristine as John always tried to be.

"Aren't you just the perfect, sympathetic friend,"

Arthur grumbled. If he were honest with himself, a part of him enjoyed it. No one had ever cared so much for his feelings in his entire life. Shinobu had been too young—and so had he, for that matter—to have a grasp on anything half so complex. The rest of him bristled at the idea of letting anyone, even a gorgeous, kind man, interrupt his independence.

John stared flatly at him as he lifted his empty suitcase down from the top of the wardrobe and set it on the chair under the window to pack. "You don't have to constantly push me away, you know," he said. "It doesn't make you any less of a man to accept the caring of another."

Arthur had just lifted his traveling bag up from the corner beside the bureau, where he'd stored it the day before, and slammed it on top of the bureau with such force that he knocked his hairbrush and a jar of pomade to the floor. "And you don't constantly have to push yourself on me, as if sentiment will solve everything."

"What else am I supposed to do to show you that I care about you?" John argued, crossing the room to throw open the wardrobe. "God sakes, Arthur. You're like an entire patch of nettles that stings anyone who dares to come near enough to touch it."

"Because I despise being touched," Arthur growled, yanking open the bureau's top drawer and plunking a handful of his undergarments into his traveling bag.

John laughed without humor. "That was not the impression I had last night."

Something about the smarmy, knowing way John made the statement boiled Arthur's blood, in more ways than one. He slammed the drawer shut and turned to John.

"Is that what you want this to be about?" he demanded. "Do you want us to have a lovely, passionate romance, like Lord Selby and Cristofori?"

"Would that really be so bad?" John asked with a frown that contradicted the suddenly tender note in his voice.

"It's not who I am, and the sooner you understand that, the sooner you will see that I can never be who you want, can never give you what you want. I am incapable of basic human connection."

Arthur was surprised by the vehemence in his voice, but it felt right. It felt as though he'd finally cracked through to the heart of the matter. John wanted romance and sentiment. He was only capable of harshness and pain.

"I don't believe that for an instant," John told him, laughing almost cavalierly.

Something inside of Arthur snapped. He would not simply stand by and let John take away the scales and the armor and the prickles that he had built up in order to survive the assault of his emotions for so many years. He could not live with John believing something about him that wasn't true.

He acted without letting himself think, crossing to where John stood at the wardrobe, slamming the door shut and nearly crushing John's hand in the process, then grabbing the man and spinning him until his back hit the wardrobe so hard it stunned him. When John was still stunned and sagging enough so that their faces were level, Arthur crashed into him with a kiss that was designed to bruise his lips and steal the air from his lungs. He took that a step further, squeezing a hand against John's throat so that he truly couldn't breathe while Arthur savaged his mouth, claiming his tongue and biting his lip. If John wanted him, then it was damn well time he discovered the truth about the man he wanted.

When he moved his hand to rip through the buttons of John's jacket and waistcoat, John gasped for breath, then coughed slightly. That was all Arthur allowed him before smacking into him with another kiss for as long as it took to finish with the buttons and shove John's jacket down his shoulders. With deft skill, he yanked John forward, throwing him off-balance, and pulled his jacket down his arms just enough to trap his arms behind his back.

He'd manhandled a lover this way in a prearranged, passionate play scene before, but with John, knowing he hadn't agreed to it and didn't know what to expect, the whole thing took on a whole new level of intensity. And arousal. Arthur jerked him away from the wardrobe and pushed John face down on the bed so that he could tie the sleeves of his jacket in such a way that John wouldn't be able to free himself easily. His heart pounded and his cock sprang to life in the confines of his trousers at John's gasp of fear.

"Is this what you've been looking for?" he growled against John's ear as he pressed the man down to the bed, yanking John's shirt out of his trousers. "Is this the beautiful, romantic love affair that you've been pining for since the moment you met me? Am I your perfect lover now?"

"I—"

Arthur didn't give him time to answer. He flipped John to his back, trapping his hands behind him in a way that lifted his hips up, and detached his suspenders before tearing his way through the fastenings of John's trousers. John gaped at him, stunned, but also more aroused than Arthur had ever seen him. The fire of lust and excitement burned brightly in John's eyes, which only spurred Arthur on more. Dammit, the man wasn't supposed to enjoy being savaged. He was pristine, perfect John Dandie.

He was the most beautiful thing Arthur had ever seen. He couldn't help but shove John's shirt up as high as he could push it with John's arms restrained behind him so that he could kiss and lick and bite John's chest and stomach. The short, sharp pants and groans that issued from John as Arthur sucked hard, leaving marks, before sliding his tongue up so that he could lave one of John's nipples and then bite it was too good. It was everything Arthur had wanted, and it was a nightmare.

John could not possibly be enjoying the point he was trying to make. He couldn't leave the confrontation before Arthur had exploded every one of his sweet little fantasies about what the two of them might be like together. The two of them were as mismatched as oil and chalk, and John had to be forced to see that.

Arthur rocked back, finishing with the fastenings of John's trousers and jerking them off as brutally as he could. Arthur couldn't decide if it was a victory or defeat when John's thick, hard cock jumped to life, slapping against his belly, already damp at the tip with precum. The sight drove Arthur wild, but not for the reasons he wanted it to. He tugged John's trousers down to his knees, immobilizing him even more, then leaned down to take John's cock in his mouth.

John let out a cry of pleasure and bucked into Arthur's mouth as well as he could with limited movement. It was carnal and raw, and Arthur groaned as he flicked his tongue over John's leaking tip before bearing down on him as deeply as he could. John moaned wildly, writhing under Arthur as if he would climb right out of his skin.

"Do you like that?" Arthur demanded, fisting John after removing his mouth, then reaching down to squeeze John's balls harder than would be comfortable. "Do you like being owned like this?" John grunted and moaned as Arthur increased the pressure on his balls until his face pinched with pain. "They're not so sweet, the things I like, are they?"

He kept his hand clamped around John's balls, then bent to take John's cock into his mouth again. The mix of conflicting sensations, pleasure and pain, had John jerking his hips and gasping, as if he didn't know what he felt. It was gorgeous, and Arthur wanted more. He wanted everything he could take from John and then some.

He could tell when John was close to coming and pushed away just before John could find that release. John protested wordlessly, but Arthur was far from done. He crouched to remove John's shoes, then yanked his trousers all the way off once they were gone. From there, he straightened again and manhandled John to his stomach with his hips just off the bed. He kicked John's legs wide apart, then grabbed his hips and jerked them up, leaving John in a completely exposed and vulnerable position.

"If you move, I'll hurt you," Arthur threatened him.

To prove his point, when John shifted just a tiny bit, Arthur brought his hand crashing down on John's arse, then a second time just because he could. John let out a sound that was far too much like ecstasy for Arthur's liking. He was supposed to be scaring the man off for good, not pleasuring him.

More determined than ever to put an end to things the hard way, Arthur grabbed the jar of ointment he had in his traveling bag and tossed it on the bed on the side John had his head turned toward. It was the only hint Arthur was willing to give about what John could expect as he threw off his jacket and undid the fastenings of his trousers. John's breath turned sharp and frantic, and he writhed against the bed.

"I said not to move," Arthur shouted, smacking his arse hard again.

John made a muffled sound as Arthur reached for the jar and unscrewed the top. Not intending to show any mercy, Arthur kicked John's legs farther apart as he slicked himself, then tossed the jar aside. He grabbed John's arse cheeks possessively and pulled them open, intending to frighten John as much as he could by indicating he had absolutely no control over what was about to happen. John's legs trembled, and his breath came in shallow pants, but when Arthur pushed hard into him, even though he met with a moment of resistance as the ring of muscle around his hole fought back, John let out a cry of pleasure the likes of which Arthur had never heard before. Before he could stop himself, Arthur had joined in with those cries of pleasure as perfect, glorious sensations shot through his entire body, bringing him dangerously close to the edge already. He leaned forward and bit into John's shoulder, but that only had John moaning and gasping for new reasons.

He didn't want it to end, especially without making his point. He pulled back, flipping John roughly to his back again, then scooped his arms under John's knees, wrenching them up until John's arse was in the air. He rested one of John's ankles on his shoulder for a minute so that he could use a hand to help guide his cock back to John's hole, but once he was deep inside again as John let out another wild sound of pleasure and surrender, Arthur grabbed John's ankles and held them up and out.

The result put John in a vulnerable and embarrassing position of openness as Arthur thrust hard into him, over and over, with everything he had. Instead of being afraid or ashamed or struggling to get free, John's face was a mask of ecstasy as Arthur fucked him. It wasn't even close to the sweet and tender sort of lovemaking Arthur had been so certain John wanted from him. It was brutal and violent, John was helpless and completely under Arthur's control, and with a cry that would probably have the inn's staff calling the police to have them taken away on charges of indecency, John came all over his stomach and chest in messy waves that surprised Arthur with their intensity. And neither of them had even been touching John's cock.

It was too much for Arthur to fight against. He grunted, tipping his head back as his orgasm slammed into him. It was far, far better than it should have been, shaking him to his soul and washing him with pleasure as he filled John. It was so much more than he thought he wanted, since the entire purpose of fucking that way was to show John how incompatible they were and how much of a villain he was.

Arthur's head was spinning and he couldn't seem to draw enough air into his lungs as he finished, still inside of John and leaning against him. For the first time in the whole, mad episode, their eyes met. John was stunned and reeling, but the fire was still there in his eyes, not as if everything between them had just come crashing down, but as if a whole new chapter had just begun.

Furious that nothing had gone to plan and pulsing with a fresh, confusing set of emotions that layered salt on the wounds of everything else he felt, Arthur pulled back with a growl. He flipped John roughly back to his stomach, slapped the man's arse hard one more time, then turned away, not wanting to see how the man's body reacted to him leaving it or to see the first pinches of anger and betrayal when John got over the pleasure and realized what they'd done. He rushed through cleaning up as quickly as he could and setting his clothes to right. From there, he tossed all of the rest of his clothes and toiletries into his traveling bag, then dashed out of the room as though it were on fire.

He didn't once look back at John. Every ounce of his effort had gone into pushing the man away, but instead, he felt tied to John now with knots he didn't think he'd ever be able to untangle.

CHAPTER 11

*J*ohn vaguely heard Arthur shuffling around the room, opening and closing drawers and throwing his belongings into his traveling bag, but he was too stunned over what had just happened to do anything about it. Stunned, breathless, and desperately attempting to maintain a hold on every physical and emotional sensation he felt in the wake of what was easily the most magnificent and invigorating sexual experience of his life.

The door opened and closed as Arthur left without a word. John could feel the tension radiating from Arthur, even though he was face-down on the bed with Arthur out of his line of sight. That tension only lessened a bit after Arthur was gone. John closed his eyes and tried to recapture it, tried to recapture the intensity of the moment, as he finished catching his breath.

His shoulders were sore from being wrenched back and held in the constrains of his jacket, but he made no move to untangle his arms and stretch. He loved the way it felt to be immobilized that way, loved the strain and the vulnerability. Parts of him stung where Arthur had bit or sucked his skin, on his back, his chest, his stomach. That sting was a revelation. But most noticeable and best of all was the deep, swollen throb of his arse.

He'd been fucked. Well and truly fucked. John didn't feel an ounce of shame for his mental use of the crude word. He'd made love plenty of times before, sometimes sweetly, sometimes with a more utilitarian aim, but he'd never been outright fucked. It had hurt like the dickens for the first ten seconds or so. His body had resisted Arthur's invasion, and the pain had been extraordinary. Extraordinarily good. Never in a million years would he have imagined it would feel so good to be choked, beaten, and violated the way Arthur had done to him.

He laughed, pushing himself into motion, rubbing his face against the unmade bed to wipe away the sweat drying on his brow, and wriggling his arms behind him to free himself from his jacket. The pain had been searing and burning, and then everything had turned glorious the moment he accepted it and surrendered. He'd felt closer to Arthur in those moments—especially after Arthur had flipped him to his back and fucked him face to face with his legs stretched out in a vee—than he'd ever felt to another man. Whatever walls he might have been tempted to put up, whatever modesty he might have attempted to maintain, was ripped to shreds by the force of Arthur's passion. It had been like touching his hand to a hot stove and being desperately aroused by the burn.

He managed to struggle out of his jacket, then discarded his waistcoat and shirt as well. They were drenched with sweat and wrinkled beyond salvation. He didn't want clothes in that moment anyhow. He rolled to his back the right way around in the bed and pulled the sheet up as if he were settling in for a long night's slumber. He needed a good, long nap after the maelstrom he'd just been through.

And yet, as he closed his eyes and let out a groan as the throb in his shoulders and arse reminded him of every second of his communion with Arthur, he couldn't drift off completely. That was what he'd been waiting his entire life for—that vulnerability, that excitement, that whisper of danger intertwined with pleasure. He almost always needed to sleep after sex, but in that moment, he felt as though he'd awakened to a new paradise. His body buzzed with sensation, his mind wouldn't settle on one thought, and his heart hammered in his chest, feeling only one thing, his need for Arthur on every level of his being.

He chuckled and lifted an arm to rest it heavily across his face so that his forearm covered his eyes. Arthur had been baiting him and toying with him for ages. He should have just given in and submitted to the man and whatever wickedness he'd wanted ages ago. If he had known how shatteringly good that kind of rough treatment could feel, Arthur's cat would have caught his mouse right at the very beginning. No wonder Shinobu had been willing to give up his entire life for—

John sucked in a quick breath and moved his arm to stare up at the ceiling. What kind of a self-indulgent bastard was he? The whole, revelatory experience had come about because Arthur had been hurting over Shinobu and over the past, and John had forgotten it already to focus on his own pleasure. Arthur didn't just need him to be some sort of sexual whipping boy, he needed him to be a sounding board and a friend. Arthur had so much unresolved hurt that John knew in his heart of hearts the man was ready to let go of, but Arthur was stubborn. He would need John's help. And once the past was finally put to rest, John would make damn certain the two of them entered the future together.

He was caught up in those thoughts, spinning the wheels in his head to come up with a way to convince Arthur to let him into his life all the way, when the door suddenly opened and a maid walked in. She seemed distracted and clearly had no idea that John was in the room, and when their eyes met, both of them yelped and flinched.

"I'm sorry, sir," the maid stammered, looking everywhere in the room but at him in the bed. "I was told this room had been vacated. I'm so sorry."

"No, I'm sorry," John said, sitting up, but holding the bedsheet to cover himself, as though he were some virginal maiden concerned for her modesty instead of a man who had just been manhandled and brutally fucked by his male lover. "I should have packed up and been gone before now."

"Oh...I...I'm sorry sir." The maid backed out of the room, shutting the door behind her.

John sighed, his face red-hot with embarrassment, and rolled out of bed. Indulgence was making him sloppy. He had a reputation to maintain and an air of propriety to recapture. He was a professional man, after all, and—

His thoughts stopped with a shiver as the remnants of his experience with Arthur slipped from his hole and onto his upper thigh. The reminder sent swirls of breathless lust through him, and he groaned at the sensation as he crossed to the washstand. Part of him wanted to be that good, upright man, but a new part of him wanted to be Arthur's wicked, dirty, vulnerable toy.

His thoughts on the subject were still so new and conflicted that he laughed and shook his head at himself as he washed up, thoroughly, and donned fresh clothes. He packed the rest away in his suitcase, including the soiled and creased items he'd been wearing earlier. Once everything was packed away and he stood in front of the mirror to straighten his tie and make certain he looked presentable, he studied his reflection with a devilish grin. He looked like the same old, dull John Dandie, London solicitor, but he could still feel the marks Arthur had left on his body and the sore stretch of his hole. He could feel

Arthur's handprints on his arse. He had secrets now that no one who gazed upon him could guess, and it felt wonderful. It made him stand a little taller, consider his reflection far handsomer than he usually thought he was, and as he made a final check of the room, picked up his suitcase, and left, it put a spring in his step.

That spring flattened a little as he made his way downstairs and returned his room key. Perhaps he and Arthur had been a bit too loud. The looks that nearly everyone, from the concierge to the other guests, gave him were knowing and hostile. John kept his head down as he paid the bill and left out the door to the beach, but as embarrassing as it was to have been found out, his heart didn't care one bit. Any one of the people at the inn likely could have called the police to cause an inordinate amount of trouble for him and Arthur, but not one of them did. It was further proof that outsiders could moralize all they wanted to, but when it came to actually taking action, they were cowards. Love had the upper hand.

Those thoughts and the deliciously sore spots of his body kept John's spirits high as he approached Cannon's back porch. The day had turned cloudy, which put too much of a chill in the air to spend time on the porch as they had earlier, but one of Cannon's maids was more than happy to greet him at the back door and to show him upstairs to the guestroom he had been given. Once he deposited his suitcase on the bed, planning to unpack it later, he had the maid show him down to the parlor that faced the sound, where Blake and Niall were finishing lunch.

"Look who has finally dragged himself back from the abyss," Blake greeted him with a sly grin, gesturing for John to sit and finish the food on the end table beside them.

"I can tell you had a pleasant plunge," Niall added with an equally cheeky look.

"I have no idea what you mean." John played innocent as he sat gingerly and helped himself to the remaining sandwiches and a glass of what he was astounded to discover was cold, black tea with ice in it.

Blake and Niall exchanged looks that said John wouldn't be able to put this one past them.

"There were rumors about strange cries coming from one of the guest rooms when I returned to the inn to pack our things," Niall said, then finished the last of his strange, cold tea.

"Perhaps some sort of wild animal was caught in the rafters," John said, taking a large bite of his sandwich so that he didn't have to look at them. It was the most delicious thing he'd ever tasted.

"Have you taken to wearing lip rouge now?" Blake asked, barely able to keep his laughter in check.

John froze in the middle of chewing, stared at him for a moment, then swallowed. Come to think of it, when he'd studied his reflection back at the inn, his mouth had been rather red and swollen from Arthur's brutal kisses.

"I paused before coming over here to have coffee," he lied. "It was too hot, and I burned my lips."

Neither Blake nor Niall believed him for a moment, but hopefully the young maid who had just entered the room to clear away the lunch things did.

"Are you quite comfortable in that chair?" Blake teased on. "Would you like a cushion? Because it looks as though your seat isn't feeling particularly at ease at the moment."

John scowled at his friend. With the maid still in the room, that little quip was beyond the pale. He swallowed another bite of sandwich and asked, "Where is Alan?"

Blake sobered up a bit, but not much, to answer, "He's gone up for a nap at his grandmother's insistence. And truly, I think he did need one, after the excitement of the morning."

Niall seemed to agree that the moment for teasing was over. "I'm concerned about Mrs. Cannon's attachment to the boy," he said, keeping his voice low even after the maid left the room with a load of dishes. "I fear she will make it difficult for us to leave with Alan peacefully."

"What do you wish to do about it?" John asked. "Should we change our plans and return to the city?" That would prove decidedly inconvenient, since he and Arthur had promised Cannon they would investigate Mr. Stone for him.

Blake shook his head with a hint of hesitation. "I want my son back, but I don't want to be rude about it.

All the same, I am counting the days until our ship for England departs."

"I could telegraph Xavier at the hotel in New York and ask him to make inquiries about whether there might be another ship departing sooner than the one we've reserved berths on," John offered. "Even if it travels to somewhere else in Europe."

"I don't think that will be necessary...yet," Blake said. He tilted his head to the side slightly, then went on with, "I suppose I should telegraph Xavier to alert him to the developments here, one way or another."

"I could walk into town and send the message for you," John said. "I'm certain I spotted a telegraph office when we arrived in Peconic."

"Would you?" Blake brightened. "That would be a godsend."

"It would be my pleasure," John smiled in return.

"I thought Arthur Gleason was your pleasure," Niall commented, back to being lascivious, since the three of them were alone once again.

John finished his sandwich and tea, deciding he trusted Blake and Niall enough to say, "Arthur was extraordinary. And you're right. I think I will need a nice soft cushion when I sit down for days to come."

Blake and Niall laughed at the off-color comment, making John feel as though all were right with the world. He got up and made a brief trip back to his guest room to unpack his things and to fetch is wallet, then left the house and headed into town. It concerned him a bit that he hadn't seen head nor tail of Arthur since arriving at the Cannon house. He was certain that was where Arthur had been heading.

Then again, Arthur had been shaken after their carnal adventure. He had packed all of his things and fled. There was nothing to suggest that he had gone straight to the Cannon house. John had yet to speak with Arthur to tell him how much he'd enjoyed being savaged. It was entirely possible that Arthur believed he'd hurt or offended him. If he thought that, he might have fled not only the inn, but Peconic and all of Long Island as well. Arthur might just have walked out of his life forever under the mistaken assumption that he'd done something John regretted.

By the time John reached the telegraph office in town, he was nearly frantic. It took every bit of his concentration to craft and send a quick message to Xavier, informing him of the unfolding events regarding Alan. All John could think about was finding Arthur and explaining that Arthur hadn't hurt or offended him, he'd changed his entire world for the better.

He went straight to the train station from the telegraph office, anxious to see what the departure table looked like and whether Arthur could have fled back to the city. As he was studying the board, however, he spotted Hiroshi speaking to a broad-shouldered man in a business suit at the far end of one of the platforms. Instinct alone told John to conceal himself. He used a wide pillar near the entrance to the platforms to stand behind, peeking around to study Hiroshi.

He was too far to hear what Hiroshi and the other man might be talking about. The conversation wasn't hostile, that much he was certain of. It seemed to consist mostly of Hiroshi speaking to the man and the man nodding and, if John wasn't mistaken, taking notes. That detail had John frowning. Hiroshi could have simply been conducting business on Cannon's behalf, delivering a message, or placing an order of some sort. Somehow John doubted it, though.

He was on the verge of moving closer when the unmistakable sound of Arthur's voice arrested his attention. He whipped around and searched, spotting Arthur walking past the train station with Mr. Stone. John's heart instantly pounded against his ribs, and he pushed away from the pillar, rushing back through the station house so that he could catch up to Arthur and Mr. Stone on the street.

"There you are," he said with a broad, likely far too affectionate smile as he jogged to fall into step with Arthur. "I've been looking for you."

"Oh, it's your solicitor friend." Stone greeted John with a smile and a tip of his hat. "Solicitor, not barrister." Stone touched a finger to the side of his nose and winked, proving he remembered.

John found the man to be a boor, but he would endure his company to discover the information Cannon wanted. Or, rather, he would endure it so that he could spend time with Arthur.

Arthur—who scowled at him as though he'd interrupted a private tea party by dumping manure on the table. "What do you want, Dandie?" he asked in clipped tones.

John's smile and excitement evaporated. He cursed himself for feeling like a debutante who had been snubbed at her first ball. After what they'd shared that morning, the least he would have expected from Arthur was the sort of sly looks and inuendo he'd gotten from Blake and Niall.

But no, there was a spark in Arthur's eyes that John could see, plain as day, no matter how desperate Arthur was to pretend he was merely frustrated with being interrupted.

"I just came into town to send a telegram to our friend, Xavier, back in the city," he said, gearing his explanation so that it made sense to Stone. "And now that I've seen you, I thought that we could all walk back to Cannon's house together."

"That's just where we were headed," Stone said, setting off again.

"I do not need your company," Arthur told John in clipped tones.

John frowned slightly. "That was not what you told me this morning."

It was a low, shameless blow, particularly since Stone walked between the two of them. John could see full well that Stone immediately picked up on the tension between him and Arthur as his smile turned more forced.

"Any conversations we might have had this morning, Mr. Dandie, were purely the result of a grievous misunderstanding," Arthur said, his voice sharp.

"I do not believe that for a moment, Det. Gleason," John replied, clasping his hands behind his back as they walked. He hoped Arthur saw the gesture and was reminded of the position he'd left John in. "In fact," he went on, "I don't believe we finished our conversation this morning. I am very much of the opinion that we'd only just begun before you departed, leaving me in a bind."

Arthur's face flushed red, and his jaw clenched. "It seems clear to me that you utterly missed the point of the argument I attempted to make," he seethed.

"And I believe you fail to so much as listen to the argument I have been trying to make on the subject for days," John fired back.

"I am not interested in your arguments, sir," Arthur insisted.

"You should be," John told him, unwilling to back down. "It is my opinion that once you resolve the argument you lost with your friend several years ago, you will see my argument for what it is, and you may even agree with me."

"I sincerely doubt that, Mr. Dandie." Arthur faced straight forward, bristling with tension. "You have never understood my viewpoint on the subject, and you never will."

John opened his mouth to fire something back, but Stone stopped and held up both hands to them. "Gentlemen, gentlemen," he said, looking horrifically uncomfortable. John should have noticed the man growing increasingly awkward since his argument with Arthur began. "It is clear to me that the two of you have things you need to discuss, and it is equally clear that I have no part of it and am only interfering by being here."

Salt was added to the wound of Stone's statement a moment later when the man glanced across the road they were walking along and spied Hiroshi driving a small cart up to the intersection ahead of them.

"Perhaps Mr. Hiroshi can give me a ride back to the house," Stone said, looking relieved as he strode forward, getting away from John and Arthur as quickly as he could. "Mr. Gleason, it has been a pleasant conversation. I will see both of you gentlemen back at the house for supper, and I do hope you've resolved your differences by then."

"Goodbye, sir." John waved to the man, his smile crumbling almost from the moment he attempted it. It hadn't been his intention to chase the man off, just as it hadn't been his intention to bring the mutinous glare to Arthur's face that his lover wore now.

"You are a cunt," Arthur hissed before turning and storming off in the opposite direction.

John stood where he was for a moment, his jaw dropping. That was absolutely the last reaction he'd expected from a man who had made his mind, body, and emotions blossom with a new dawn of experience just hours before. He wasn't going to stand for it either. Arthur had no right to open him up like a lotus blossom, then walk away from him and hide himself away in his own, ancient problems.

CHAPTER 12

*E*verything in Arthur's life had been so careful and so controlled, and then John Dandie happened. He should have known better, should have read the signs when his infatuation with the man turned into something more than a passing fancy. Now, there he was, storming away from some insignificant, American town on a cloudy, April day with the tall, blond Adonis following him like a tune he couldn't shake from his head.

"Arthur, do not walk away from me," John called after him, striding closer with each second.

Arthur could hear the frustration in his voice. His chest felt tight, knowing he was the one who had put that frustration there. Pain was supposed to be controlled, something he could wield to get his way and satisfy someone else. It wasn't supposed to be a wild, untamed thing that got away from him and left everyone in its path bleeding.

"Arthur," John's voice was even sharper as he caught up and fell into step by Arthur's side. "You cannot avoid this forever. Eventually, you need to voice your thoughts and emotions aloud so they stop eating you from the inside out."

"Are you offering to eat me out?" he snapped, knowing full well it was avoidance. "Because if you are, I'll take you up on your offer."

John made an impatient sound and tried to grab Arthur's arm to stop him. Arthur shook away from his touch, but slowed his steps and turned to look at John, even if it was with a glare.

"You're too late," John said, an uncertain smile pulling at the corners of his mouth. "I already know your tactics to avoid speaking of things you don't wish to speak about."

They were far enough from the town, and no one was on the road near them, so he stopped and whipped to face John. "If you already know that I do not wish to discuss a topic, why do you bother accosting me with it?"

John pursed his lips and rested his hands on his hips for a moment. "You really are the prickliest and most aggravating man I've ever met."

"I have good reason to be," Arthur muttered, walking on again. John clearly didn't want to get to the point, so there was no reason for them to stop idly on the roadside for a chat. "You interrupted my investigation of Stone," he growled as John fell into step with him again. "I had him talking about his father and the way he took over the man's operation. I was close to discovering the things Cannon wants to know."

"By talking to Stone?" John blinked.

Arthur sent him a withering look over the obvious question. His scowl was dampened somewhat by the fact that John looked extraordinarily handsome in the subdued, Long Island light. His shoulders seemed broader, and he walked with more purpose than he usually did. Frankly, Arthur was surprised that he could walk comfortably at all after what he'd done.

His face heated at the memory. He'd lost control of himself, something he considered a mortal sin. And John had groaned in ecstasy, taking whatever he'd dished out. It was embarrassing. It was astounding. It made Arthur want more, much more. He might have been the one who spilled himself inside of John, but it felt as though John had somehow infused him with his soul. He both loved and despised the fact that the two of them had a bond that he wouldn't simply be able to dismiss.

"Oftentimes, the simplest way to glean the information a client needs is simply to ask," he said, fighting with everything he had to keep the conversation about business. Everything else was too raw. "I'll follow it up with a few, official inquiries if I need to, but most people are more than happy to talk about themselves and to give you all the information you want to know."

"So you intend to make friends with Stone and ask him all the questions Cannon feels he can't?" John asked.

"Precisely." Arthur nodded.

He took a breath and glanced up at the sky as they kept walking. Some of his tension siphoned away. He and John made good business partners. They both had quick minds. Whatever mistakes he'd made that morning, they still made a good team when it came to gleaning information from people. That much hadn't changed.

"I think your friend, Hiroshi, is up to something," John said after they'd been silent for a minute or so.

"He is not my friend," Arthur barked, a little too forceful. He blinked as John's statement sunk in, then asked, "What makes you think that?"

John glanced back to the town, receding in the distance, and nodded. "I saw him talking to a man in a business suit back at the train station. They looked as though they didn't want to be disturbed."

Arthur's brow went up, and he, too, glanced back to the town, as if he could see what John saw. "Do you remember what the man in the suit looked like?" Perhaps there was a connection to the man Hiroshi had met with at The Slippery Slope.

John shrugged and winced. "Tall, broad shoulders. Dark hair. He was rather nondescript."

It wasn't much help. The man at The Slippery Slope fit that description, but so did half of the men in the world. Even if they were the same man, there was no way to know who he was or what they had discussed. There was no way to know anything at all. He wouldn't put it past Hiroshi to be up to something, though. The man was a criminal, and if Arthur had his way—

"We need to talk about this morning," John said when they were far out on the road, away from everything, wrenching him out of his thoughts.

Arthur scowled at him even as his heart thumped harder in his chest. "There is nothing to discuss. I simply disabused you of the notion that I am some tender-hearted yet tormented lover from a fairy story, and that the two of us discussing my past will be the antidote to every wicked and miserable feeling inside of me."

"Is that what you did?" John asked with a wry grin and cleverly narrowed eyes.

Arthur should have known from that look and the heat he could practically feel rolling off of John in waves that his plan had backfired.

"You're a fool for thinking me anything other than a rapacious villain," he grumbled, refusing to look at John and picking up his pace.

John waited a few beats, almost until Arthur let his guard down again, before saying in a quiet voice, "This morning was the single most exciting and satisfying sexual experience of my entire life."

Chills ricocheted through Arthur, sending his blood pumping hard through his veins, making his cock take notice, and filling him with the visceral urge to give it all to John again and more.

The bastard had to make it worse by going on with, "I never knew it could be like that. I've always assumed the ordinary was good enough for me, that I had no interest in anything more. You showed me a different way, and

I...." He paused. Arthur peeked at him, struck with even more desire at the way John's mouth hung open and his eyes blazed as he scrambled to put his thoughts into words. "I want more of it," he said in a near whisper. "I want you to tie me up tighter. I want you to fuck me harder and deeper. I want you to force me to do things that frighten me. But I want to talk to you about how you make me feel too. I want to feel the storm with you, but I want us to bask in the afterglow too. Frankly, I don't think that's too much to ask."

Arthur clenched his jaw so hard he thought his teeth might shatter. Everything John had just described felt like heaven. It felt like things had been when Shinobu had first shown him that his baser instincts could be beautiful instead of damaging. He knew exactly where John was, exactly what it felt like when you accepted a part of yourself that defied everything convention said you were supposed to feel, and when you embraced your need for more with both arms. It was beautiful and humbling to be that catalyst for John, to be there at the very start of what could be his journey of a lifetime.

And it hurt. It hurt so much that it was driving him mad.

"If you were as clever as everyone is always telling me you are, you'd forget everything that happened, forget the way you feel, and go back to your sweet, good life," he grumbled. "You're only going to be hurt by things you don't understand."

"Stop telling me that I don't understand you," John

shouted so suddenly that Arthur missed a step. John grabbed Arthur's arm and forced him to face him. "I *do* understand you, Arthur. Far more than you give me credit for."

"You don't even begin to understand me," Arthur fired back at him. "You couldn't possibly."

"I understand that you have been scarred by a death you feel responsible for," John said. "I understand that you like control as a way to cope with the guilt. And I understand that I have blasted all of that to smithereens by becoming a part of your life that you cannot walk away from, especially not now, no matter how badly you want to. I understand that you have been fighting a bitter war to push me away because I frighten you, what we have frightens you. But you cannot push me away, Arthur. I am here to stay."

Panic washed over Arthur as John gripped the sides of his face and leaned in for a kiss. Panic caused him to shout out wordlessly and shove John away with as much strength as he could manage.

"You're wrong," he shouted, agitated to the point of hyperventilating. "So I fucked you this morning, so what? Do you think I actually cared about you when I was trying my best to hurt you in the most humiliating way I could? Do you think that I've wanted more in these last few months than to embarrass and humiliate you? Nothing gives me greater pleasure than humiliating a good man who thinks he's so high and mighty. Now look at you. I bet you'd drop to your knees in the mud right here and suck my cock if I asked you. And you think that's love? Affection? A relationship?"

He hated every word that spewed from his lips and wanted to tear his lungs out to keep him from saying any more. He wanted to rip his traitorous heart out and stomp it into the ground for daring to feel love again after the agony of Shinobu. He knew pain better than most men, but he was on the wrong side of this pain, and he couldn't take it.

John glared back at him in the brittle silence that followed Arthur's terrible words. Arthur wasn't the only one who had been turned inside out, but damn him, John seemed to still have the upper hand in the whole thing, in spite of Arthur's best efforts.

"You are an utter shite sometimes," John seethed, visibly shaking for a moment. Then he turned and marched back the way they'd come, clearly indicating some sort of a parting of the ways between them.

Arthur didn't stay to watch John's retreating back. He stormed forward, hands balled into fists at his sides. John had gone his way, and he would go his own. It was exactly what he wanted. So why did it feel as though he now had a gaping hole in his chest? Why did he want to turn around and run to John, to apologize for the words he didn't mean, with every fiber of his body? He wasn't a young man anymore with his head spinning because of his first serious love affair. He wasn't naïve enough to believe everything would be sunshine and primrose for him and John as he'd believed it would be for him and

Shinobu. He felt like an old man well before his time, burdened by the knowledge that love was a curse and not a gift.

He'd barely pulled himself together by the time he returned to the Cannon house. His thoughts and emotions still roiled through him, but at least he'd been able to school his outward appearance to calm. He even managed a cheeky wink for one of Cannon's maids as he entered the house through the kitchen with the hope that by doing so, he wouldn't run into Lord Selby or Cristofori before he made it to his guestroom.

It was a stroke of luck—though he didn't know what kind—that he nearly ran headlong into Hiroshi as he reached the doorway to the main part of the house. The moment the two of them were face to face, the air between them crackled.

"Did you learn anything of interest from Stone?" Arthur asked, falling back on the joint task Cannon had assigned them.

"Perhaps I did," Hiroshi said in clipped tones. He clasped his hands behind his back as though that were the only thing stopping him from strangling Arthur.

"If you learned anything of importance, we need to discuss it," Arthur insisted. "Cannon wishes us to work together for his benefit."

"And you would share whatever information Mr. Stone told you with me?" Hiroshi asked, sniffing with derisive laughter.

"I would work for the benefit of the client who hired

me," Arthur insisted. Without wanting to, he wished John were there. John was the perfect buffer and the ideal man to wheedle information out of an arse like Hiroshi.

"Mr. Cannon is my employer," Hiroshi said in a bitter voice. "But then, you always have been inclined to steal things that do not belong to you."

Fury pulsed through Arthur's veins. "Shinobu was his own man," he seethed. "As Cannon is as well. You cannot change the past, and if you do not have a care, you will destroy what you have in the present by clinging to old grudges."

Arthur flinched as soon as he finished speaking. Even though he'd spoken the words, they rang in his head in John's voice. It was exactly the advice John would have given him about his own situation.

"You have so many things still to answer for," Hiroshi hissed, not seeing the impact Arthur's words had on himself. "And you will pay for them."

He tried to step past Arthur, but as he did, Arthur called out, "Who was the man you were speaking to at the train station?"

Hiroshi's back went stiff, and for a moment, he stood stock still. Arthur waited, but he didn't turn around. He sucked in a breath and kept on walking.

"I will discover who that man was," Arthur continued to accost him. "And the man at The Slippery Slope. You're up to something, Hiroshi, and you know full well that I do not stop until I get what I want."

Hiroshi continued to walk way in spite of Arthur calling after him. As far as Arthur was concerned, that was all the proof he needed that Hiroshi was involved in something he shouldn't be. Then again, it was Hiroshi. The man's nature was to be involved in things he shouldn't have been.

Arthur shook his head and continued on into the house, doing his best to avoid Lord Selby when he heard the sound of the man's voice down the main hallway. His mission with Lord Selby was done. The man's son had more or less been returned to him. The case in front of him now was not only the one Cannon had given him, it was an additional investigation. Whether he liked Cannon or not, the man was employing him. He had a responsibility to discover if a member of his staff was involved in criminal activity of some sort. He had true and just cause to investigate Hiroshi now.

And John. Whether he liked it or not, the ties that held him to John were too firmly in place for him to untangle himself. He'd let his pain get the better of him. He'd lost control. It was a cardinal sin to forget himself the way he had. John wouldn't be dissuaded by any effort Arthur employed to push him away. The only way he could pry John from his heart to restore the equilibrium in his life would be to apologize to the man, be as sweet as honey to him, and wait for him to grow bored, as he inevitably would.

CHAPTER 13

*N*ot once during the trip to America thus far had John felt anything but completely focused on his mission to return Alan to Blake. Even with a few loose ends to tie up, John was certain that mission was now complete. And now all he wanted to do was go home.

Long Island felt like a prison as he spent the rest of the afternoon walking up and down the shore around Cannon's house, chewing over his thoughts and emotions as though they were particularly sticky toffee. It aggravated him to no end that the more in love with Arthur he fell, the more that love hurt. He could see clearly what the matter with Arthur was. Arthur was haunted by his past and refused to let it go. It made him surly and defensive, and the more John reached out to him, the more Arthur snarled and snapped to fight him off. Even though, underneath all of those prickles, it was apparent

170

that Arthur wanted him. After walking aimlessly for nearly two hours, John found himself wondering how long he could allow himself to be tied to that speeding carousel, going around in dizzying circles, until it became too much for him to take.

He wasn't certain how he was going to face Arthur at supper or what he would be able to say to the man—or hold back from saying—in a public setting, but as he joined his hosts for supper, sending a quick look down the table at the relatively small company for the evening, Arthur wasn't there.

"You don't know where Gleason has gone off to, do you?" Blake asked once John had taken his seat and was served by one of Cannon's liveried servants.

John blinked across the table at him. "I was hoping that you had seen him."

Blake and Niall exchanged a look as subtly as they could. "The two of you haven't had a disagreement of some sort already, have you?" Niall asked.

"Oh, they had a real hum-dinger of an argument earlier," Stone said in a boorishly loud voice as he reached into the center of the table for the salt without asking someone to pass it.

Blake and Niall—and everyone else seated at the table—turned to Stone with surprised looks. "They did?" Blake asked.

John scowled, hardly daring to guess where the conversation would go.

"I ran into Mr. Gleason in town earlier, and we got to

talking," Stone said, adding too much salt to the already well-seasoned meat on his plate. "Then Mr. Dandie came along, and the two of them really got into it."

"I'm terribly sorry you were made privy to an ongoing dispute Det. Gleason and I have, which had nothing to do with present company," John said as politely as possible.

"I wasn't even listening to what the two of you were saying, to tell the truth," Stone said with a huff. "But boy, were you two sore with each other."

"Is there some sort of trouble?" Cannon asked.

John wanted to wince at the alarmed look Cannon—arguably his employer, at the moment—stared at him. "No, sir," John said with a calm incline of his head toward Cannon. "It was a silly dispute, if I am honest. One having to do with—" he stumbled, scrambling to think of something that would explain him bickering with Arthur, "—with a matter of business. I have been attempting to convince Det. Gleason to attach himself to my law office for the purpose of assisting my clients. He has resisted the idea."

Blake and Niall sent each other surprised and impressed looks. "I could most certainly see that sort of a partnership being beneficial to the both of you," Blake said. John had no idea whether he was actually speaking of a business partnership or whether he meant a more personal alliance.

"But the two of you clearly hate each other," Stone said with a genuinely baffled look. He huffed a laugh and said, "You could have started a fire with the sparks between those two earlier."

John reached for his wineglass to hide the flush he felt rising to his face. Thank God for the ignorance of men like Stone who mistook one emotion for its polar opposite.

Cannon stared at John with a calculating expression, though. John had to take a second gulp of wine for fortification when Cannon glanced to Blake and Niall with the same sort of calculating look. The very last thing they needed now was for Cannon to turn squeamish as he figured out the nature of all the men who were guests in his house, not just Blake and Niall.

"I was quite impressed with the decorations that have already been put up in the center of town," John quickly changed the subject, glancing to Mrs. Cannon with a smile. "Are you involved in the festival on Saturday, other than your plans to attend it, Mrs. Cannon?"

Mrs. Cannon seemed more than happy to become the center of attention. "I have been part of the planning committee, yes, Mr. Dandie."

She proceeded to tell everyone at the table about every committee meeting she had had recently, about the activities the festival would offer, the entertainment that had been hired, and even some of the gossip among the ladies of Peconic. John smiled and feigned interest, if only to keep the woman talking so that all other conversation was forgotten. He was the only one pretending interest, and soon Cannon fell into conversation with

Stone as Blake and Niall began whispering to each other.

Supper ended shortly after that, on Cannon's order. John grimaced at the idea of spending an evening closeted away with the other men, drinking port and smoking cigars, as Cannon seemed to favor. He considered it a stroke of luck when Blake asked for Alan to be brought down so that the two of them could spend time together before the boy's bedtime. Mrs. Cannon insisted on being there to enjoy Alan's company as well, which John could see clearly was her way of attempting to coax Alan into liking her more. That was a hopeless cause, however. Alan adored his papa.

"I can only hope that when the time to part does come," Niall murmured to John as the two of them stood near the fireplace, watching the subtle tug-of-war, "that Mrs. Cannon doesn't make it overly difficult."

John huffed an ironic laugh. "I'm beginning to see that love is, in essence, overly difficult."

Niall sent him a wry look. "Is it love, then?"

John let out a long sigh and rubbed a hand over his face. "I don't know." He shrugged. "I feel it. I want it to be. He makes me feel that way."

"But he's also a prickly bastard with a sadistic streak who enjoys tormenting you," Niall finished his thought with a lopsided grin.

Again, John laughed. "You don't know how true those words are."

"He'll come around," Niall insisted, thumping John's

shoulder. "Blake did eventually, even though it took ten years."

John winced. "I'd rather it didn't take that long with Arthur."

"It won't." Niall seemed relatively confident.

John still wasn't certain. He took his leave of the others and made his way up to his guestroom, completely exhausted. At some point, Arthur would have to screw his courage to the sticking point and make the decision to be happy himself. John could offer him all of the care and affection in the world, but it wouldn't do a lick of good if the man continued to wallow in his past. He knew it, he was convinced Arthur knew it too, but doing something about it was an entirely different kettle of fish. The fact that Arthur was avoiding company, avoiding him, didn't seem to be a good sign, though.

Hard on the heels of those thoughts, he stepped into his guestroom and discovered Arthur there in his room, sitting on the bed, back against the pillows at the headboard, shoes off, reading a book.

"I was beginning to wonder if I'd ever see you tonight," Arthur said, as cool as you please, not looking up from his book.

John clenched his jaw and turned to check whether the door had a lock. It did, so he turned it, then stepped slowly toward the bed, unbuttoning his dinner jacket. "Funny, I was just wondering the same about you," he said with a scowl.

Arthur glanced lazily up from his book and fixed

John with a leonine smile. "I didn't feel much like company this evening," he said. "I had Cannon's cook send a plate up to my room and gave every indication to the staff that I was feeling poorly and would retire early for the night."

"But you chose to retire to my room instead." John moved to sit in a chair beside the room's bureau so that he could remove his shoes.

Arthur closed his book and set it on the bedside table, then swung his legs over the side of the bed. He didn't get up, though, before saying, "I have a few theories about what Hiroshi might be up to by meeting with strange men in noisy Bowery clubs and Long Island train stations."

John tugged off his second shoe, sending Arthur a surprised look, his jaw still clenched. "And this is what you've been doing all day while avoiding me? Revenge investigating the man who you believe ruined your life?"

Arthur's expression went downright thunderous for a moment before he smoothed it out. "Hiroshi was an underhanded bastard ten years ago, and I believe he is still an underhanded bastard now. I asked the maid who brought up my supper how long Hiroshi has been employed by Cannon, and she said he's only been the butler for two years now. Cannon likes the idea of an exotic butler, and Hiroshi came recommended by a business associate."

"So?" John shrugged, standing to move his shoes to the wardrobe and to remove his waistcoat. "The upper classes hire new staff all the time. Recommendations are a good way to find the right staff."

"The man who recommended Hiroshi, a Mr. Alfred Brendel, has been in competition with Cannon for the last two years, and in several cases, he has snatched business deals right out from under Cannon's nose at the last minute," Arthur said.

John's hands stilled on his waistcoat buttons. "And you think Hiroshi has something to do with that, with Brendel?"

Arthur shrugged and spread his hands wide. "Espionage is not just for battling nations these days. Industrialists are forever planting moles in each other's ranks to feed them inside information." He stood, stepping over to John to finish with the buttons of his waistcoat and to undo his tie.

John's pulse sped up, and his skin tingled where Arthur's hands touched, even though he still had his shirt on. "What is your aim, then?" he asked, cursing the fact that his voice cracked in the middle of his question.

Arthur glanced slowly up at him, his mouth spreading into a sultry grin, heat in his eyes. "What do you think?" He rested his hands on John's chest as soon as his tie hung loose around his neck.

The bastard was deliberately using sensuality to knock him completely off-balance. And damn him, it was working. But two could play at that game.

"I think you're settling for petty revenge by gathering enough evidence to have Hiroshi fired, rather than digging deep into your own emotional turmoil to come to grips with your past," he said. "And by doing so, I think you're selling yourself short. Hiroshi is an inconsequential gnat compared to you."

Arthur's clever grin dropped. He lowered his gaze to his hands, which he kept on John's chest. His expression morphed further until Arthur wore a pinched, troubled frown. "I don't trust Hiroshi," he said, lowering his hands to his side without looking at John. "I never have. He thinks of only one person, himself. I wouldn't wish him on an enemy, and while Cannon is not precisely my friend, he doesn't deserve to have his business undermined."

"You're still avoiding the real issue," John said, keeping his voice firm. It was a rare moment where he felt as though he had the upper hand over Arthur, so he intended to latch onto it. "Hiroshi can hang, for all I care. Pursuing any sort of grudge against him does nothing to help you recover from a traumatic past."

Arthur snapped his gaze up, narrowing his eyes at John. The tension that radiated from him was sharp, bitter, and entirely typical of everything John had come to know about Arthur.

A moment later, as Arthur let out a breath, that tension evaporated. John could swear he saw the moment Arthur's thoughts turned.

"I'm not as adept with emotional nonsense as you are," Arthur said in an uncharacteristically quiet voice. "I have never been the sentimental sort that you have always seemed to be."

"I would argue that point," John said, resting a hand on Arthur's shoulder. He took a risk and slid that hand up to cradle the side of Arthur's face, forcing Arthur to look at him. "You feel things deeply and you are nostalgic for the past. I would call that sentimental."

Arthur shook his head, but John refused to let his hand be dislodged. "That is not sentimentality. There is nothing soft about me."

"Oh, I think there is," John said, lowering his voice to a purr.

He took another risk by clasping both hands on Arthur's face and leaning in to kiss him. He deliberately made the kiss sensual and sweet instead of the rough, exciting kisses they'd shared so far. He wanted to try something with Arthur, to test a theory, and to test Arthur's limits. If he was right, then Arthur would show a side of himself that John knew was there, but which Arthur usually ran from.

Arthur was hesitant. John had to kiss him long and deep, coaxing his lips apart with supernatural patience as resistance radiated from Arthur, even though he didn't move a muscle. Arthur didn't need to thrash and squirm to fight what John wanted to give him. At the same time, as John lowered his hands to push Arthur's unbuttoned jacked off his shoulders and work through the buttons of his waistcoat, he could feel Arthur's heart racing.

He pushed things further, stepping into Arthur and

forcing him back until his legs bumped against the side of the bed. Arthur might like brutality and domination—and John had to admit he loved it too and wanted to explore more of it—but John was determined to find out what the man thought of sensuality and passion. He trapped Arthur against the bed, pulled off his waistcoat and tugged Arthur's shirt out of his trousers, then slid his hands along the firm, lean lines of Arthur's torso.

"This is not how I generally go about things," Arthur protested, gripping John's arms as he moved to sweep Arthur's shirt over his head, preventing the motion.

John shrugged. "You got to do things your way this morning. I get to do them my way now."

Arthur stared up at him with a look that was almost comically suspicious. John didn't laugh, though. He continued his movements, surprised that Arthur actually let him pull his shirt off and toss it aside. He was doubly surprised when Arthur let him kiss him again, and when he made a sound of longing as their tongues slid against each other.

That simple sound fired John's blood. Perhaps the way to Arthur's heart was through tenderness after all. He never would have guessed it of the irritable man, but then again, everyone grew tired of the fight eventually. Better still, as John continued undressing Arthur, he was treated to the full sight of his body, which he'd never managed to see before. Arthur had still been fully dressed when he'd fucked him silly that morning, and even in the times they'd been forced to share a room—on the ship, at the hotel in New York—Arthur had never exposed himself. His small frame was muscular and defined instead of simply slender, as John had expected. Arthur's body was every bit a man's body, complete with dark chest hair that narrowed to a line pointing from his naval downward. Better still, when John unfastened Arthur's trousers to see where that line led, he was treated to the hot spear of Arthur's generously-proportioned cock springing straight up.

"You didn't tell me you were so beautiful," John hummed, pushing Arthur's trousers down over his shapely arse. Undressing the man was like unwrapping a marvelous gift.

"Don't be an arse," Arthur growled. "I've a body just like any other man."

"This is not just like any other man," John said, sliding his hands around Arthur's arse, then up his sides to toy with his nipples.

"I don't like this," Arthur huffed. "I don't like being fondled like some sort of overripe fruit."

"Yes, you do," John insisted, stroking his hands down Arthur's belly and reaching for his balls and cock. "As for overripe fruit," he peeked mischievously at Arthur's eyes as he brushed his fingers across the precum beading on his head, "you are juicy."

Arthur barked a sound that could have been a laugh, but also a groan of pleasure. "If you ever say something so ridiculous to me again—"

John didn't let him finish. He slanted his mouth over

Arthur's, stealing the words and the air from his lungs. Arthur was magnificent at playing the aggressor, but John could play that game as well. He kissed Arthur until he felt the man's resistance wane, then pushed him back to the bed, lifting his feet so that he could tug Arthur's trousers off.

The carnal mood was suspended for the length of time it took John to shed the rest of his clothes and climb into bed with Arthur. As soon as they'd positioned themselves the right way around between the sheets, Arthur attempted to muscle his way into having the upper hand, but John pushed him firmly to his back and kept him there as he treated Arthur's mouth to another, searing kiss. As he did, he wedged his way between Arthur's thighs and let his hands rove over every bit of skin he could reach.

"I don't like it this way," Arthur insisted again. His voice held more force, but the way his cock strained against John's as they ground together told a different story.

"Yes, you do," John repeated his earlier insistence. "You're just unfamiliar with it."

"I don't bottom," Arthur growled, raking his nails down John's back as if to prove his point.

John sucked in a breath at the scintillating pleasure-pain, then growled as he kissed Arthur hard. "Who said anything about bottom?" he panted as he moved away from Arthur's mouth, kissing his way down to the man's chest so that he could lave and suck his nipples. "Does this feel like I'm dominating you?"

"Yes," Arthur said, gasping for breath. He gripped handfuls of John's hair as John kissed his way down Arthur's belly, rubbing his cheek against Arthur's prick. Arthur gasped again and said, "No. I don't know. It's not...I don't...."

He grunted but failed to finish his sentence as John nudged his face between Arthur's legs and drew one of his balls into his mouth. It was exactly the sort of thing John imagined Arthur ordering him to do if he were playing the role of dominant bully, just in a different context. John wasn't surprised at all to discover how much he liked directing all of his energy into giving Arthur pleasure, even if it had the potential of coming at the expense of his own. He shifted to draw his tongue up Arthur's shaft, earning a moan and a shudder from Arthur as he did, then closed his mouth around his flared tip.

It was good in ways John couldn't begin to comprehend. Arthur was just a bit too big for him, and while having so much in his mouth alarmed him, he bore down more than was comfortable on purpose. It was a baffling paradox that the way Arthur fisted his hands in John's hair and jerked deeper until John choked had John so aroused he was already close to coming. It shouldn't have been that way. Fear and discomfort should not have had him moaning with pleasure, but with Arthur, they did.

He couldn't take it for long, though. When the

gagging started to feel like too much, he pulled back and spread himself over top of Arthur again, catching his breath for a moment, then kissing his mouth again.

"Still feel like a bottom?" he panted as he reached between them, closing his hand around both of their cocks together.

"No," Arthur admitted. It was one syllable, but it was the most beautiful thing John had ever heard. It was made even better when Arthur grasped John's arse in both hands, pulling his cheeks apart and slipping his fingers towards John's hole. "Do you have anything slippery on hand so I can take this?" he asked.

"No," John sighed, disappointed in the word when it came from his lips.

"Fuck," Arthur growled.

John laughed in spite of himself. "The whole world is conspiring against you today," he said, gazing fondly down at Arthur. "It's a bloody shame that you're being forced to make love instead of fucking me."

Arthur snarled in answer, grabbed the back of John's neck, then yanked him down for a kiss.

It was bizarrely beautiful. Neither of them were able to fully get what they wanted, but making do had fantastic consequences. They stroked and fondled each other, letting their hands speak while their mouths were busy. Arthur couldn't simply assert his dominance by penetrating John and coming inside of him. He was forced to kiss and tug on John's balls, grind against him, and stroke his cock as John gave the same right back.

And somehow, it was magical. The fire built slowly but surely, and by the time they were both primed and ready, sweating and panting, lips swollen from kissing, cocks already dripping in anticipation, John felt as transported with new sensations and excitement as he had that morning under entirely different circumstances. He and Arthur seemed so connected that they were able to communicate without words that the end was near, and they stroked their cocks together, hands clumsily bumping into each other but getting the job done anyhow, as they erupted into orgasm, first John, then Arthur. The sticky mess they created was pure poetry, as far as John was concerned, and they shamelessly continued to stroke and coat each other's flagging pricks with the aftermath as they came down from the high of bliss.

When even that was done, John was beyond content to roll to his back and let out a sigh of perfection.

"Don't you dare leave this bed to go back to your room tonight," he told Arthur, laying a hand on Arthur's chest as it rose and fell in a desperate attempt to regain his breath.

"I won't," Arthur promised.

John grinned over the fact that Arthur sounded dazed. Good. The man needed to be dazed more often. Perhaps it would stop him from being such an aggravating bastard. He laughed at his thought as he closed his eyes, more content than he'd been in a long time.

CHAPTER 14

*A*rthur slept far better than he should have, all things considered, and in the morning, as the first light of dawn filtered through John's curtains, he awoke to find himself nestled cozily against John, his back to John's chest. For the first few, bleary waking moments, Arthur smiled, liking the feeling of John's larger body against his and John's arm over his side, his hand near Arthur's heart.

The moment he realized that he had ended up as the smaller spoon, however, everything within him rebelled. He was *not* a small spoon. He was not a small anything. And he damn well wasn't going to lie there pretending that he and John were some darling, precious, lifelong pairing, like half the men of the Brotherhood seemed to want these days. He was not some pet to be tamed and thrust into a cage of—

He took a deep breath when John stirred against him,

186

still asleep, brushing his half-hard prick against Arthur's backside. Alright, perhaps there were some benefits to domestic bliss after all. Damn John for being so physically alluring, and for not only putting up with him when he was behaving at his worst, but for lapping up his petulance like it was...well, like it was other things he had half a mind to force John to lap up next time they played. The very fact that he took it as a given that there would be a next time was infuriating on one level...and deeply satisfying on another, like those blissful days right after he and Shinobu had—

Arthur's eyes popped open as though someone had fired a gun next to his ear and his throat constricted. He hadn't thought about Shinobu once since slipping into John's room the evening before. He'd betrayed his own determination to never fall in love again and dishonored Shinobu's memory by entrusting himself to John the way he had. His heart pounded against his ribs and his throat constricted in horror, but worst of all, his mind couldn't shake the image of Shinobu weeping and pleading with him not to leave him behind the day that Arthur had told him he was returning to England. He was doing it again, in his heart this time. He was leaving Shinobu after promising to stay with him forever. How could he be so callous a second time?

As soon as John was settled and snoring lightly, Arthur peeled himself away from the man's tempting body and slipped off the far end of the bed. He fought to steady the tremor that made his hands unsteady and to breathe away the remembered horror of discovering Shinobu dead. Rationally, he knew it wasn't the same thing, that he had every right to love another man. His wounded heart wasn't open to rationality, though. He'd killed a man by leaving him once before, and he'd be damned if he put his heart in danger of repeating that mistake, no matter how lovely John was.

Making as little noise as he could, he washed what was necessary to wash, dressed in his discarded clothes from the night before, unlocked the door, and crept back down the hall to his own room. Once there, he allowed himself to scowl and frown at the maelstrom of emotions that battered him like a ship against rocks. He washed in earnest and shaved, dressed in fresh clothes, then mussed up his bed so that whatever maid Cannon's housekeeper sent to tidy his room would think he'd spent the night there. He hesitated once that was done instead of leaving the room and going straight downstairs, though. What was he supposed to do with his life now? He'd trapped himself in a corner. Being with John grated on every nerve he had and made him feel out of his depth. It was a betrayal of everything Shinobu had died for. But not being with John put him on the receiving end of all the pain, a position he wasn't used to. Leaving was a wound he wasn't ready to inflict on himself yet.

There was nothing for it but to go downstairs and join the others for breakfast. The whole muddle would be easier to handle once he had coffee anyhow.

He wasn't particularly surprised to find the only

person already in the breakfast room—which faced a view of the sound that hinted it would be a lovely day—was Stone.

"There you are," Stone greeted him with a smile as Arthur approached the sideboard where several, covered dishes were already in place. "We were all worried about you last night, Mr. Gleason."

Not for the first time, Arthur was tempted to inform the man that he should be addressed as "Detective", but it hardly mattered. In fact, it might help lull the man into complacency and get him to open up.

"I was feeling unwell last night," Arthur said with what he hoped was a gracious smile. He fixed a plate of sausage and eggs, then joined Stone at the table. "It was nothing a good night's sleep couldn't cure, though."

"It wouldn't have had anything to do with your scuffle with Mr. Dandie, would it?" Stone asked with a teasing look.

Arthur figured there was no harm in giving the man a sheepish look. "I'm afraid Mr. Dandie and I can be like oil and water at times."

"Yes, partners can be like that."

Arthur almost choked on his first bite of eggs at Stone's words. "Partners?" he managed to wheeze as he quickly poured himself a cup of black coffee and gulped half of it down.

"Your secret is out," Stone said with a wink. "Dandie informed us at supper last night that the two of you are considering going into business together."

Arthur let out a long hum as if to say, "Oh, *that's* what you're talking about." What he actually said was, "The matter is still up for consideration."

Stone shrugged and cut into the slab of ham on his plate. "I was that way when I took over my father's mine and got the idea into my head to buy up the others. I didn't get along at all with the owner of the first mine I bought, Bristol. But in business, it's not about making friends, it's about making money."

Arthur's pulse sped up—partially because he knew he was on the verge of Stone spilling everything that Cannon wanted him to discover about the man, and partially because it was at that very moment that Hiroshi decided to enter the room with what looked like a fresh tea tray.

Arthur pretended not to notice Hiroshi. "And that's your primary aim in business?" he asked Stone. "To make money?"

"Well, to make alliances," Stone continued. "There is a difference between friends and allies. I learned that quite some time ago. To build a business empire, a man needs three things—a good idea or product, a savvy sense of how to bring that product or idea to market, and allies to lift the idea or product even higher." He nodded.

Arthur broke into a genuine smile, mostly because Stone had just proven himself to be exactly the sort of businessman Cannon wanted for his ally. At the same time, he was wary of the fact that Hiroshi seemed to be lingering in the room unnecessarily, listening in.

"I'm sure Cannon will appreciate all of this," Arthur said, intending to wrap up the conversation so that he could pick it up again when Hiroshi wasn't around.

Stone dashed that hope immediately by leaning closer to Arthur and saying, "Between you and me, I'm not certain Cannon is the right kind of ally for me."

Arthur's brow shot up in alarm. Hiroshi gave up the pretense of being busy with his butler duties and was now clearly listening in.

"He isn't?" Arthur asked, shifting as close to Stone as he could in the hope that the man would lower his voice to the point where Hiroshi couldn't overhear without being obvious.

Stone shook his head. "I like my business partners to be forthright and transparent in their dealings," he said. "I don't appreciate any of this beating around the bush business. I'm never going to decline an offer to spend a few days at the seaside, but I prefer to keep my negotiations in a boardroom."

"I see," Arthur said. Hiroshi was inching toward them, his eyes ablaze with interest. Arthur felt as though he needed to learn more, but he could hear voices approaching in the hall. "Are you going to proceed with the deal Cannon is offering?" he blurted, glancing desperately to the doorway.

"I don't know," Stone confessed. "I've had another offer—"

Stone snapped his mouth shut and focused on his breakfast plate a moment later as Mrs. Cannon swept into the room, little Lord Stanley in her arms, Lord Selby and Cristofori following her. Both men wore frowns.

"Madam, we agreed that Alan would spend the morning with me," Blake said in exasperation, following Mrs. Cannon around the side of the table, then attempting to take Lord Stanley out of her arms.

"We agreed on no such thing," Mrs. Cannon said, struggling to keep the boy in her arms, even as he whined and wriggled and tried to go to his father. "Now, Alan, be a good boy and stay with your grandmama."

"No, I want Papa," Lord Stanley sobbed. As soon as Lord Selby had him, the boy buried his face against the man's shoulder.

Mrs. Cannon made a whimpering sound herself and glared mutinously at Lord Selby. "This is not what we agreed upon at all, your grace. Not at all."

"If the boy wishes to be with his father, he should be with his father," Cristofori argued.

A moment later, Cannon strode into the room, effectively ruining any chance Arthur might have had to pry more information from Stone.

"Could we please enjoy one hour of peace, at least, in which to eat our breakfast?" Cannon boomed, glaring at the cluster of his wife, Lord Selby, Lord Stanley, and Cristofori. "We can all be civil, can't we?"

"But Douglas," Mrs. Cannon started to argue.

Cannon held up his hand. "I will not discuss the matter before I've had my coffee.

The room had gone from nearly silent to bustling

within a minute. Stone leaned close to Arthur and *humphed.* "If you ask me, there's a bit too much domestic drama in this house for me to be fully comfortable going into business with Cannon."

Arthur wanted to shout for everyone to be silent and to get out so he could have a word with Cannon. Cannon needed to know that his prize business catch, the man he was on the fence about wanting to connect himself with, was having reservations about him. That was precisely the sort of thing Arthur had been hired to find out. At the very least, he needed to figure out how to convince Cannon to step out of the room so they could have a word. But just as he glanced Cannon's way, trying to catch the man's eye to indicate he'd discovered something, Hiroshi moved smoothly to the head of the table where Cannon sat and offered to pour the man's coffee. Chances were, he would be able to whisper in Cannon's ear, thus beating Arthur at his own game.

Arthur shifted as it to push his chair back and stand, but at that precise moment, John entered the room, and it was as if the air had left Arthur's lungs. For some reason, John was positively radiant that morning. He wore a bright smile that accented all of his best features, he was freshly shaved and groomed, and maddeningly, his blue eyes seemed to shine with happiness—at the precise moment he met Arthur's eyes. It felt as though someone had lit an entire box of firecrackers in Arthur's chest. He felt the heat of them rise to his face, painting his cheeks, and he felt the blast stiffen his cock, making

193

his trousers far too tight for him to rise from the table without being obscene. But along with the arousal came guilt like nothing Arthur had ever known. A man had killed himself for his love, and just like that, he was ready to forget that sacrifice for a pretty face and a nice arse?

"Good morning, every—" John started his greeting, eyes still dancing amorously in Arthur's direction, when a sharp scream from Lord Stanley brought not only John's greeting to an end, but silenced every other conversation in the room as well. Arthur had never been so relieved to be yanked out of his thoughts.

"Let me go!" Lord Stanley wailed as he tried to wriggle away from the tug-o-war between Lord Selby and Mrs. Cannon. The boy was now fighting everyone.

"Both of you will unhand the child at once," Cannon boomed. Both Lord Selby and Mrs. Cannon glared at him. "Let the boy sit in his own chair at the table. Give him some food and leave him alone to eat it. When he's done, let him choose whom he'd like to be with." He stared at his wife, as if warning her not to fuss if that person proved to be Lord Selby.

Surprisingly, both Mrs. Cannon and Lord Selby did as Cannon asked. As far as Arthur could tell, Mrs. Cannon did so because she felt cowed, but Lord Selby did because he saw the wisdom of Cannon's command and knew he would win in a contest for the boy's affections. Settling Lord Stanley only went so far to calm the room, though. Mrs. Cannon and Lord Selby continued their battle silently as Cannon rolled his eyes and glanced to the side of the table where Arthur and Stone sat.

"Do you see what I have to put up with?" he asked.

"Sir, if I might have a word with you," Hiroshi stepped in, sidling up to Cannon's side.

Arthur's eyes went wide in alarm. A part of him whispered that it didn't truly matter who informed Cannon that he was about to lose a business deal, as both he and Hiroshi had been tasked with the same mission, but pride, Hiroshi's previous suspicious behavior, and the memory of all the misery the man had caused Shinobu wouldn't let Arthur drop the matter so that Hiroshi won. Arthur glanced desperately to John, trying to communicate wordlessly that John should engage Cannon's attention.

John was slow on the uptake. He seemed more interested in claiming the seat at the table next to Arthur than taking his bloody head out of the clouds and focusing on the job they were supposed to be doing.

"Oh, what in the devil do you want now?" Cannon bellowed at Hiroshi, bringing the other conversations buzzing around the room to a stop once more.

Hiroshi cleared his throat and leaned close to Cannon. "Sir, there is a matter of great importance—"

"Not now," Cannon snapped. "I just want to have my coffee and eggs. Leave me be, man!"

Hiroshi reeled back as though Cannon had slapped him. Arthur smirked at him, which caused Hiroshi to glare. The man couldn't do anything to contradict

Cannon, though, and in the end, he was forced to stiffen his back and leave the room, since he didn't really have any business there.

"I demand that we enjoy the rest of our breakfast in peace," Cannon went on, attempting to marshal his patience. "Please."

No one at the table dared to say a thing. Arthur counted his blessings. He might still be able to get the upper hand on Hiroshi by catching Cannon after the meal was over.

That proved to be the least of his worries, though. As everyone focused their attentions single-mindedly on eating in order to avoid incurring Cannon's wrath once more, John reached for Arthur's leg under the table, squeezing his thigh a little too close to the bits that mattered. Arthur was already tense from the confrontation and fumbled his fork, dropping it noisily onto his plate as he did.

"Excuse me," he mumbled when Cannon glared at him. As soon as Cannon went back to his breakfast, Arthur kicked John under the table. Just because the man had coaxed him into a night of sweet, ordinary lovemaking didn't mean he could—

"Dear God, what are *they* doing here?"

The question was issued in an offended squeal by none other than Lady Selby as she marched into the doorway of the breakfast room, dressed in silk and feathers, as if she'd just come from a night at the theater. Ian Archibald trailed a step behind her. His expression pinched to fury at the sight of Lord Selby and Cristofori.

"Annamarie!" Mrs. Cannon jumped up from her place beside Lord Stanley, where she'd been trying to coax the boy into eating the toast with jam she'd prepared for him instead of the eggs and bacon Lord Selby had presented to him. "What are you doing here, my love?"

"We've come for the festival weekend," Lady Selby said, sashaying into the room as though she were a heroine in a melodrama. She kissed both of her mother's cheeks as the two met, then she went on with, "How could you possibly stoop so low as to eat at the same table with the likes of *them*?" She wrinkled her nose at Lord Selby and Cristofori.

Arthur sucked in a breath. He had a bad feeling the already tumultuous situation in front of them was about to take a turn for the much worse. Ironically, part of him wished he still had John's hand on his thigh.

"My dear, your husband—that is, your soon to be former husband—is here to take your son away with him forever," Mrs. Cannon said, as if appealing to Lady Selby's maternal instincts to intervene.

"And why shouldn't he? Caring for the boy is so much harder than I imagined it would be, and I don't wish to do it anymore," Lady Selby said, leaving her mother to parade over to her father so that she could kiss his cheek. "Hello, Papa."

Cannon stared warily up at her. "Do not make more trouble than we already have here, darling," he growled.

"*I* am not making trouble," Lady Selby insisted. "Whoever invited those two abominations into your house is the one who made trouble."

"Abominations?" Mrs. Cannon glanced from her daughter to Lord Selby and Cristofori in confusion. "My dear, whatever do you mean?"

"This is better than a vaudeville show," Stone snorted, leaning back in his chair to watch the drama unfold.

"Mama, don't you know?" Lady Selby blinked at her mother as though the woman were simple. Arthur winced, bracing himself, as the blasted woman went on with, "Blake and that horrible playwright are lovers. That's why I left him and why I want a divorce."

Dead silence fell in the room again. At least, until Stone burst out in laughter. Cannon glared at him, as did Lady Selby.

"No, my dear, you must be mistaken," Mrs. Cannon said. "If the duke has a lover—" She stopped cold as the truth hit her, then clapped a hand to her mouth, scandalized. "Oh, no. No! Douglas." She raced up the table toward her husband as though she'd spotted a rat at Lord Selby and Cristofori's end of the room. "They're abnormal! You cannot let abnormal men take my grandson away. Heaven only knows what they'll do to the poor boy."

"I think it would be best if we left," Lord Selby said, standing and reaching for his son.

"No!" Mrs. Cannon shrieked. "Douglas, tell that horror to unhand my grandson at once!"

"Mama, just let the boy go," Lady Selby sighed. "I don't want him anyhow."

"But I do," Mrs. Cannon shouted. "He should be mine." She started back down the table toward Lord Stanley.

Lord Stanley screamed and practically leapt into Lord Selby's arms. "Papa!"

Stone made a sound and pushed his chair back from the table. "I think I'd better be the one to go," he began.

"Silence, everyone!" Cannon shouted. "No one is leaving this room or this house until this matter is settled, do I make myself clear?"

CHAPTER 15

They had been so close. So close to everything going right—Blake getting his son back, Cannon getting a solid business partner, and John ending up with Arthur in his arms and his bed at last. So close, and then, as usual, Annamarie crashed into the scene like a broadside fired at a frigate, shattering the whole thing to splinters.

"Papa!" Annamarie gasped, holding a hand to her chest and gaping at Cannon in offense. "I do not appreciate you speaking to me in that way. I am a duchess, after all."

"You have been doing everything within your power for months now not to be a duchess anymore!" Niall shouted at her from the other side of the table.

John couldn't blame the man for losing his temper, but not only did his outburst send Alan into a fresh, new wave of wails as he clung to Blake's neck—and Mrs.

Cannon into sobs as well as she watched, most likely drawing some sort of unkind and sordid conclusion—it had Cannon's moustache quivering with rage and his face turning so red John genuinely feared the man might fall into a heart attack.

"Not another word from anyone," Cannon bellowed. He turned to his daughter. "Annamarie, what are you doing here and why do you feel the need to cause trouble wherever you go?"

"I came to tell you that dear Ian and I are to be married," Annamarie said, clasping Archibald's arm with a simpering grin. "As soon as you force Blake to finalize our divorce."

Archibald simpered back at Annamarie, but the moment she turned away from him, he looked as though he might be sick. Mrs. Cannon groaned and flopped into the nearest chair, burying her face in her hands.

John cleared his throat gently and stared at Cannon.

"Do you have something to say?" Cannon barked.

"Your daughter has been in possession of divorce papers for quite some time, sir," he said. "She has yet to sign and return them."

"I lost them," Annamarie said with a shrug. "It's very unfair." She paused, then added, "And Ian said I shouldn't sign anything until Blake pays me."

Cannon sighed and closed his eyes, as if praying for patience. "I will handle the legalities in my daughter's name from now on. Can you provide me with another set of documents?"

"I can, sir," John said with a nod, glad he'd thought to bring duplicates. He'd done so precisely because Annamarie was such a flibbertigibbet.

"That problem is solved, then," Cannon said. "Annamarie, *you*." Cannon narrowed his eyes at Archibald. "Get out of my sight at once."

"I have unpacking to do anyhow," Annamarie said, tilting her head up with a smile, as if she'd won the argument.

"Wait!" Mrs. Cannon called. "You must stay and help me to convince your father to fight for little Alan."

"No! I want Papa!" Alan burst into tears all over again.

Blake glared at Mrs. Cannon as he rubbed Alan's back, and he and Niall started out of the room.

"Wait!" Mrs. Cannon called again, shooting to her feet as though she would stop them.

"You heard the boy, Mama," Annamarie said, already on her way out of the room with Archibald. "He wants to be with his father. Let him."

"But darling...."

Mrs. Cannon rushed out of the room after Annamarie. Blake and Niall departed with Alan a few steps behind them.

John glanced to Arthur, interested to see what he thought of the whole situation. After the night before, he felt like the two of them had reached a new level of understanding. What they'd shared had been beautiful and scintillating. Not just the pleasure, but the way they'd made a connection on a whole new level. Even though Arthur had left before he'd awakened—which he'd told the man not to do, damn him—he felt as though they'd turned a corner, and the future was now theirs for the taking.

But Arthur's look was distracted and closed off, cold. The spark of wicked amusement he'd expected to see in Arthur's expressive, blue eyes simply wasn't there. Instead of making even a little bit of an effort to see the situation as funny, Arthur turned straight to Cannon and asked, "Sir, may I have a word with you?"

Cannon looked exasperated. Before he could say anything, however, Stone dabbed his mouth with his serviette, tossed it on his empty breakfast plate, and stood. "That's enough for me," he said. "Cannon, it has been a pleasure staying with you, but I believe your family business trumps your industrial business at the moment."

"Stone, wait." Cannon took a step toward the man as Stone left the room.

John held up a hand to Cannon and said, "I think I can handle this. It appears as though Det. Gleason has something he'd like to share with you."

"You don't need to—" Arthur began.

John was in the hallway, chasing after Stone before Arthur could finish his sentence.

"Mr. Stone, please wait." John caught up to the man halfway down the hall. "Might I have a word with you."

Stone stopped and turned to him with a humorless

laugh and a roll of his eyes. "Never thought you'd find yourself in the middle of a French farce by accepting old Cannon's invitation to stay, did you?"

John read the man's mood quickly and played along. "Not at all."

They were near one of the rooms that had an exit to the back porch, and as the morning was shaping up to be pleasant, at least where the weather was concerned, John gestured for Stone to accompany him outside.

Once they were there, John opened the conversation by saying, "I'm terribly sorry that my client's personal difficulties have interrupted your business holiday. Now that you have met Lady Selby, you can see the difficulty we've been having securing this divorce."

Again, Stone laughed humorlessly. "I can see your reasons for requiring a divorce as well." He shook his head. "These modern vices perplex me. I don't know what it is that turns decent men into monsters who would rather sin infamously with other men than stick to a pretty wife and a normal family."

John did his best to swallow a burst of incredulity. "In all fairness, sir," he said, "you are mistaken if you believe this variation in tastes is a modern invention. Men like Lord Selby and Mr. Cristofori have been woven into the fabric of society since the dawn of man. They have made vital contributions to the development of civilization. Why, Socrates himself—"

"Spare me the history lecture," Stone cut him off. It was probably a good thing as well. "Maybe perverts have been meddling with things since early days, but what has Socrates done for civilization lately?"

John's jaw dropped. He couldn't believe what he was hearing...and yet he could. When one rejected the truth, the only thing to fall back on was stupidity.

"I am done here," Stone went on, stepping past John as though he would go back inside. "Tell Mrs. Cannon—"

He didn't get any farther before Arthur came shooting out the door to join them.

"And just what do you think you're doing?" Arthur demanded of John.

John was so surprised by the hostility of the comment that he reeled back. "I was having a conversation with Mr. Stone, attempting to assuage his troubled thoughts after the scene he just witnessed."

"You were not asked to do so." Arthur stepped right up to John, radiating anger.

John was at a complete loss and could only work his jaw wordlessly for a moment, scrambling to know what to say or do. Things had been so good just a few, short hours before.

"Is everything all right?" he asked as soon as his thoughts settled enough to make speech possible. "Has Cannon said something to upset you?"

"I think I'll just let the two of you get on with whatever argument you're clearly still having," Stone said with a roll of his eyes, attempting to sidestep around them to reenter the house.

"No!" John and Arthur shouted at the same time,

which only served to make Stone flinch back as though they'd fired shots at him.

"I'm terribly sorry, Mr. Cannon," John told the man, wincing over his own misstep. "This argument with my colleague is nothing. We should be addressing your concerns."

"I should be addressing Mr. Stone's concerns you mean," Arthur hissed at John.

"Should you?" Stone asked, looking increasingly uncomfortable by the moment.

John felt as though they'd stepped out onto a crumbling ledge and were about to plunge to certain doom at any moment. That feeling of disaster grew ten times worse when, of all people, Hiroshi stepped around the corner of the house, walking fast.

As soon as Hiroshi saw the three of them on the porch, his quick gait stopped dead, and he stared at the three with wide eyes. For the briefest moment, he glanced back over his shoulder, as though at someone he'd just been speaking to, then his expression went perfectly blank. The porch had a small set of stairs leading off that side, and whatever Hiroshi had been planning to do, he changed those plans and marched up onto the porch.

"Mr. Stone, is there something I can help you with?" he asked with perfect manners.

"Yes," Stone said, taking a step toward him. "You can help me pack up my things and get out of this madhouse."

"Mr. Stone, wait." John stepped into the man's path

again. "There must be some way we can appease you."

"Appease him?" Arthur argued. "As if it is your job to soothe the ruffled feathers of any man who does not fit into your definition of geniality?"

John blinked at Arthur, baffled as to why, of all times, the man would choose now to throw something like that in his face. "I only wish to see Mr. Stone settled and satisfied with the situation he now finds himself in," he argued.

"Let the man have his own opinions on things." Arthur turned toward Stone. "I am sorry if my friend has offended you with his high-handedness. Perhaps it would be best if we were to take a stroll on the beach to talk things through."

"Arthur," John snapped. "Now is not the time for a walk."

"Oh." Stone drew the single syllable out, taking a large step back and glancing warily between John and Arthur. "Oh, I see what this is all about now." He raised both of his hands, looking as though he would either try to settle everyone to calm or ward John and Arthur away. "An argument. I see now. The two of you have been having an *argument*. It would make perfect sense, though, wouldn't it? I mean, if Lord Selby and his friend are that way, it would be only natural—if I can even use that word now—that they would hire a solicitor and a detective who are just like them. I see now." He glanced between John and Arthur as though either one of them might attack at any moment.

"Lord Selby is not Det. Gleason's employer," Hiroshi added, a victorious light in his eyes. "Mr. Cannon is the one who has hired him."

Stone balked, turning to Hiroshi. "Cannon? Hire a queer detective? Whatever for?"

"To investigate you, sir." Hiroshi bowed to the man.

John gaped at Hiroshi, incredulity stacking on top of the frustration and anger he already felt. "Hiroshi," he warned.

It didn't do a lick of good.

"Cannon has been investigating me?" Stone was visibly offended. "Whatever for?"

"To determine whether you would be a safe business partner or whether you are little more than a backwoods ignoramus who had a lucky break in business, as Mr. Cannon said."

"How dare you?" Arthur seethed, looking as though he would throttle Hiroshi.

"No, how dare Cannon," Stone snapped. "This is positively the last straw. I have never been so insulted in all my life. If Cannon thinks I would lower myself to go into business with him after this, then he's the ignoramus, not me. Good day to you all."

Stone marched back into the house, and this time John didn't make a move to stop him. He could hardly believe what he'd just witnessed. Stone might have had good reason to be alarmed by everything that had been revealed that morning, but Hiroshi was an outright traitor for pushing the man over the edge and sending him on his way. The bastard barely acknowledged John or Arthur at all once Stone dashed into the house. He merely grinned as though he'd gotten his revenge and walked in after Stone.

"I cannot believe any of what just happened," John said, aghast, turning to Arthur with wide eyes.

"Believe it," Arthur growled, pacing away from John. "Your meddling caused the whole thing."

It was an unexpected blow, and John flinched, eyes going wide. "Where is this venom coming from?"

Arthur stopped a few yards down the porch and turned to glare at John. "Investigating is my realm. Cannon hired me to handle Stone."

"He hired both of us," John insisted. "As a team. I thought we worked well together as a team."

He knew he'd made a grave error in touching on the tender subject at the very moment that the two of them had experienced a set-back, as evidenced by Arthur's cold reaction.

"You are far too concerned with forming teams and alliances and...and...."

"Relationships?" John suggested when Arthur fumbled for the word.

Arthur clamped his jaw tight and stormed right up to him, stopping when they were so close John could feel the heat radiating from him. "Stop mistaking a night in bed together for a relationship. Be both got what we wanted. Stop making more of it than it is."

"Stop running from the truth," John hissed back at

him, grabbing Arthur's arms. "I can see in your eyes that you're lying to yourself. I can see that you're hurting yourself by denying the one thing that you truly want. I have been extraordinarily patient in my efforts to help you along, but every man's patience has its limits."

John considered it a miracle and a sign of progress that Arthur let him get through the entire speech without interrupting or pulling away. That didn't mean he and Arthur had completely turned a corner yet, though. He could still feel resistance pulsing through Arthur, could still see the fear and the need to fight in Arthur's eyes.

"Now is not the time for this conversation," Arthur said in a hoarse voice, pulling away from John. He turned to walk down the porch, speaking as he went. "Cannon has just lost his business partner. Stone might see fit to inform Cannon of our—" For a moment, John was certain Arthur was going to say "relationship", but he finished with, "proclivities" instead. "And now that Lady Selby is here to ruin things, as she always does, we have Mrs. Cannon's insistence on keeping Lord Stanley to deal with."

Arthur paused three-quarters of the way down the porch, bending to pick up a small scrap of paper that had blown up against one of the wicker chairs.

John let out a breath and scrubbed his hands over his face. "You're right," he admitted, hating the way it squeezed his chest with anxiety to let something so vital go so easily. "I apologize for pressing the matter when too many other things require our full attention. But Arthur," he took a few steps toward his lover as Arthur frowned at the slip of paper in his hands, "we cannot brush things between us aside and treat them as secondary for much longer. It is eating you from the inside, and my heart cannot take...." He scowled. "Arthur, are you even listening to me?"

Arthur glanced up at him in alarm. "I think we've got the bastard," he said, his alarm taking on a vicious gleam.

John frowned. "I beg your pardon?"

"Hiroshi. I think we've got him pinned like a butterfly specimen." Arthur thrust the slip of paper at John.

John took it, gaze still focused on Arthur for a moment, still bristling with frustration over the man's uncanny ability to ignore his feelings, and the lengths he would go to in order to avoid even a hint of the things that needed to be resolved between them.

The writing on the paper arrested those thoughts for a moment.

"The plan is nearly complete. Brendel will make a counteroffer to Stone within days. Payment forthcoming."

John didn't know what to think. He wasn't surprised. It was like Arthur had said the day before. Industrial espionage was increasing every day. But compared to the things that truly mattered, compared to the tenuous grasp John felt he had on Arthur's heart, the matter was nothing but an excuse.

He thrust the paper back at Arthur. "Well done," he said without any enthusiasm.

"This has to have come from Hiroshi, though

whether he was the recipient or whether he sent it...." He pressed his lips together for a moment and stared at John. "Why are you not pleased with this development?"

John stared at him for a few, painful seconds before shaking his head. "Have fun playing spy," he sighed, walking for the stairs that would lead him to the beach.

"John where are you going? This is an important lead," Arthur called after him. "I can take this to Cannon and prove that Hiroshi is playing him for a fool."

"You mean the way you're playing me?" John asked without turning around. He did glance over his shoulder once he reached the boardwalk. "This is all just another excuse to stay in the past, Arthur. You're never going to be free until you cleanse Hiroshi and Shinobu from your thoughts. And until you do, I fear there is no room for me."

It hurt more than John anticipated to say so.

"John," Arthur called after him, his voice dark with frustration, and then worried when he called again, "John!"

John merely shook his head and kept walking. Perhaps there was something to be said for a nice, boring love affair with a good, uninteresting man who wouldn't jerk his heart around as though it were bound in chains. Perhaps he couldn't change who he was after all. He couldn't change unless Arthur was willing to change with him.

CHAPTER 16

*E*ach time Arthur tried to do what he thought should come most naturally to him and push John away in favor of work—and more importantly, out of respect for Shinobu—it backfired worse than the time before. Not just in terms of John walking away from him. He'd half expected that when he ignored John's obvious attempt to discuss feelings and probably snuggle up and pretend they were giggling misses who wove daisy crowns for each other like they were—

No, that wasn't fair.

He blew out a breath as he watched John's retreating back disappear around the corner on the beach. He wasn't supposed to ache with regret when John walked away from him, he was supposed to be relieved. It was supposed to assuage the guilt, not make it worse. John wanted things that Arthur couldn't give him, as evidenced by the night before.

That was also unfair. The night before had been beautiful and erotic. Rather, it was his thoughts when the reality of morning hit him that had provided all the evidence he needed to prove he couldn't be John's sweetheart.

He turned around and headed into the house, needing something to help clear his head. He could argue with himself about John, the nature of their connection, his responsibilities to Shinobu's memory, and the night they'd spent together all he wanted, but the fact was that being together with John the way they'd been—neither of them particularly dominant or submissive—had been enjoyable. Sleeping with John as the small spoon hadn't been half bad. The possibility of working with John, not only in an attempt to fix things with Cannon where Stone was concerned, but in the future as well, was intriguing.

No, it wasn't. It went against everything Arthur thought he knew about himself, everything he'd allowed himself in the wake of the disaster he'd caused with Shinobu.

He stopped when he reached the front hallway of Cannon's house and let out a loud, frustrated growl. So loud and ferocious, in fact, that he inadvertently frightened a young maid, causing her to drop the traveling bag she carried down the stairs.

"I'm sorry," Arthur instantly apologized. "I'm so sorry."

He didn't know what he was doing anymore. He

rushed to help the maid retrieve the traveling bag as it bumped down the rest of the stairs, but it didn't do any good. He was convinced he should be talking to Cannon about Stone and his suspicions where Hiroshi was concerned. But more urgently, he knew he needed to speak to John and somehow make things right. He needed to be honest with the man, tell him there could never be anything between them the way John wanted, his heart was too ruined.

No, he needed to swallow his pride, put the pain of his past and his youthful folly with Shinobu behind him, and admit that the sort of relationship John seemed to be after would actually suit him just fine.

But he couldn't. Not after what he'd gone through with Shinobu. He couldn't give his heart away like that again.

John wasn't Shinobu, though. Arthur had been a much younger, much less experienced man back then. He'd learned things since, he'd grown. John was so much more of an equal to him than Shinobu ever was.

"Sir? Sir, are you quite all right?" the maid asked.

Arthur blinked, realizing that he'd picked up the traveling bag without handing it to her as his tumultuous thoughts brought him to a complete standstill. He handed the bag over with a sheepish look. "I have no idea," he told the young woman honestly.

"I never expected a whirlwind would come through the house when I woke up this morning," the maid whispered, a look of camaraderie in her eyes as she stepped past Arthur. "First chance I get, I'm having a cigarette out by the kitchen door. You can join me if you'd like," she whispered, making eyes at him.

Of all things, that cheeky invitation from Cannon's young maid put a smile on Arthur's face and let him take a deep breath. "I just might," he winked at the girl. He wasn't the only one whose head was spinning at the moment.

That point was proven further half a second later as Lord Selby and Cristofori came marching down the stairs, their suitcases and bags in hand. Strangely, Lady Selby followed them.

"Honestly, this whole thing has gotten terribly out of hand," she said, unable to see the way Lord Selby and Cristofori rolled their eyes at her. "You don't need to go on my account."

"We are not going anywhere on your account, Annamarie," Blake said with a sigh. When he spotted Arthur, he nodded. "We're going back to the inn. Mrs. Cannon has made it clear she does not want us residing under her roof anymore."

"Are you certain the inn still has a room available for you?" Arthur asked, stepping aside as the two men pushed past him, heading for the door. Lady Selby remained on the landing halfway down the stairs, likely so that she could remain several feet above them all.

"If they don't, we'll figure something else out," Cristofori said.

"And what about Lord Stanley?" Arthur asked.

JUST A LITTLE RIVALRY

"Oh, I still plan to spend as much of my time as possible with my son before we leave. And we're leaving just after the festival," Lord Selby said, then added, "We'd leave before, but Alan's heart is so set on attending the festival."

Arthur nodded, but was prevented from saying more as Stone came thundering down the stairs next, a suitcase in one hand and one of Cannon's male servants with armfuls of other traveling bags behind him.

"And tell Cannon that I do not want word of this to be spread all around the city," Stone was in the middle of saying, though Arthur couldn't determine to whom he was speaking.

"You can tell him yourself," Cannon said, striding into the foyer from one of the adjacent hallways.

Lord Selby and Cristofori exchanged nods, then headed out the front door and on their way.

Stone paused in the foyer to glare at Cannon. "I have never been so insulted in all my life," he said. "It's bad enough that you would let your family problems interfere with our potential working relationship, but hiring a private investigator to vet me? All because you think I am an idiot?"

Arthur winced.

Cannon looked as though someone had suddenly thrust an iron pole up his arse. "What is the meaning of this accusation?" he boomed, his voice a little too high. "I have done no such thing."

"Your butler informed me of it, sir." Stone sniffed at

Cannon. "I'll see myself out. I've already sent one of your servants off to fetch your carriage. Giving me a ride to the train station is the least you can do."

"I don't understand," Cannon growled, frowning. "My butler told you I hired a private investigator?"

Cannon would have done a better job at feigning ignorance if he hadn't scowled at Arthur.

"Good day, sir," Stone said, then turned to march out the door.

As soon as he was gone, Cannon turned to Arthur as though he were ready to commit murder. "You," he hissed, starting toward Arthur.

"Sir, I think it would be best if we spoke in private," Arthur said.

"I think it would be best if we didn't speak at all," Cannon said. "You delayed me this morning with some nonsense about Stone having cold feet, and now he's gone." He stood a little straighter, pointing at the front door. "The door is open, sir. I think it would be best if you used it."

"Hiroshi is double-crossing you, sir," Arthur blurted, getting it all out on the table. "He has been false with you this whole time, and I believe he is actually employed by someone else as a mole in your house."

Cannon stopped short in his move across the hall. He narrowed his eyes at Arthur. "Prove it."

Arthur held up the slip of paper he'd found on the porch. "We should speak in private, sir."

Cannon quivered angrily on his spot for a moment

before blowing out a breath, shaking his head, and striding down the hall, gesturing for Arthur to come after him. Several doors down, Cannon motioned for Arthur to join him in what turned out to be a small, stuffy office.

As soon as Cannon shut the door behind him, he said, "I will give you five minutes to prove your case, otherwise, I will toss you out on your ear."

Arthur bristled. Cannon had no business being so short with him. He would have made a rude gesture and walked out of Cannon's house and his life for good, leaving the man to his fate, but pride, his bone-deep need to see things through, and his determination to see that Hiroshi was thwarted pushed him on.

"I found this on your porch, sir." Arthur handed him the note. As soon as Cannon opened it and read, his eyes went wide. "More than that, yesterday, Mr. Dandie and I spotted Hiroshi speaking to an unknown man in a suit at the Peconic train station. Even before that, before we arrived on Long Island, I saw Hiroshi at a club in New York, speaking to a man in a business suit who looked out of place for the particular sort of club we were attending."

Cannon snapped his eyes up from the note in his hands, glaring at Arthur. "How did you know it was my butler if you had yet to come out here?"

Arthur winced slightly, regretting the fact that he couldn't avoid telling Cannon the full truth. "Sir, I was already acquainted with Hiroshi from the time I spent in Japan."

That surprised Cannon. "You were in Japan?"

"Ten years ago, sir." Arthur nodded. "When I was a member of Her Majesty's Navy. I knew Hiroshi back then as the owner of a brothel and a petty criminal."

Cannon narrowed his eyes. "How do I know you aren't lying to me?"

"Why would I?" Arthur asked honestly. "You hired me to look out for your best interests. That originally involved investigating Stone, but I discovered that you have a deeper problem—a member of your staff. You can either believe me and trust the note in your hands, or you can disbelieve me and have me thrown out."

Cannon was silent for a long time. He stared at Arthur. He stared at the note in his hand. He clenched his jaw and stared at the wall.

Finally, he said, "I won't throw you out. Not yet. But I want you to prove to me that these accusations you have made against my butler are true."

"I will endeavor to do so to the best of my ability, sir," Arthur said with a curt nod. "And I can assure you, my abilities are extensive."

Cannon didn't seem impressed. "If you fail to prove Hiroshi has been working against me," he said, "I will ruin you. I am a powerful man, Det. Gleason. Don't think I can't do it."

"I am quite certain you can, sir." Arthur bowed to him.

Cannon dismissed him, and once he was out of the room, Arthur let out a shaky breath. He didn't truly think

Cannon could ruin him, but he wasn't in the mood to find out for certain. He needed solid proof that Hiroshi was everything Arthur knew him to be, and that he was at least partially responsible for Stone's defection.

The only way to do that was to do what he did best—investigate. And investigation meant that he had to return to the city. Blessedly, it wasn't that long of a train journey back into the city, and trains departed and arrived fairly frequently on Long Island. Arthur spent the rest of the day combing through whatever public records he could find about immigrants from Japan, searching for tangible proof of Hiroshi's background. He hadn't told anyone where he went, though, and on such short notice, the number of records he was granted access to was pitifully small. Taken together, it meant he had to return to Peconic on the last train to leave that evening empty-handed.

At least the whole misadventure meant he had been able to avoid both John and Hiroshi all day. It was well after midnight by the time Arthur crawled into his own bed in his own room. All he wanted to do was sleep so that he could face whatever new miseries life had for him on the day of the festival, but in the end, he wasn't even capable of that.

He lay in bed, staring up at the ceiling, wondering if John was thinking about him in his bed at the other end of the hall. He wondered why he was spending more of his sleepless hours thinking about John than Hiroshi. Or even Shinobu, for that matter. Especially Shinobu.

For years, Shinobu had occupied all of his restless, middle-of-the-night thoughts. He'd sworn he wouldn't forget the man, sworn that their love would continue beyond death. Those promises had seemed so important and so vivid to the young man he'd once been.

Now, everything was muddled. Essentially, until Hiroshi had slammed into his life once more, Arthur's memories of Shinobu had faded into a shroud of love and guilt that he'd worn without thinking about it. For months now, he'd spent his sleepless hours coming up with ways to vex John or imagining all of the wicked things he could do to the tall, handsome, good man while beating himself off. He'd been able to separate the two things in his mind and heart.

Since arriving on Long Island and having his past dredged up from the deep, where it had been almost buried, he'd been acutely aware of the promises he'd once made to Shinobu and the pain of their past together, but would he have thought of those things if Hiroshi hadn't been there to remind him? Would he and John eventually have drifted together anyhow? They had certainly wanted each other long enough. Would he have let Shinobu's memory go without the pain and the soul-rending if Hiroshi hadn't torn the scab off of a partially-healed wound?

Deeper, more frightening thoughts hit Arthur as he tossed and turned, as far from sleeping as could be. Was he simply a coward? He'd protected his heart for so long that he'd convinced himself that he didn't need love, only satisfaction. Was he using work and the past simply as a way to stop himself from feeling beholden to another man? And if that was what he was doing, it certainly wasn't fair to John. Was he a cruel man at heart, as he'd thought he only pretended to be when playing with a willing partner? Would John continue to love him once he saw the truth?

Arthur tossed and turned, fighting to avoid the maelstrom of questions that shook the very foundation of what he believed about himself for the rest of the night. By morning, he was exhausted inside and out. He got up, washed, and dressed for the festival in spite of it all, determined to make himself as pleasant as possible. Instinct told him he should go back to New York again, he should find the information he needed to prove Hiroshi was working against Cannon. He should be professional, and certainly not more concerned with matters of the heart—particularly not his own heart.

He had the sinking feeling he was a disgrace, that he had let everyone down—Shinobu, Lord Selby, Cannon, and especially John—but he had no idea how to rectify the situation.

"You look wretched this morning," Cristofori teased him with a grin as they walked into town for the festival.

Lord Selby and Cristofori had arrived at the Cannon house first thing to escort Lord Stanley to the festival. Mrs. Cannon had protested fiercely that the event was something she and her grandson had been looking forward to. Lord Stanley had cried, Cannon had just barely convinced his wife and Lord Selby to take Lord Stanley together in one of his carriages, and everyone else had been left to walk into town behind them.

Except John. John had been busy sorting out the divorce papers with Lady Selby and Cannon when Arthur had come down for breakfast, and, coward that he was, Arthur had slipped out of the house with Cristofori before speaking to him.

"He'll come along eventually, you know," Cristofori told Arthur after catching Arthur glancing back at the house over his shoulder for the fifth time in a minute.

Arthur blew out a breath and faced forward, shoving his hands in his pockets. "I was not designed to carry on love affairs," he grumbled. "I'm shite at it."

"I think we all are, until we find someone who changes that," Cristofori said sympathetically. When Arthur didn't say anything else, he went on with, "So what's the problem?"

Arthur glanced warily at him and said, "John wants me to be someone I'm not."

Cristofori hummed sagely. "Just as I wanted Blake to be someone he wasn't."

Arthur winced. It wasn't quite fair of him to assume he was the only man who had difficulties in love or pain in his past. "The two of you sorted it out," he said.

Cristofori laughed. "After ten years of misery." He reached out and thumped Arthur's shoulder. "You'll be fine. The more time you spend talking to John about these things, the better off you'll be."

Arthur grunted. "I detest talking about things. Talk only brings confusion and misery."

Cristofori shrugged. "Then just fuck instead." When Arthur gaped at him, he laughed and went on with, "It's speaking without words. Blake and I have resolved more than a few arguments in our day without words."

"I wish," Arthur grumbled.

In fact, he did wish he could sort things out with John that way. He rather felt as though he could sort a great many of his most troublesome thoughts out in a horizontal position with John. With or without restraints and whips. Cristofori had a point about speaking without words.

Arthur continued to chew on those thoughts once they reached town. The entire place was brightly decorated with flowers and bunting. Booths and activities had been set up all along the main street, and people from every walk of life were there enjoying the sights, sounds, and tastes that were available to them. Arthur clearly understood why Mrs. Cannon had been so adamant that Lord Stanley attend. At least half of the games and activities that had been set up were perfect for children of the boy's age. Arthur spotted Mrs. Cannon and Lord Selby continuing their emotional tug-o-war with the boy once he and Cristofori had wandered around for a few minutes, taking in the sights.

Not long after Cristofori parted ways with Arthur to join Lord Selby, Arthur spotted John striding into the colorful chaos. He couldn't decide whether it was a bad sign or a good one that his heart squeezed and his spirits felt lighter at just the sight of the man. John truly was too handsome for his own good. Part of Arthur wanted to wrap the man up in tight bonds and paint the word "Mine" across his brow because of it, but at the moment, after his conversation with Cristofori and his restless night of tormenting thoughts, he was convinced at this point that he had to earn it.

Arthur winced and turned away from John, buying himself some time by purchasing a cone of roasted, seasoned nuts from a vendor set up near where he stood. He despised the idea of earning his place by any man's side, writhed in discomfort at the notion that he needed someone else in his life, and was outright terrified of driving another man to his death, as he'd done with Shinobu. But John deserved better than what little he'd given so far, and if he was ever going to be able to look at himself in the mirror again, he had to do something.

"Haven't I seen you around here before?" he asked as he approached John from behind, deliberately surprising the man—and also deliberately behaving as though nothing at all were out of the ordinary between the two of them.

John jerked slightly at being surprised and twisted to face Arthur. Arthur smiled as fetchingly as he knew how, then held out the paper cone of nuts like a peace offering.

"What is this for?" John asked suspiciously. His eyes flashed, though, hinting to Arthur that he was ripe for forgiveness.

"I thought you might like to eat some nuts," Arthur teased him.

John made a snorting sound, like he was trying not to laugh, and schooled his expression into a frown. "That is the oldest, most tired joke known to man," he drawled, snatching the cone from Arthur's hand. His eyes continued to shine in spite of his expression.

"I'm not very original," Arthur confessed. "Not when it comes to jokes. I'm not particularly good at this sort of thing either." He waved his hand in John's general direction. "Something I'm certain you've noticed by now."

"Then you need to practice," John said, seemingly nonchalant as he picked through the nuts, popping a few into his mouth. "Practice makes perfect."

Arthur turned to lean against the edge of the porch next to where they stood. "Practice either makes perfect, or, if someone is truly inept at something, it causes them to hurt themselves and end up dead. Or for someone else to end up dead."

John's brow shot up. "That's taking things to extremes, don't you think?"

Arthur stared hard at him, fighting down the wave of frustration that came with John missing his point. There were few enough people immediately next to him that he could stare at John and say, "Shinobu ended up dead."

John's sly expression hollowed out. "God, Arthur, I'm sorry. That's not what I meant at all."

"I know." Arthur held up his hands with a sigh. "I just wanted to remind you that even though it may not seem like it on the surface, even though it may not feel obvious to you, I am playing for the highest of stakes."

And that was it. That was the summation of everything that had been tormenting him for days, for years. He'd gambled with high stakes and lost once before. It wasn't cowardice or fear that was holding him back from trusting John with his heart; it was experience. He knew it, he'd figured it out at least a dozen times already, but the aggravation of life and love was that it became necessary to have the same epiphany several times before it truly took root.

"Can you forgive me for being a prickly and broken bastard, riddled with guilt and uncertain whether I am deserving of a second chance?" he asked John in a casual voice while actually feeling as though he'd slit his wrists open and bled all over the man's feet. "Could you still want me even though—"

His words dried up and his mouth hung open as he spotted Hiroshi slipping through the crowd and up the stairs leading to the post office across the street. The post office which also contained the telegraph office, if Arthur remembered correctly.

He jerked to stand straight, heart pounding. Years of instinct as a detective had taught him to look for the signs when someone was about to make the move that would do them in. Hiroshi had that look. Arthur had to act now, or he might lose his chance to prove the man's duplicity to Cannon forever.

"Excuse me," he told John as he strode away, his focus solely on Hiroshi.

"Arthur!" John called after him, clearly annoyed.

Arthur felt the sting of his tone, but he kept moving forward. In spite of the layers of his soul that had been peeled away and the revelation of everything he felt for John, he had to finish up this last part of his past before he could charge headlong into his future.

CHAPTER 17

*J*ust like that, Arthur was gone. Again. John took a step as if he would follow the bastard, but stopped when a group of excited children shot past him, blocking the way. John let out a baffled, irritated breath and gaped after Arthur's retreating back as he nearly leapt into the post office. Once again, it seemed as though anything and everything had taken precedence in Arthur's mind except for him, and what was he left with? A sack of nuts.

Clenching his jaw tight, John mashed the top of the paper cone holding the nuts closed, then raised the bundle, wanting nothing more than to throw it into a window that would shatter spectacularly as a representation of his frustration.

"If you're not going to eat them, give them to me," Niall said, walking swiftly over to where John stood.

The arrival of his friend was like a splash of cold

water to John. He lowered his arm and sighed. "Here." He handed the nuts over to Niall as he stopped beside him. "I don't think I have the stomach for anything Arthur has deigned to give me anymore."

Niall hummed and nodded slowly, as if he could guess exactly what the problem was. "It's come to that, has it?"

John frowned, crossing his arms and leaning back against the porch railing where Arthur had leaned earlier. "It shouldn't have come to anything," he grumbled. "I shouldn't have been such a damn fool and let myself be led by the nose the way I have been."

Niall tilted his head to the side and looked at him strangely before shifting to lean against the railing by John's side. To any outsiders, the two of them would have looked as though they were simply observing the activity of the festival and commenting upon it. "Is that what's happened? You've been led by the nose?"

John sent him an irritated, sideways look before saying, "That is what it is beginning to feel like. I was perfectly happy before, living my life in peace, reestablishing my business in London, sticking close to the things I knew."

"Were you, though?" Niall asked. "Happy?"

John's frown deepened. "Of course, I was. I had work, friends, enough money for a holiday now and then."

"Did you have all of that in Liverpool?"

John could tell Niall was driving at something. He

wanted to end the conversation then and there, but he owed it to his friend to be honest. "I did," he said, sensing where the conversation was going. He grabbed the nuts away from Niall and popped one into his mouth sullenly.

"Then why move back to London?" Niall shrugged.

John let out a breath and dropped his arms to his sides with it. "Because I was restless," he confessed. "Because there didn't seem to be a reason to stay after my relationship ended."

"Because London is exciting and full of interesting people and experiences?" Niall suggested.

"I know you're implying that I wasn't as perfectly happy as I thought I was, that I was searching for something," John said, his back aching as though he'd let go of a heavy weight after straining himself.

Niall merely grinned. "Good. Then I don't have to attempt to prove that point. And now, can you guess my next point and save me the trouble of proving that?"

"Yes," John sighed, rubbing his forehead. "That Arthur hasn't led me into anything. That I've taken myself along this path of frustration and misery by chasing after a man with a checkered past who is so afraid of being hurt by love again that he runs and runs until—"

He was forced to stop talking as a trio of young women with bright smiles, stars in their eyes, and their whole lives ahead of them crossed a little too close to him and Niall for his comfort.

Once they had passed, John didn't have the heart to continue on down the same path of conversation.

"There's no point to anything now, is there?" he said, opening the cone of nuts again and eating a few without savoring them. "Just now, for example," he said with his mouth full, "he was saying such lovely things, asking for understanding, but the second Hiroshi showed his ugly face, he was off like a shot, chasing the past instead of looking to the future."

"Yes, what is the connection between those two?" Niall asked with genuine interest.

John finished chewing his mouthful of nuts and swallowed. He bought some time by closing up the cone and shoving it in his jacket pocket before saying, "They knew each other in Japan, right after Arthur left the navy." John shuffled his feet, face heating as he worried about the implication of sharing Arthur's business without permission. "Suffice it to say there are more details that I cannot speak about, but Hiroshi was Arthur's rival for the affections of a young man named Shinobu."

"Ah," Niall said, as though he understood.

John shook his head, and raised a hand to warn Niall that he didn't yet understand. "Shinobu committed suicide, and Arthur has always blamed himself."

Niall blinked, his eyes going wide. "Oh, that is a different kettle of fish. A sad one as well."

"He's told me the whole story, and I maintain that Arthur is not to blame in the least—"

"—but of course Arthur doesn't see it that way," Niall finished the thought.

"Now I believe he feels he needs to make certain that Hiroshi gets his just deserts over the whole matter, but...."

He let his thought go with a sigh and shook his head. He stared at the door to the post office, wondering if or when Arthur or Hiroshi would come out again. Surely, they had to have had whatever confrontation Arthur was hungry for by now. John was half surprised an entire, violent scene hadn't unfolded, spilling from the post office to the street.

"I am not inclined to play second-fiddle to a dead man," John said at last, pushing away from the porch railing, but feeling as though he had nowhere to go. "Nor am I inclined to forever rank lower than a grudge."

"And have you told Arthur that?" Niall asked.

John blinked at him. It seemed like the most obvious question in the world. "I feel as though I have," he said, then shrugged. "How many times does a man need to hear an ultimatum before he understands that it is an ultimatum?"

Niall hummed as though he were considering the question seriously, then said, "Perhaps roughly the same number of times that a man comes to the conclusion that he will not accept shabby treatment before he becomes willing to actually walk away from that treatment."

John winced as though Niall had slapped sense into him. Niall was right. If he truly was at the end of his patience with Arthur, he had to be genuinely willing to walk away from the man to preserve his sanity and his heart instead of making hollow threats.

"I suppose I know what I have to do, then," he said, hating the very thought of actually letting Arthur go. Neither of them would be able to find peace if he didn't, though.

He stepped away from the porch railing, but before he'd gone more than two steps, an almighty cry split the air, and when John frowned and searched for its origin, he found Alan screaming his poor little head off as Blake held one of his hands and Mrs. Cannon the other, both trying to take the boy in different directions.

"For heaven's sake," Niall hissed under his breath, striding past John and heading toward the fray. John kept right behind him as they approached the squabble and Niall demanded, "What is going on here?"

"Papa!" Alan wailed, trying to pull away from Mrs. Cannon's hand.

"I am attempting to take the boy for ice cream, as I promised," Mrs. Cannon said, her voice at such a high pitch that she sounded hysterical.

"And I say that my son has had far too many sweets already this morning," Blake countered, emphasizing the fact that Alan was his son to the group of curiosity-seekers gathering around to see what was the matter.

"He's a child, he should have sweets," Mrs. Cannon argued.

"Too many will make him sick, then he won't be able to enjoy anything," Blake argued.

"I want to go with Papa," Alan cried. He gave up his fight and stood between the two warring adults, weeping.

235

It didn't help matters that he also cried, "I want ice cream."

"You see?" Mrs. Cannon declared, her chin tilted up in victory. "He wants his grandmama."

"He said nothing of the sort," Blake huffed, "and frankly, ma'am, I have reached the end of my rope where this battle over my son is concerned."

Blake's declaration had perhaps the opposite effect from what he wanted. Even more people gathered around to see what the trouble was, including Cannon himself. The man strode up through the gathering crowd with an exasperated frown. John had been tempted to intervene in the dispute, but the arrival of Cannon held him back.

"Roberta," he boomed, marching up to his wife and Blake, "let go of the boy's hand this instant."

"But Douglas," she protested, looking as though she might burst into tears. It dawned on John that the apple might not have fallen far from the tree where Annamarie and her mother were concerned. At least he knew where Annamarie got her dramatic streak. "The boy should be ours. You know what kind of a man his father is," she added in a low hiss.

She let go of Alan's hand, but at precisely the moment when Alan would have launched himself at his father, Mrs. Cannon's maid arrived with a dish of strawberry ice cream. Alan lunged hungrily for it as Blake looked on, incensed.

"I will tell you what sort of a man I am, Mrs.

Cannon," he said, stepping protectively toward his son while Alan dove into the ice cream. "I am the kind of man who has risked everything and spared no expense to travel halfway around the world to retrieve his son. I am a humble, flawed man who knows that he has made mistakes in his life, but who has tried with deepest sincerity to put those mistakes to right. I have incurred scorn from my peers and moved my family to a protected home as a result. I am the sort of man who gives everything for those he loves, and who would gladly exchange all of his earthly riches to ensure that his family is safe and happy. I have allowed Alan to stay with you out of respect for your position as his grand-mother, but I am afraid that concession has come to an end. I will be returning to the city with my son this evening, ma'am, and I expect you to respect my wishes as Alan's father."

Mrs. Cannon burst into tears. "Douglas, do some-thing," she appealed to Cannon.

"Let the boy go, Roberta," Cannon said, clearly still frustrated, but not without compassion. "He was not ours to have in the first place. He belongs with his father and his sisters. He clearly wants to go home."

"Can we go home, Papa?" Alan asked, gazing up at Blake as though home were a treat much better than ice cream.

"We can go home now, my darling," Blake told his son with a relieved smile. "We can finally go home."

"He can't go like that," Mrs. Cannon said, sniffling.

She nodded to Alan's shirt. "He's already spilled ice cream all over himself."

Indeed, he had. To John's eyes, it looked as though more of the ice cream had ended up on Alan's shirt than in his mouth.

"I'll take him home, clean him up, have his things packed, and we'll be on our way," Blake said.

"No, no." Mrs. Cannon held up a hand and made a face as though she were a martyr. "I will take my grandson home. It will be the last time we have together."

Blake glared at the woman in suspicion, but before he could say no, Cannon stepped in with, "I will accompany them to make damn certain that my wife follows my wishes in this matter."

Mrs. Cannon sent her husband a withering stare, as though he had thwarted her plans. "Very well," she said, turning her nose up and sniffing again.

That was the end of the confrontation, and, John hoped, finally the end to Blake's pursuit of his son. Niall stepped closer to Blake to have a murmured word with him, to which Blake nodded. They watched the Cannons and Mrs. Cannon's maid walk Alan to the end of the street, where several carriages were parked, then as they climbed into one of them.

John shook his head over the whole thing. He was on the verge of searching out something to occupy his mind among the festival booths, however, when he spotted Arthur racing out from behind one of the buildings behind the row that held the post office, charging toward Cannon's carriage.

John's chest tightened as every thought and emotion he'd had while speaking to Niall came back to him. He launched into motion, striding down the street at a pace that would allow him to intercept Arthur. It was long past the time for the two of them to lay all of their cards on the table.

"Arthur!" he called out once he was close.

Arthur slowed his run—particularly as Cannon's carriage had already lurched into motion and was now too far away for Arthur to catch it—then stopped entirely, leaning his hands against his knees for a moment to catch his breath. As soon as John came within a few feet of him, he breathlessly asked, "Did you see Hiroshi? Did the bastard get into the carriage with Cannon?"

"No," John said, straightening his back and summoning all the courage he could. "I did not see Hiroshi. I would be quite content never to see the bastard again in my life."

Arthur must have sensed John's frustrated tone. He straightened, facing John with a wary look. "I nearly caught him handing off a letter of some sort to the same gentleman we spotted at The Slippery Slope," he panted. "Miraculously, the young lady who works at the post office identified him as a Trevor Wallace, a man in the employ of Brendel. I have my proof that Hiroshi is working for Cannon's rival."

"I don't give a damn," John said, shaking his head.

"Hiroshi and Cannon and Brendel can rot, for all I care. The only thing that concerns me is the fact that the man I love feels the need to walk away from me in the moments when I need him most, and that he would rather embrace revenge for wrongs suffered in the past than reach forward to a new life with me."

Arthur recoiled, clearly stung by John's words. "You don't understand," he said, still catching his breath, his face pink, and his eyes glassy with emotion. "This is it. This is the moment we've been waiting for since rediscovering Hiroshi. I have him now. Cannon will certainly—"

"Is this truly the moment you've been waiting for?" John demanded, taking a step toward him. Arthur was so surprised by the movement that he stepped back. "Because the moment I have been waiting for is the one where you pull your head out of your arse and recognize the gift that I have been attempting to hand you at great personal risk." He stepped closer still and lowered his voice so that any stray passerby wouldn't be able to hear him.

"I do not give my heart away lightly, Arthur," he went on. "It has recently occurred to me that I have never truly given it away at all. Yes, this terrifies me, as I know it terrifies you, but to me, it is worth it. Or, at least, it might have been worth it if you had been more willing to share your past with me instead of making a half-hearted effort, then running off mid-explanation. I may be intrigued by the idea of you wrapping me up in chains and bending me to your will, but I absolutely refuse to let you yank me around on those chains without any promise of devotion or a future together."

"John, I can't—"

"For God's sake, stop telling me what you can't do," John hissed, thoroughly done with the whole thing. "Either do it or don't. Commit or leave me alone. There is no middle ground anymore. I deserve better treatment than what you have given me so far, and that is the end of that."

John took a step back, terrified that he'd come off sounding more like a child than the determined man that he was. But no, it was not childish to stand up for oneself. It was not childish to demand fair treatments, especially to demand it of someone he was fully prepared to give his life to. He was satisfied with everything he said, so he met Arthur's eyes one final time, then turned and marched back into the bustling activity of the festival.

It wasn't until he was a block away from where he'd left Arthur that his heart began to thunder against his ribs and he couldn't draw a full breath. He'd attempted to be brave, but walking away from Arthur was the most frightening thing he'd ever done. He wasn't certain it was the right thing either. Worst of all, he had no idea if Arthur would come after him or if that was the end.

CHAPTER 18

*H*e'd deserved that. As Arthur watched John walk away, noting the tension in his shoulders and the stiff way he walked, he knew that he'd deserved the telling-off that John had just given him. He hadn't been fair to the man, not from the start. He'd held John to an impossible standard from the moment they'd first met, held him up against Shinobu and the fantasy born of young love that he'd been clinging to. It was time for him to be honest with himself and admit that there could be something deep and special between him and John, and that the love he felt for John was not a betrayal of Shinobu, it was merely a sign that his heart had healed and was ready to love again.

He glanced in the other direction, down the road leading out of town to the houses facing the sound. He could still see Cannon's carriage in the distance, and if he didn't catch up to that carriage, if he didn't race to

Cannon with the information he'd discovered, not only would Hiroshi get away with everything he had been up to, Cannon would suffer for it.

With a frustrated growl, Arthur swept his hat from his head to shove his fingers through his hair, glancing toward John again. The last thing he wanted in that moment was to be forced to make a choice.

He let out a heavy sigh and slammed his hat back on his head. John was a grown man with a steady head on his shoulders. He could handle a bit of disappointment. Shinobu had been little more than a boy with a too-sensitive soul who had believed he would have no choice but to return to a life of being used. He hadn't even tried to see things another way. John would always find a way out of whatever sticky situation he landed in, which meant Arthur could trust him not to do anything drastic while he handled one last bit of business.

He set out down the road toward Cannon's house, jogging as much of the way as he could without pushing himself into exhaustion. He was already exhausted enough from carrying the burden of his past for so long, but now he could see the end in sight. He could practically feel the bonds slipping away from his heart as he pushed closer and closer to seeing that Hiroshi got what he deserved at last. One last push and he could put the past behind him and focus on the future, focus on John.

The Cannon house was relatively quiet once he arrived. Cannon had given most of the servants leave to attend the festival, since he and his wife planned to be there for most of the day anyhow. Stone was gone now as well, as were Blake and Niall. The halls rang with Arthur's footsteps as he charged through the house in search of Cannon. He was tempted to call out to the man, but since he'd lost track of Hiroshi in town, there was a decent chance the man was in the house, and Arthur was loath to alert him that the game was over.

Fortunately, he found Cannon in his study, exactly as he'd hoped.

"What the devil is the matter with you?" Cannon asked, glancing up from the letter he was reading through as he stood by one of the room's two, small windows. "You're drenched with sweat."

"I had to run to catch up with you," Arthur panted, marching boldly into the room. "Sir, I believe I've discovered everything that proves Hiroshi is, in fact, working for your competition, working for Brendel."

"What is this?" Cannon boomed, dropping his letter on the desk and striding over to Arthur.

Arthur nodded as he caught his breath. "I observed him, just now, at the post office in Peconic, speaking to a man who the postmistress has identified as an employee of Brendel. It was the same man I observed him speaking with at the club in New York."

Cannon scowled, crossing his arms. "How does this prove Hiroshi is a traitor?" he demanded. "You've given me nothing but circumstantial evidence."

"I would hope I've given you enough to justify a search of the man's room," Arthur said. "If you are uncertain, the postmistress has said she would gladly identify the man Hiroshi was speaking to."

Cannon's scowl deepened as he studied Arthur through narrowed eyes. Arthur was beside himself with impatience. The longer they waited, the more likely it was that Hiroshi would figure out a way to either turn the situation in his favor or escape entirely. And if there was one thing Arthur knew, it was that he couldn't stomach the idea of letting the bastard get away for a second time. Who knew what other crimes Hiroshi had committed in the years since Shinobu's death? Who knew how many crimes could be stopped if Arthur was able to somehow bring the man to justice?

"I'll search his room," Cannon said at last, starting toward the door.

Arthur could have shouted in victory. Finally, someone was going to do something that might actually mean justice was served. He followed Cannon out of the office and down the hall toward a small doorway that led to the servants' section of the house. Unlike houses in England, the servants in Cannon's house didn't have their private rooms in the attic. The entire western quarter of the house was dedicated to kitchens, workrooms, and staff bedrooms. Only the cook and a kitchen maid were present as Cannon stormed through that section of the house and up to a floor containing bedrooms, and Arthur wasn't certain they even noticed.

Cannon knew exactly which room belonged to his butler and pushed it open without knocking. Both he and

Arthur were surprised to find Hiroshi in the room, scribbling something on a piece of stationary at a small desk in the corner. The moment Cannon entered the room, Hiroshi gasped and dropped his pen in shock, standing so fast he bumped the desk and splashed ink from his inkwell onto the blotter.

"Sir, this is an invasion of my privacy," Hiroshi said, his face flushing a dark red.

"You work for me," Cannon said. "You have no privacy."

Under other circumstances, Arthur would have found that sentiment offensive. As it was, he nearly cheered when Cannon crossed the room to snatch up the letter Hiroshi had been writing. He glowered as he read it, then threw it back on the desk.

"What is the meaning of this?" he asked, gesturing to what Arthur now realized was an entire folder of correspondence, and a ledger to boot.

"These are my private things," Hiroshi said, shifting restlessly and looking as though he wanted to shove Cannon out of the way. "You have no right to look at them."

"You've been working for Brendel this whole time," Cannon boomed, tearing page after page of correspondence from the folder. "It's all right here. The Stone deal. The McGregor deal?" He took out one paper in particular and shook it in Hiroshi's face. "The Wyoming deal? This is treachery, man! Explain yourself."

Arthur rocked back, leaning against the doorframe,

exhilarated beyond belief that Hiroshi's downfall had finally come.

Hiroshi gaped like a fish for a few moments, gesturing wildly, before seeming to give up and accept that he was defeated. "Only a foolish man believes himself to be invincible when surrounded by stronger and smarter men." His words were mostly for Cannon, but he glanced to Arthur with bitter hatred as well.

"So you admit that you have been working for Brendel?" Cannon demanded.

"I have," Hiroshi said, tilting his chin up, as if there were some sort of honor in admitting that he was a spy.

Cannon quivered with rage. "You were right," he told Arthur, not looking pleased. "You were absolutely right, sir." He spun back to face Hiroshi. "You will leave my house immediately. Pack your things and get out. I will not pay you for the final days of your employment with me as it has become quite clear you have swindled me out of far more money than you are worth. And if I ever come across you or your name again, I will make it my business to ensure that you are disgraced, deported, and decapitated, if I have my way. Do I make myself clear?"

"Yes," Hiroshi snapped the single syllable.

"You disgust me," Cannon growled before turning and storming out of the room.

His abrupt departure left Arthur alone with a seething Hiroshi.

"Everyone gets what they deserve in the long run," Arthur said with a vicious grin, straightening and standing in the doorway, blocking his departure just as he had blocked Hiroshi's underhanded plans.

Hiroshi glared right back at him, undeterred. "That is something you would do well to remember yourself, Gleason," he hissed. He took a step toward Arthur. "If you think that I will let you get away with crushing my life like this, you are mistaken."

"I have done nothing, Hiroshi," Arthur insisted. "You dug this grave for yourself by your actions."

"Yes," Hiroshi said with a sudden, bitter smile, "as I dug Shinobu's grave all those years ago."

Cold prickles shot down Arthur's neck and back, and his stomach turned.

"You didn't know that?" Hiroshi said, almost gloating. "You didn't know that I was not only the one to hold Shinobu as he died, I cared for his body after. I was the one who arranged for him to be buried. I performed the funeral rights. You fled for your precious England, abandoning the soul of the man you claimed to love."

"There was nothing left that I could do," Arthur said, cursing his voice for sounding so hoarse. "The authorities did not want an Englishman involved in the death of a Japanese citizen. They didn't want the diplomatic problem it might have caused."

"That was my doing," Hiroshi growled. "I didn't want you involved. I always get what I want in the end." He laughed at the stricken look in Arthur's eyes. "So you see, I loved him more than you after all. You were merely a distraction to him. I am the one who owned his heart."

An old, scarred part of Arthur believed him. He remembered the pain he'd felt when he'd been forced to abandon the scene of Shinobu's death, forced to leave everything that he'd felt and experienced behind. He'd failed the man he loved in so many ways that he'd spent years wondering whether he'd been right to declare his love to Shinobu and take him away from the life he knew at all.

But a newer, wiser part of Arthur rejected the idea. He'd been young. His love for Shinobu had been true. He'd been up against forces that he never could have anticipated. He'd done the best he could under trying circumstances with a young man who hadn't been any better about making good decisions than had been.

He let out a breath, removing his hat, which he'd forgotten to take off earlier, and brushed a hand through his hair. What had been the point of holding onto everything for so long?

"Fine," he said, glancing up at Hiroshi, feeling strangely calm. "You win. It's what you've wanted all along, isn't it?"

Hiroshi shifted uncertainly. "I have always won," he growled, as if attempting to be strong and powerful when he now felt uncertain. "You were never strong enough or honorable enough to stand up to me."

"No, I wasn't," Arthur said, even more weight dropping off his shoulders. "I should have seen that much sooner. I shouldn't have wasted years of my life blaming myself for a battle that I never would have won in the first place."

Hiroshi's confusion grew, and he scowled at Arthur. "So you admit that I am the superior man?"

Arthur wanted to laugh. "Far from it," he said. "Because you haven't let it go."

"I will never let it go," Hiroshi growled, taking a threatening step toward Arthur once again. "I will dog you until your dying day. I will make your life a living hell. I will not rest until I have sought my revenge for Shinobu."

"Then you lose," Arthur said, shrugging halfheartedly. Hiroshi blinked in frustrated confusion, so Arthur went on with, "The past is behind us, Hiroshi. I've spent the last ten years of my life clinging to it as if it were Shinobu's corpse. He's never coming back to either of us, though. There will never be life in that story again. And we dishonor his memory by refusing to live the sorts of lives he would have wanted us to live."

"You know nothing," Hiroshi scoffed. "You are a disgrace if you think that there is honor in forgetting."

"Not forgetting," Arthur said, shaking his head. "I will never forget Shinobu and the love we shared. I will never forget the courage he showed in leaving you, or the well-intentioned mistakes I made in forcing him into a situation he wasn't ready for. I cannot go back and save him, but I can go forward and honor his memory. He took his own life, and that was his decision. I cannot take my own life in spirit by failing to live to the fullest every day."

Hiroshi snarled, more confused than ever. "You have taken my life from me today."

"No." Arthur shook his head, strangely calm. "I changed your life today. You've been fired from a job for cheating your employer. You're still alive, you're still free, and if I'm not mistaken," he gestured to the table piled with correspondence, "you have another employer who will probably find a new job for you. I've ruined nothing."

He sucked in a breath as his old thoughts dissolved and new ones slammed into him.

"I almost ruined everything," he said quietly, his heart squeezing in his chest, glancing out the window as the sunny morning. "I had everything handed to me in a beautiful package, and I've come within inches of discarding it, as though it means nothing. It doesn't mean nothing," he said. "It means everything."

"I do not know what you are talking about," Hiroshi growled, losing more and more of his certainty and his anger by the moment. "You are a fool, Gleason, and you will always be a fool."

"Probably," Arthur said, plunking his hat back on his head. He turned to go, knowing he didn't belong where he was anymore, and also knowing where he did belong, whom be belonged with. "Have a good life, Hiroshi," he said. "And thank you for taking care of Shinobu when I couldn't."

The sentiment must have been wildly unexpected,

because Hiroshi pulled back with a grimace, as though he had no idea what Arthur meant, but was still threatened by it. Arthur no longer cared what he thought. He'd said the last of what he needed to say to the man. As he left the hall and headed down the stairs, he glanced up, as if having a final word with Shinobu and thanking him for their time together. He was ready to let the whole thing go, though, and somewhere nearby, John was waiting, if it wasn't too late to make things right.

He was stopped halfway down the stairs by a child's tired whine in the hallway just below. The staircase turned on a landing, and he was able to lean over the railing just in time to see Mrs. Cannon's maid carrying a sleepy Lord Stanley quickly through to the kitchen as Mrs. Cannon followed them.

"Hurry, Lucy, hurry," Mrs. Cannon hissed. "The next train leaves in only an hour."

Arthur rushed the rest of the way down the stairs, pursuing Mrs. Cannon and her maid through the kitchen. "Madam, stop!" he called out just before the pair reached the door leading outside.

Mrs. Cannon yelped and whipped around to face Arthur. "You cannot stop me, sir," she said in a high-pitched voice. "Alan is my grandson, and I will not have him going back into the care of that despicable man."

"That despicable man is his father," Arthur insisted, "and he loves the boy dearly."

"So do I," Mrs. Cannon argued, "and I can care for him far better than a man like Lord Selby."

"No, madam, you cannot," Arthur said.

"Leave me alone," Mrs. Cannon huffed, pushing her maid to carry Lord Stanley outside.

As soon as they opened the door, Arthur spotted a carriage waiting for them just on the other side. He growled in annoyance and hurried after them, but Mrs. Cannon had planned things well enough that before Arthur could so much as raise a hand or call out to them, the carriage was moving forward.

It felt as though the mad carousel was starting up all over again. Arthur called after them, already knowing the carriage wouldn't stop. He hesitated for only a moment, glancing back at the house and contemplating whether to dash inside to alert Cannon to the potential kidnapping or to follow the carriage to see if he could stop it himself.

In the end, he chose to go forward, moaning in complaint as he broke into a jog yet again, and followed the road back into town. The best thing for Lord Stanley in that moment was to alert Blake to what was happening. If the train didn't leave for an hour, there was still ample time to intercept Mrs. Cannon. Besides, John was still in town, and more than anything Arthur had ever wanted in his life, he wanted to take John up on his challenge and tell the man that he was finally ready to embrace the future, a future with John.

CHAPTER 19

*T*here was no better way to cause a man to fall in to paroxysm of doubt than by issuing an ultimatum to the man he loved without any idea what would happen next. It took every bit of courage—or perhaps stupidity—that John possessed to walk away from Arthur after saying his piece. It took even more strength not to turn around after he'd gone three steps and run back to Arthur to say he was sorry, he was being too difficult, and he would give Arthur all the time he needed to overcome the heartache of his past, if only the two of them could be together.

The restless energy that pulsed through John after the scene was so intense that he just kept walking, no idea where he was going, no longer seeing the festival at all. The town was decorated quaintly and its citizens wore smiles and did their best to engage John in any number of activities, or to sell him every sort of treat he could imagine, but he was too anxious to smile back, and the half bag of nuts in his jacket pocket was all the refreshment he needed, because it had come from Arthur.

"You're being a sentimental fool," he cursed himself as he reached the far end of town. He supposed it was true that love made fools of all men.

And yet, when he turned around to glance back over the distance he'd traveled, he didn't see a single sign of Arthur. It wasn't as though he'd expected the man to chase after him and shadow his every move, but he was disappointed to be alone all the same.

He turned back, crossing through the sweetly decorated houses and businesses, dodging children who laughed and ran this way and that with their friends, and avoided the simpering, flirtatious young women who seemed to think the festival was an excuse to find themselves new beaux. They were most certainly barking up the wrong tree if they considered him a likely candidate. As he walked, he searched for Arthur in the crowd, but once again, the slippery bastard was gone without a trace.

"Have you seen Gleason?" he asked Blake and Niall when he spotted them at a small table eating some bizarre American delicacy called a "hot dog", for some ghastly reason.

"Oh, so it's back to 'Gleason' again?" Niall asked with a far-too teasing grin.

John huffed impatiently. "It verges on being nothing at all at this point. Words were spoken, an ultimatum was issued—quite stupidly, I might add, because someone gave me the impression ultimatums were a good idea—" he glared at Niall, "and now the blighter isn't anywhere to be found."

"You frightened him away?" Blake asked, one eyebrow raised warily. He turned that look on Niall. "Did you encourage him?"

"I told him to stand up for himself," Niall said.

John's frown darkened. Perhaps he wasn't being fair to Niall, but he refused to consider that he had been the one to damage things, not when Arthur was the one who kept backing away. "Have you seen him?" he asked, too frustrated to treat the situation lightly.

"Not since earlier," Niall admitted, catching on to John's mood. "In case you hadn't noticed, we've been a bit preoccupied ourselves."

"I've purchased tickets to return to New York tonight," Blake said. "I took the liberty of purchasing one for you as well, though if you decide you want to stay here—"

"Not at all," John cut him off before he could finish his sentence. "In fact, I want nothing more than to return to Cannon's house to pack my things and be done with this place."

"I understand the feeling entirely," Blake said in a flat voice.

John saw no reason to wait. He nodded to his friends, then walked off toward the road that would take him back to the Cannon mansion. He encountered a stroke of luck when the driver of a small cart containing some of Cannon's staff invited him to ride back to the house with them. Not only did that save John the strain of walking the whole way yet again, it gave him the feeling that he was actually moving forward, that he was getting somewhere, perhaps in his life as well as in his attempts to move on from the interlude on Long Island. And he was determined to move on, one way or another. In his heart, he hoped he could move on with Arthur instead of without him.

The Cannon house was oddly quiet when John walked through the front door and headed up the stairs to his guestroom to gather his things. The only sounds echoing in the massive building was the extremely faint echo of raised voices from the part of the house John was reasonably certain held the kitchen. He didn't envy whichever servant was being told off, but it was no longer his problem. The entire blasted Cannon family was no longer his problem.

No sooner had that thought entered his head as he reached the top of the stairs when he nearly ran headlong into Annamarie.

"Oh! Good heavens," Annamarie gasped, pressing a hand to her chest. "I didn't see you there, Mr. Dandie."

"No, I'm certain you didn't," John said.

He attempted to step around Annamarie, but she fluttered a bit and told him, "I wasn't doing anything I wasn't supposed to, I swear."

"I'm certain you weren't." John smiled curtly and tried to move on again.

"Don't tell Mama that Ian and I are sharing a bedroom and, well, a bed," she said in a whisper.

John wasn't certain whether he wanted to smile indulgently at her or roll his eyes. "You are a grown woman, Lady Selby. As soon as you sign the papers I have given your father, you will be a divorcee and free to remarry whomever you like." John paused. "Provided you are not a member of some church that does not allow those things."

Annamarie laughed as though he'd said something ridiculous. "I am a member of no church, sir. I abhor all of those rules against perfectly normal things, like having your own way and enjoying nice things."

John arched an eyebrow, wondering if those rules Annamarie abhorred were the Ten Commandments.

"And I signed those papers this morning," she went on. "Papa made me do it before everyone went to the festival. I believe he was planning on returning everything to you so that you can file them with the proper authorities as soon as possible, when you return to England or some such."

It was the first bit of good news John had heard all day, and as a result, he broke into his first genuine smile in what felt like ages. "Thank you, Annamarie," he said, daring to address the woman by her given name. "You've done a very good thing by signing those papers and setting both yourself and Blake free."

Annamarie sighed and leaned against the wall. "I never should have married Blake in the first place, you know," she said with a surprising amount of candor, as if, after all this time, John was her friend and not the man who had hounded her for months on behalf of her soon-to-be former husband. "Marrying Blake was the most foolish thing I've ever done."

As much as part of John wanted to wave the woman off and march away from her forever, John's curiosity got the better of him. "How so?" he asked, crossing his arms and leaning against the wall opposite her.

Annamarie sighed, glancing down the hall as though she were gazing into the past. "It's all very romantic and exciting, isn't it?" she asked. "The very idea of the English aristocracy and all those titles and estates and protocol. It's like gazing into some sort of fairy tale with knights in shining armor and princesses in castles."

"That has not been my experience of the British upper classes at all," John said with a wry grin.

"No," Annamarie agreed emphatically. "That was most certainly not my experience either. I thought it would be such a lark to be a duchess, to be a grand lady in a sweet, old fashioned country. I thought everyone would circle around and adore me and hang on my every word." She closed her eyes and smiled, breathing in what John was certain she must have thought was her fairy tale.

A moment later, she let her breath out with a disappointed huff. "It's not like that all, is it."

"No, it is not," John agreed.

"There were so many things I was expected to do," Annamarie complained. "Producing an heir with a man who could hardly stand to touch me, for one. And there were so many rules about how I was supposed to behave, what I was meant to say to people, everything I was supposed to remember. I couldn't care less about judging who grew the best flowers in the county, or attending inane theatrics put on by local primary school children, but those were the sorts of things I was expected to do. The *only* things I was expected to do."

"Yes, my lady, those are the day-to-day expectations of a duchess," John told her, pitying the woman more and more. She had been entirely out of her depth as Lady Selby.

"Marrying into the English aristocracy was all the rage with my friends," Annamarie went on with a sigh. "They were all so envious of me when I announced my marriage to Blake. But do you know who I envied the most?"

"Who, my lady?" John asked.

"Millicent Hardy," Annamarie sighed. When John looked confused, she went on with, "She was in my class in finishing school, and when we graduated, she married a clerk who worked in her father's accounting firm. A clerk! Can you imagine?"

John kept his mouth judiciously shut.

"But they were in love," Annamarie continued with a shrug. "So very in love. They still are all these years later. Ian and I dined with them the other evening, and it was almost disgusting to see how much they still adore each other. And Orville has risen up to be a partner in the accounting firm. He is not a wealthy man by any stretch, but he does well for himself."

She paused, smiled, then added, "Orville offered Ian a job, and Ian accepted. Once I've received word that my divorce is final, Ian and I will be married and live in New York permanently."

"I...I'm very happy for you," John said, surprised that he actually was happy for her.

Annamarie fixed him with an astoundingly serious look and said, "I should have married Ian right from the start. I loved him all those years ago, but I let pride get the better of me. And it made me so unhappy that I ended up causing a great deal of harm to so many people."

She blinked rapidly, tears coming to her eyes that appeared to startle Annamarie herself as well as John. John reached into his inner pocket and pulled out a hand-kerchief for Annamarie.

"I have not been a good person, Mr. Dandie," she said as she dabbed her eyes. "I did wrong by my husband and I dislike my own children. I never wanted any of them in the first place. I should have let them go sooner. All I ever wanted was Ian."

She sniffled and blew her nose. The unladylike nature of the sounds she made felt oddly like the first time John had ever seen her be honest with him.

"Love is a funny thing, isn't it?" she asked, dabbing her eyes again. "I had it in front of me all along, but I let pride and greed get in the way of having it." She paused, then asked, "Have you ever been in love, Mr. Dandie?"

Considering the circumstances, John felt he owed it to Annamarie to answer honestly. "Yes, I have. I am."

"Then don't let anything stand in the way of that love, particularly your own pride," Annamarie went on. "Look at the mess I made by turning my back on Ian when I shouldn't have." Her expression grew even more solemn as she said, "Look at how I stood between two people who loved each other for ten years. I do not understand that love, but it is none of my business. And look how happy Blake and his...his friend are now." She pinched her face as though she still thought Blake and Niall's love was wrong, but then shook her head.

"Too many things can stop people who love each other from being together," she went on. "Pride, position, money, stubbornness. But none of them are worth it. If you haven't told the woman you love how much you adore her, I urge you to do so as soon as you can. They send telegrams across the ocean now, you know. And if she is angry with you for going away or giving your attention to someone or something else or doing any of the stupid things I have done, please forgive her. Learn from my mistakes and be gentle and forgiving with love. You will both be so much happier in the end."

John was floored. Never in his life would he have expected to receive such beautiful and meaningful advice from Annamarie Cannon Williamson soon-to-be Archibald. "My lady, I do believe you are right," he said.

"I'm always right," Annamarie said with a cheeky grin, tilting her head up. She offered John his now damp handkerchief back.

John held up a hand, refusing it. "Keep it," he told her. "As a memento of our acquaintance."

"We haven't exactly been friends, Mr. Dandie," she said with a sly look.

"No," John agreed, "but as it happens, you've just told me something I very much needed to hear."

He didn't want to make the same mistakes Annamarie had. He loved Arthur, not in spite of his rough edges and the prickles cause by the pain he'd endured, but because of them. All of those hard angles and gruffness were what made Arthur exciting, what aroused John. He wouldn't have any of those things if not for the heartaches of his past. Perhaps issuing an ultimatum to Arthur wasn't the wisest move on his part, but at least it had enabled him to be clear about what he wanted. Now it was his turn to clarify what Arthur needed in order to feel secure about giving his heart away. The last thing John wanted now was to let pride stand in the way of something potentially beautiful, like Annamarie had.

"I think I'd better go on with my business," he told Annamarie, nodding and turning to head down the hall.

"And I'd better make an appearance at the festival before people start wondering what I've been doing at home all day," Annamarie said, glancing to her bedroom door, her cheeks turning pink.

John grinned, no doubt in his mind that Ian Archibald was somewhere on the other side of that door.

He headed down the hall, but before he could go more than a few steps, a maid came running up the stairs. She exclaimed wordlessly at the sight of Annamarie, then caught her breath and blurted, "Miss Annamarie, it's your mother."

"Mama?" Annamarie grasped the maid's arm. "Has something happened to her? Is she ill?"

The maid gulped as she caught her breath, then said, "She's run off with your son. She's taken the little tike to the train station. I think she's trying to run away with him."

"Mama!" Annamarie exclaimed in an indignant tone. She turned to John. "Did you hear?"

"I did," John said with a glower, abandoning his plans to pack up his things. He strode down the hall to join Annamarie and the maid as they hurried back downstairs. "How long ago did they leave? Do you know for certain they were heading to the train station?"

"Cook and I saw them," the maid said. "She's definitely trying to take the boy away."

They raced downstairs and along the hall to the kitchen. John wasn't certain if interviewing the matron who served as the Cannon's cook would do any good when time was of the essence, but it was a starting place.

No sooner had they reached the kitchen hallway than John was nearly bowled over by Hiroshi. The man tore down the stairs with a large suitcase in one hand and a smaller bag in the other.

"Out of my way," Hiroshi growled, looking as though he were on his way to commit murder as he plowed through the hall and the kitchen, then out the door at the far end.

John didn't have the time to question what the bastard was up to. His heart rushed instantly to thoughts of Arthur, but Arthur was still nowhere to be seen. There was nothing John could do but hurry along to the kitchen.

"What is going on?" he demanded as he strode through the kitchen door to the small courtyard just outside, where all of the kitchen staff seemed to be assembled.

A carriage pulled away a moment later, and John caught sight of Hiroshi inside. He ignored the man's departure, turning to the cook instead.

"Mr. Hiroshi has been fired," the cook said. "And Mrs. Cannon has run off with Lord Selby's son."

"Do you know where she's taking him?" John asked, already moving to follow the carriage into town, even if he had to walk the whole way.

"Away, sir," the cook said with a shrug. "She doesn't want Lord Selby to have him, so she and Lucy took the boy to the train station."

That was all John needed to know. He set off at a jog, cursing the fact that he had to cover the distance on foot —again—which would slow him down, but it had to be done. The sooner he reached town and found Blake and

Niall, and the sooner they all made it to the train station, the sooner they'd be able to close this mad chapter of their lives. And with any luck, now that it appeared Hiroshi was out of the picture, John would be able to set things to right with Arthur and finally come to the under-standing they'd needed to reach all along.

CHAPTER 20

*I*f Arthur never had to run a mile again in his life, he would be glad for it. He was certain his feet were covered in blisters as he dashed back into the fringe of festival-goers at the edge of town, and that his shoes would never be the same. Everything depended on speed, though. Mrs. Cannon had a head start by traveling in a carriage, and even though the train that could potentially whisk her and Lord Stanley away to the city had yet to arrive at the Peconic station, Arthur still felt as though time were not on his side.

His sense of urgency mounted even more just as he dodged around a group of boys aiming slingshots at a row of cans lined up on a fence and another carriage whipped past him. He wasn't certain, but he thought he spotted Hiroshi glaring out the window of that carriage. He was completely done with Hiroshi now, though—a fact that surprised him. Now, his sole focus was on finding Lord Selby and Cristofori and alerting them to Mrs. Cannon's flight.

"My lord!" he called out when he finally spotted Lord Selby and Cristofori watching a man who had several trained dogs in tutus dancing in circles.

The dogs lost their concentration at Arthur's sudden shout and started barking, which caused their trainer to bark as well. That disrupted the entire show, leaving half the audience glaring at Arthur for causing the disturbance, and the other half laughing uproariously over the whole thing.

Arthur ignored them all, pushing his way through men in bowler hats, women holding up dusty parasols, and children who were eager to play with the dogs, once the show descended into chaos. "My lord," he shouted again as Lord Selby and Cristofori turned to him. "You have to come at once. Mrs. Cannon is attempting to run off with your son."

His words were like shots fired over Lord Selby's head. He grabbed Cristofori's sleeve, in spite of the attention they were already getting, and dashed away from the center of the crowd to meet Arthur in the middle of the street.

"How dare she?" Cristofori hissed. "I thought Cannon was supposed to be supervising her?"

"He was distracted with business," Arthur told them, feeling momentarily guilty for the part he'd played in that regard. "He found it necessary to fire his butler."

"So you got rid of that villain, did you?" Cristofori asked with a grim smile.

"I did, but now is not the time for that story." Arthur set off toward the train station, gesturing for the two men to come with him. "Mrs. Cannon is desperate. I don't believe she has the wherewithal to hide your son from you forever, but the sooner we intercept her and convince her that she's in the wrong, the sooner we can bring this whole thing to an end."

And the sooner they brought everything to an end where little Lord Stanley was concerned, the sooner Arthur could turn his attention where it belonged, to patching things up with John and giving the man the attention he deserved. The possibility of that caused Arthur to find the energy to keep running when he was already drenched in sweat, his feet aching, and his lungs tight from breathing so heavily as he ran.

"They must be here somewhere," Arthur said as they mounted the stairs to the train platform at the edge of the stationhouse. He could already hear a train's whistle in the distance, signaling that time truly was running out. Whatever train was coming wouldn't stop for more than a few minutes in a town as small as Peconic.

"Perhaps there is a waiting room they're hiding in," Cristofori suggested. "Or perhaps they're waiting in a carriage."

Arthur nodded at both suggestions, but his attention was arrested a moment later as he watched Hiroshi climb up onto the platform at the other end of the stationhouse.

It seemed mad, it felt like a contradiction of all the conclusions he'd just come to about letting go of the past and putting his full effort into his future, but if Hiroshi had even the slightest clue where Mrs. Cannon and Lord Stanley were, then Arthur was willing to face him.

He broke away from Lord Selby and Cristofori and strode across the platform, dodging the few passengers waiting for the train. As the whistle sounded again, closer this time, Arthur picked up his pace.

"Do you know where Mrs. Cannon is?" he demanded of Hiroshi as he drew near.

Hiroshi snarled, holding back whatever answer he might have until Arthur came closer. He set his bags down on the edge of the platform and reached into the pocket of his jacket.

"Answer me," Arthur demanded. "Do you know where Mrs. Cannon is? She cannot run off with Lord Selby's son. The game is up for her, and—"

Before he could finish his sentence, Hiroshi lashed out and grabbed his arm, yanking him off the platform and around a corner. Arthur nearly lost his footing and crashed to the ground at the suddenness of the move, but just barely managed to remain on his feet. Hiroshi dragged him across the rough ground beside the station to the far side of a small outbuilding, shielding him from the view of both the passengers waiting on the platform and the festivalgoers. He slammed Arthur up against the building, and just as Arthur opened his mouth to protest and call Hiroshi every name he could think of, in English and Japanese, Hiroshi drew a revolver from his jacket and pointed it at Arthur's head.

"I told you revenge would be mine," Hiroshi growled, pulling back the hammer.

Arthur went very still. The entire world seemed to fall away, except for the fury in Hiroshi's eyes and the cold metal gleaming in front of him. He breathed, forcing himself to appear calm, and looked Hiroshi in the eyes.

"If you kill me, your victory will be short," he said in a quiet voice. "A hundred people will hear the gunshot and come running. You will be arrested and found guilty of murder. You will spend the rest of your life in prison. How do you think a man like you would be treated in an American prison when he is found guilty of murder? Meanwhile, I will be reunited with Shinobu in the life that comes after this one." He paused, continuing to stare at Hiroshi without blinking. "Is that what you consider victory? Is that what you consider revenge?"

Hiroshi growled and snarled. He pushed into Arthur, grinding him against the rough side of the outbuilding. He muttered a curse in Japanese, then jerked back, letting Arthur go.

"Give me the gun," Arthur said, extending his hand to Hiroshi. "You don't need it. It will be bad for you if you're caught with it."

"Give it to you so that you can shoot me in the back?" Hiroshi hissed.

"I just told you, any murder that is committed right here, right now, would be a death sentence for the one who fired the gun, no matter who that is," Arthur said. "I have too much to live for to kill you."

The train's whistle sounded so close that it drowned out the end of Arthur's speech. It might have drowned out any gunshots as well. A moment later, the train's engine slid right next to them on the track as the train screeched to a stop. The engineer pulled a cord to sound the whistle again, then glanced to the side, spotted the confrontation between Arthur and Hiroshi, and exclaimed, "Hey!" in shock.

Hiroshi flinched at the shout. He jerked briefly toward the conductor, then quickly thrust the revolver at Arthur. A split-second later, he dashed out from behind the outbuilding, ran for his bags, which still rested on the platform, then sprinted to board the train and was gone.

Arthur let out a heavy breath, then fumbled with the gun, releasing the hammer, then fumbling to open the barrel with shaking hands to remove the bullets. He couldn't catch his breath as he realized how close he'd just come to dying. It was all he could do to step around the corner of the outbuilding and lean against the side facing the tracks as the train chugged into motion again. Arthur clutched the revolver in one hand and held his other hand to his thundering heart as the train pulled away from the station. As the passenger cars passed, he caught his last glimpse of Hiroshi glowering at him from one of the seats, and then the man was gone from his life forever.

John was too exhausted and out of breath to apologize to the people he shoved aside indiscriminately as he ran the last few yards to the Peconic train station. The train had just arrived at the platform, and as the porters opened the doors, a flood of people disembarked. John frantically scanned the passengers waiting to board for Mrs. Cannon, her maid, and Alan, but didn't see them. He did spot Blake and Niall, though.

"Blake!" he called out, dodging the departing passengers as he dashed onto the platform. "Niall!"

They both turned to see him, but before either could say a word, Mrs. Cannon burst out of the station, heading for the train, dragging Alan behind her. Her maid attempted to push Alan along, but she was weighed down with traveling bags.

"Stop right there!" Blake shouted, lunging toward his son.

Mrs. Cannon screamed as though she were being attacked. In her shock, she dropped Alan's hand. The boy made a break for it, shooting toward Blake and leaping into his arms as Blake embraced him.

A second after that, Hiroshi sprinted onto the platform from the scrub beside the station, grabbed two bags that were sitting unattended on the edge of the platform, then dashed toward the train, zipping past Mrs. Cannon as he did.

"Hiroshi!" Mrs. Cannon yelped. "Where are you going? I demand you help me with my grandson this minute!"

Hiroshi ignored the command, leaping onto the train just as a conductor blew his whistle and bellowed, "All aboard!"

"Wait, no!" Mrs. Cannon shouted. "I have a ticket for that train."

"Then you'd better board, ma'am," the conductor advised her.

"Not without my grandson," Mrs. Cannon insisted.

"Sorry, ma'am," the conductor said, stepping onto the train himself, then signaling to the engineer at the front. A moment later, the train lurched into motion and started off.

"No!" Mrs. Cannon called after it, then burst into tears.

"How dare you attempt to kidnap Lord Selby's son?" John demanded. His nerves were raw, and his heart still pounded from running. Beyond that, he had lost all patience for the woman's shenanigans. It was time she realized she'd lost.

"It's all right, John," Blake said in a much calmer voice that John ever could have managed. "I have Alan and I'm not letting him go. It's over."

John took a breath and tugged at the hem of his

jacket, then rolled his shoulders to steady himself. "It is over," he said.

Blake turned to Mrs. Cannon. "I'm taking my son home," he told the woman with heroic calm. "This has gone on long enough. I will send my friends to pack Alan's things and bring them back to the station, but neither Alan nor I will return to your house. In fact, I have half a mind to purchase tickets for the very next train to come through and let the others follow us later."

"But you can't," Mrs. Cannon wept. "He is my grandson."

"Come along, ma'am," Mrs. Cannon's maid said. She sent Blake a look of apology and mortification as she stepped forward to rest her arm around Mrs. Cannon's shoulder. "Let's go back to the house and have a nice cup of tea, shall we?"

Mrs. Cannon wailed, but she let herself be led off by the maid.

John breathed a sigh of relief, feeling as though the whole ordeal was finally, *finally* over, but a hint of movement near the outbuilding beside the tracks caught his eye.

In a split-second, John's heart was back in his throat, and every emotion he had came barreling to the fore as he saw Arthur leaning against the small building, a gun in his hand.

"No!" he shouted, racing toward the end of the platform. In his panicked haste to reach Arthur, he leapt off the side of the platform rather than taking the stairs, stumbled a bit as he landed on uneven ground, then darted the rest of the way to the man he loved. "No, Arthur, don't do it! It's not worth it."

Arthur jerked in surprise at the sound of John's cry and whipped to face him. "John?"

"I'm sorry," John gasped, reaching for Arthur. He had so much momentum behind him that he pushed Arthur around the corner of the small building as he grabbed his shoulders. "I'm sorry that I tried to force things with you," he said. "I'm sorry if it is all too much, too soon. I know that you are still reeling from the past. I know that you loved Shinobu and that his death was hard on you. Just please, give me the gun."

Arthur blinked at him, baffled, and immediately handed the revolver over, handle first. "John, I wasn't—"

"Please, just hear me out," John gasped, taking the gun and opening the barrel to empty the bullets. It puzzled him when he discovered the barrel was already empty, but he ignored it, dropping the gun entirely so he could grip Arthur's shoulders.

"I'm sorry that I've been such a demanding arse these last few days," he panted, pouring his heart out. "It's just that I love you. There, I've said it. It doesn't feel particularly manly to gush with these sorts of emotions. I have generally avoided feelings that are too strong or too taxing, but I cannot avoid it any longer. I love you. I think I've loved you from the moment we first met. You terrified me with your confidence and the wicked glint in your eyes, but I loved it. No one has ever challenged me like you do."

"John, you don't need to—"

"No, hear me out," John cut him off again, holding up one hand for a second before grabbing his arms again. "I know that I need to be patient. I know that your past is important to you, that Shinobu meant so much to you. I know that your work is important as well, as is mine. Everything has just seemed so heightened these last few days, and after what happened between us, all of what happened between us, I just didn't want to hold back for another moment.

"I want to be with you," he rushed on, lowering his voice a bit. "I want to be with you your way, to learn everything wicked and dangerous that you like. I want to be with you my way too, tender and passionate. I want to be with you every way, in work, in play, and in life. I think we could do it. I think we complement each other perfectly. I think we can work out all of our differences. I think our differences are what make us so exciting together. But if you need time, if you need to do some-thing, anything, to find peace with Shinobu's death and everything he meant to you, then I'm willing to wait. I'm willing to do anything to have you, just don't ever consider killing yourself, like Shinobu killed himself, please."

Arthur's eyes went wide. "That's why you would assume I'd take my own life? Because Shinobu did?"

John blinked, suddenly terrified that he'd misread the

entire situation and made a damn fool of himself. "You had a gun, and you looked terribly distressed."

Arthur stared at him even harder, then burst into a laugh. "You daft man. I took the gun from Hiroshi before he flew off on the train. He was planning to kill me, but I talked him out of it."

"He...*what*?" A whole new wave of fury filled John.

"It's all right," Arthur reassured him, shifting so that he was the one gripping John's arms and holding him still. "I don't think he would have gone through with it anyhow. He's a petty criminal, not a murderer. And he's gone now. You saw me breathing a sigh of relief. You saw me letting the past go, once and for all. There is no possible way I would even come close to ending my own life. Not when it has just begun."

"You wouldn't?" John panted, unable to catch his breath for an entirely different reason now.

"No, you madman," Arthur laughed. "The past will always be a part of me. Shinobu will always have a place in my heart, just as your past lovers will always have a place in your heart. But the past is the past, and I have finally been able to see that. I have finally been able to see that because you helped me to see that. You helped me to see that I have been holding on to something for far too long and that the time has long been past for me to let go of it. I've let go, John. I've let go, and now I'm clinging to something else, someone else." He glanced to his hands on John's arms as if to prove his point.

"So, you...you're ready to move forward?" John asked

with a sheepish look. "Even though I am a ridiculous fool who has behaved like a complete nitwit?"

"I wouldn't have you any other way," Arthur said.

"Truly?" John blinked as though he didn't believe it.

"Absolutely," Arthur said with a saucy wink. "You've given me so, so many things to punish you for. We're going to have quite an interesting time once I have you on your knees, making amends for everything."

John's insides quivered dangerously, making him suddenly self-conscious of the fit of his trousers and the look he knew painted his face. "I cannot believe I'm about to say this, but I'm looking forward to it," he said in a hoarse voice.

"Of course, you are," Arthur said with a fond grin. "Just as I'm looking forward to learning how to be a soft and sentimental dolt."

John let out a breath, relieved and touched beyond words. "Something tells me this won't be the last fight we ever have," he murmured, stepping closer and clasping Arthur's face in his hands. He peeked around to make certain no one could see them. They weren't completely alone, but as far as John was concerned, whatever he did next was worth the risk.

"The beauty of bickering is in the making up after," Arthur growled, sliding his hands around John's waist under his jacket.

"And I'm certain we will become quite adept at that art in no time," John said.

He leaned in, slanting his mouth across Arthur's and

stealing a kiss that could land them both in heaps of trouble if they were seen. He didn't care, though. Arthur's mouth was warm and welcoming under his. Their tongues worked perfectly together, and the sighs they both let out were heavenly. Both of them had worked damn hard to earn that kiss, and not even the threat of disaster was going to stop John from claiming it, from claiming Arthur as his own and being claimed in return. Love was worth the risk every time.

CHAPTER 21

*J*ohn had never been so happy to see the
hustle and bustle of an overcrowded city
that he barely knew in his life. Even though
the train journey had taken only a little over an hour, the
return to New York felt as though it had taken a lifetime.
After the scene at the Peconic train station, Blake had
taken Alan back to the inn while he packed his and
Niall's things, and Niall had returned with John and
Arthur to the Cannon house so the rest of them could
pack. Mrs. Cannon had been in such a rush to run away
with the boy that she'd only taken a few changes of Alan's
clothes with her and nothing else.

Mrs. Cannon was, unsurprisingly, remorseless and
wept the entire time after Niall strongarmed her into
giving him, John, and Arthur a ride back to the house in
the carriage. Once they'd reached the house, the woman
was faced with her husband's wrath, as Annamarie and

the maid had informed him of what had happened. John was passionately against the mistreatment of women in any form, but even he had to admit that Mrs. Cannon deserved whatever lecture her husband gave her in a voice loud enough that John could hear it from his room as he packed his bag.

From there, they had to go through the usual kerfuffle of making certain everyone had everything they needed, traveling back into Peconic, meeting up with Blake and Alan, then waiting for the next train into the city. Alan had napped while Blake packed, which meant he was wriggly and impatient, and he wanted to explore more of the festival, which was still going on as they lingered on the train platform. It didn't matter how over-joyed Blake was to have his son back, telling a five-year-old boy he couldn't have another ice cream or play with the other children—who somehow all had colorful streamers they were waving around—was a recipe for misery.

But the train finally arrived, they all bundled aboard, and shortly after suppertime, they were all blissfully back at the Fairmount Hotel, just off of Central Park, reunited with Xavier Lawrence and his young man.

There was another addition to their party as well.

"Lord Selby, I'd like you to meet my sister, Anya," Zander Plushenko said, resting a hand on the shoulder of the tiny, blond girl who stood beside him, leaning against his leg.

She looked as though she wanted to hide her face

against Zander's side, but made a brave effort to dip into a charming curtsy and whisper, "How do you do?"

Blake smiled broadly and bowed to her. "I am quite well. It is a pleasure to meet you, Miss Anya."

The girl peeked up at her brother with wide, sparkling eyes, then turned back to Blake, "Are you a prince?" she asked in an awed voice. "Zander said you were a prince."

Blake laughed, crouching in front of her to be at her level. "I'm a duke, not a prince. But I'd like to be your friend. I have two little girls myself who are close to your age, Greta and Jessie."

"I like those names," Anya said. "Where are they?"

"They are at home, in London," Blake said.

"Where we are going soon," Zander added, squeezing Anya's shoulder.

"I'm certain they will be so pleased to meet you," Blake said. "And if you don't mind boys, you can meet my son, Alan, right now." He twisted to gesture for a sleepy Alan to step forward from where he had been leaning against Niall's leg and yawning.

Alan perked up at the sight of Anya, staring at her with his big, blue eyes.

"Alan, say hello to Anya," Blake prompted him.

"You're very pretty," Alan told her in a hushed voice.

Anya merely giggled, hiding her face against her brother's side in earnest. "Thank you," she mumbled. "You're pretty too."

John covered his mouth with his hand to hide his grin

and glanced to Arthur. Two darling children meeting for the first time was not the sort of thing he would have thought Arthur would be at all moved by, but to his surprise, Arthur smiled at the charming pair as though they were a complete delight.

When Arthur caught John grinning at him, his cheeks gone pink, Arthur frowned slightly—an expression that did not meet his eyes—and said, "What?" with a shrug. "I'm not made of stone, you know."

John sent him a mock smirk and rolled his eyes. "You could have fooled me."

Arthur was standing close enough that he could jerk out his elbow and gouge John's arm. John pretended to be wounded, but then laughed it off.

"It looks as though we have more than one set of children to contend with," Niall drawled, shaking his head teasingly at John and Arthur.

"Not children," John corrected him. "Merely happy people who are glad that a long and trying time has finally passed."

He didn't just mean the time it had taken to track down and reunite Alan with his family. In spite of all his efforts to help—and all the ways he'd inadvertently stood in the way—John was certain beyond a doubt that Arthur had successfully put the pain of his past behind him as well, or at least begun to. Even though it was well after dark, it felt like a new day was dawning.

"Well, now that we all have our rooms," Niall said, "I suggest we retire for the night. Our passage home doesn't leave for another two weeks, but I, for one, would enjoy touring this fine city without the pressure of a lost child hanging over my head."

"Agreed," Blake said with a deep sigh. "But only after a very long, very relaxed night of sleep."

"If you'd like," John offered, "I can telegraph Stephen and Max in the morning to let them know we have Alan back. I'm certain your girls would be glad to know they will be reunited with their brother soon."

"That would be magnificent," Blake said with a deep breath of relief, standing and picking up Alan as he did.

"Can we go to the zoo tomorrow, Papa?" Alan asked as he threw his arms around Blake's neck and rested his head against his shoulder. "I kept telling Mama I wanted to go, but she said no and be quiet."

"Of course, we can go to the zoo," Blake said, smiling at his son with so much love that it nearly made John misty-eyed. Alan leaned in, cupped his hands around Blake's ear, and whispered something. Blake's smile grew, and he turned to Anya to ask, "Would you like to go to the zoo with us tomorrow, Miss Anya?"

"Can I?" Anya's face lit up, and she glanced up to her brother.

"You absolutely can, sweetheart," Zander said, ruffling her hair. He glanced across to Xavier and said, "That might give the two of us some time alone that we haven't had for a few days." He winked, and Xavier turned an adorable shade of puce.

"And with that, I think it truly is time for us all to

retire for the night," Arthur said, sending John a knowing look. "Come along, John," he said with just a hint of command.

It was enough of an order to fire John's blood, even though he laughed outwardly and pretended they were just joking.

"I still can't believe you were bold enough to ask for a second key to my room instead of booking one of your own," John murmured as they headed up the stairs to the fourth floor.

Arthur shrugged. "As I've learned of late, hotel staff will either come up with whatever excuse in their own minds that they need in order to explain away something they don't want to know, or else they have seen so many unusual things that they have become inured to the idea of anything else untoward happening."

"There's nothing untoward about the two of us sharing a room," John scoffed as they stepped out onto the fourth-floor hallway and headed along to their door.

Arthur paused as they reached it and leaned cockily against the doorframe while John fit the key in the lock. "You haven't seen what I plan to do in there yet," he said, arching one eyebrow.

John felt his neck and face heat, and he couldn't stop himself from bursting into giddy laughter as he pushed the door open. Just because the majority of the stress and strain between them—and between the present and the past—had been resolved, didn't mean Arthur no longer left him feeling a scintillating sort of fear when he made comments like that. As much as John hated feeling out of his depth, he was aroused by not knowing what to expect from Arthur. As intimidating as it could be, he hoped they would always feel that way about each other.

"Do you have any plans for once we return to London?" he asked, setting the room key on the bureau near the door, then unbuttoning his jacket once the door was shut and locked behind them.

"I'm not entirely certain," Arthur said, crossing the room to undress near the washstand by the window. "Someone suggested there was a solicitor's office that might be in need of an investigator on staff."

John's brow inched up, and he turned to Arthur as he tossed his jacket aside, then leaned against the bureau to remove his shoes. "You'd actually consider that?" he asked. "You'd be interested in going into business with me?"

"I'm interested in going into you in every way, John," Arthur teased him from across the room.

John heated even more. He wasn't sure where to look or what to do with his hands. He certainly wasn't used to feeling so devilishly bashful and in over his head the way Arthur made him feel. "Are you certain you won't get bored?" he asked, arching one eyebrow.

Arthur tossed his jacket over the chair by the window and moved slowly toward John as he unbuttoned the cuffs of his shirt. "I am entirely certain that I will not get bored," he said. "I am an inventive and imaginative person, you see. I know how to keep myself entertained."

John smiled, more in relief than anything else. When Arthur continued to stalk toward him, he sat against the edge of the bureau and opened his legs so that Arthur could stand between them. That brought Arthur right to his eye level, or more importantly, his mouth level.

"You are not as boring as you think, John Dandie," Arthur whispered before slanting his mouth over John's.

The man was devilishly good at kissing. The way he devoured John's mouth with the perfect mixture of rough demand and soft lips had John melting like wax in no time. He moaned deep in his throat and slipped his arms around Arthur's waist, pulling him closer. That small gesture of possession and control fired something in Arthur, who countered by thrusting his tongue into John's mouth in a way that lay claim to whatever it touched. He fisted a hand in John's hair, tugging just enough to show dominance without hurting too much. And John loved it.

"Take your waistcoat and shirt off," Arthur murmured his command, already helping with the buttons. "I have something in mind for you."

"Is this part of your effort never to get bored with me?" John asked in a husky voice, flickering one eyebrow.

Arthur responded with a laugh and a glint in his eyes that had John hard as iron and desperate to remove his trousers as well as his shirt. "You cannot even imagine all the things I plan to do with you," he said, pushing John's waistcoat and suspenders off his shoulders. "Some of those things I'm certain you've never heard of. Some of them are obscene. Some of them will leave you feeling so very dirty."

John caught his breath, his heart pounding furiously against his ribs. "I should not be aroused by those suggestions at all."

"But you are," Arthur finished his thought. "Even though they frighten you. And that's why I will never, ever grow tired of you."

He emphasized his point by sweeping John's shirt up over his head, then stroking his hands across the hard planes of John's chest and stomach. The way Arthur sucked in a breath and drank in the sight of his naked torso left John grinning. It wasn't just Arthur who affected him. He had just as much of an intoxicating effect on Arthur, which evened the odds between them a bit.

"You'll have to be gentle with me as you introduce me to all these new things," he said, working open the buttons of Arthur's waistcoat.

"Gentle? Me?" Arthur peered wickedly at him.

John tugged Arthur's shirt out from his trousers, then spread his hands along Arthur's sides. "You have gentleness in you as much as I have it in me to do everything you command."

"Do you think so?" Arthur asked with a teasing look, then, as John nodded, said, "On your knees, then."

The zip of excitement that John had felt before, when Arthur fucked him in their room at the inn, returned. He didn't understand it, but that didn't lessen his enjoyment of the feeling at all. He slipped off the bureau and went to his knees in front of Arthur. He was by far the bigger of the two of them, but it felt so good to look up to Arthur.

"It's a shame I don't have any of my toys with me," Arthur said, detaching his suspenders from his trousers. "We'll have to make do with what we have." He flickered one eyebrow at John, then said, "Arms straight up."

John sucked in a breath, then did what Arthur said, holding his arms up over his head. Arthur finished unbuttoning his suspenders from the back of his trousers with one hand, then used one end of his suspenders to tie John's hands together. The thrill of that tiny bit of immobility was just what John needed.

"That should do," Arthur said with a grin, stroking the side of John's face. "Are you still interested?"

"Very much so," John said, letting out a rough breath.

Arthur's grin grew broader and wickeder. "Good. Then I have something for you."

He quickly slipped out of his shirt, then unbuttoned his trousers. John sucked in a breath as he pushed his trousers down over his hips and his prick leapt free, already hard and eager. John's mouth instantly began to water, and when Arthur glanced from his cock to John with one eyebrow arched, John didn't hesitate for a moment.

There was something scintillating and, if he dared admit it, fun about attempting to capture Arthur's cock with his mouth but not his hands. It took a level of coordination John wasn't certain he had, and on top of that, he was certain Arthur kept moving just enough to make him work for it. It was most definitely a trick to assert power, but that strange and new part of John that liked the power Arthur had over him thrilled to it.

When he finally closed his mouth over Arthur's tip enough to suck him in and hold him in his mouth for a moment, Arthur groaned in approval. "That's a good lad," he sighed.

John's eyebrows flew up, and he glanced up at Arthur—managing to keep hold of Arthur's cock in his mouth—almost unable to stop himself from laughing. He was well into his thirties and hadn't been called "lad" in over a decade. Something about hearing Arthur say the word now made him feel young and randy, and as soon as Arthur's gaze gained some focus and he met John's eyes, John bore down on his cock, taking him deep.

Arthur flinched in surprise and gasped, then let out a long moan and tipped his head back in pleasure for a moment. It was the most gratifying feeling John had ever had, knowing he was pleasing the man he loved, and it spurred him on to more daring deeds. He moved intensively on Arthur, sucking him and swallowing, and daring himself to take the man beyond what he thought he could endure. And it was clear Arthur loved every moment of it.

Until Arthur stopped him with a hand on John's head. When John glanced up questioningly at him,

Arthur asked, "Do you want to take this further? Are you ready for that? For a bit of rough treatment?"

The genuine concern and honest question nearly had John groaning with enthusiasm. He had no doubts that whatever Arthur defined as rough treatment could become very rough indeed, but every fiber in his body longed for it. The excitement and arousal that coursed through him now was what he'd been missing his entire life. He'd spent so long trying to be in charge of everything that he'd never stopped to consider the glory of being utterly vulnerable and helpless.

He nodded up at Arthur, his breath coming in shallow pants through his nose, communicating with his eyes that he truly was ready for whatever Arthur wanted.

"If it gets to be too much, genuinely too much, say 'mercy', do you understand?" Arthur asked.

John nodded, shifting restlessly, anxious and aroused.

Arthur sent him a devastatingly naughty grin. "Good," he winked. "Good lad."

He fisted his hand in John's hair again, harder this time, and clamped a hand around John's bound wrists, then pushed his cock deeper into John's mouth, all the way to the back of his throat.

It was instantly too much, and John gagged, but Arthur didn't let up, and John was surprised to find that he didn't want him to. Arthur thrust harder and faster, vocalizing his pleasure as he did, fucking John's mouth so deep that for a moment he couldn't breathe. But still he went on, claiming John as his, until saliva dribbled from

John's mouth as he choked on Arthur's cock enough to heave.

"That's it," Arthur panted, tugging John's hair and pulling his wrists up until his shoulders ached from the position. "That's a good lad."

It was all an astounding, heady, magnificent paradox. John had never been used in such a way before, but once Arthur pulled back for a moment to allow him to breathe, the tip of his cock resting just inside of John's lips, he found he wanted more. He wanted all of it, the physical sensations of Arthur's cock filling his mouth and pressing him beyond his limits, his own prick throbbing for release in the confines of his trousers, the sensation of being controlled by another man, the fear, and the deep, pulsing love he felt for Arthur for awakening him to every new sensation.

He sucked Arthur's cock deeper into his mouth, teasing it with his tongue, before Arthur asked anything more of him, which brought a light of pure, carnal delight to Arthur's eyes.

"Oh, you're eager for it, aren't you?" Arthur asked, beginning his merciless assault again. "You like choking on my cock, don't you?"

John somehow managed a slight nod and what he hoped was an impish look as he opened his throat to take more of Arthur.

The whole thing was mad. Arthur jerked mercilessly into his throat, wrenching John's arms in a way that had him crying out. But it was so good. He gagged again, his eyes streaming involuntarily, but he worked just as hard as Arthur to give them both what they wanted. The sense of surrender that shuddered through John was like heaven, and he groaned with it.

He was so transported with desire that he gasped in shock when Arthur stepped away from him, suddenly leaving his mouth free.

"As much as I'd like to finish this way," Arthur gasped, tugging John to his feet, "that pert little arse of yours is calling my name."

"Whatever you want," John panted, stumbling toward one of the room's two beds when Arthur jerked him that way.

Arthur surprised him again by laughing. "I want so many things right now that I can't keep them all straight in my head," he said as he quickly shed the rest of his clothes. Once he was done with his own, he pushed John to his back across the bed, then tugged his trousers off as well. John was so blissfully happy to have his aching cock free that he groaned with delight.

"I want to string you up until you're completely immobile and fuck you until you weep my name," Arthur went on, shifting John so that he lay the right way around on the bed, then reaching up to grab the loose ends of the suspenders binding his arms. He pulled hard, stretching John's arms again, and tying the suspenders to the bedstead. "I want to spread you wide so that your cock and balls and hole are mine to do with as I please, and I will do wicked things to them," he promised with a villainous grin, pushing John's legs apart as wide as they could go and wider, until his feet were hanging off either side of the bed.

He cupped his hand around John's balls and squeezed just past the point of comfort, tugging as he did. More surprising than the shock of mild pain was the fact that John liked it. He liked it and wondered what other terrifying things Arthur might do to the most sensitive parts of him that he would also like.

"I want to mark up that delicious back and arse of yours with welts that will take days to fade," Arthur went on, "and hear you weep with pleasure while I do it." He hinted at the future by closing his mouth over a spot on the top of John's inner thigh, sucking and biting so hard that John bucked against him, then moaned at the titillating sensation, knowing it would leave a large red mark.

"Yes," John gasped, his imagination running wild as his sense of propriety and decorum went flying out the window. "Yes, I want all of it," he groaned—gasping even harder when Arthur sucked on one of his balls. "I want to try it all."

"Good," Arthur said in a downright wicked voice. He licked his way up John's rigid, leaking cock to close his mouth over its tip for a moment, sucking away the precum. It was only a fleeting, tantalizing taste of pleasure before Arthur slid his way up John's body so that he could kiss his mouth. The kiss was searing, but Arthur laughed and muscled himself above John when it was done so that he could gaze down at him and say, "This is why I love you, you know."

John's brow shot up. "You love me?"

Arthur laughed harder. "Of course, I do, you dolt." He settled above John in such a way that he could grind his hips against John's, rubbing their cocks together and causing John to moan. "I love the way you are so serious and earnest about your job and the clients you serve," he said, emphasizing the point with a kiss. "I love how good you are and how pure-hearted." He punctuated that with a longer kiss. "I *love* the fact that such a good man is so open to doing such wicked things," he said next, his voice taking on a diabolical tone as he reached between them to stroke John's cock. Another kiss, and he continued with, "I love that you accept me as I am, and that you never once gave up on me, even though I was consumed by the past, even though I was a selfish bastard."

"You weren't selfish," John panted, his body on fire with need. "You were heartbroken. There's a difference."

"And you put my heart back together," Arthur smiled, stealing his longest kiss yet. When he raised himself above John again, he grinned roguishly and said, "That is why I fully intend to spend the rest of my life taking you apart."

He kissed John long and lingeringly. John's heart swelled with affection and longing. It also raced with excitement at the thought of being taken apart for the rest of his life. He was already desperately enamored with everything that Arthur was doing now, and he knew that wasn't even a fraction of what the man could do.

Arthur scooted back a bit, grabbing John under his knees with both hands and yanking his legs up until he was positioned like a frog on his back, his arse tilted up and on full display. Then he left John in the position with the command, "Hold that position. Do not close your legs or lower that fine arse of yours one bit."

John was certain he looked utterly ridiculous with everything hanging out as it was, but he did exactly as Arthur commanded, keeping himself spread and on display as Arthur climbed off the bed and went to his suitcase. John nearly shouted for joy when Arthur took out a small jar of Vaseline and brought it back to the bed. The anticipation of watching Arthur slowly, painstakingly unscrew the lid and toy with the contents of the jar, peeking lasciviously at John the whole time, had John panting and desperate, and unsure whether he wanted to laugh or beg Arthur to get on with things and fuck him already.

Arthur must have known what the anticipation was doing to John's. He took his sweet time slicking his cock, then bringing a little extra Vaseline on his fingers as he climbed back onto the bed and knelt between John's legs.

"You're getting a little sloppy with this position," Arthur told him, one eyebrow raised. "I'm not convinced you truly want it."

John couldn't help but laugh out loud, even as his legs shook and his cock dripped in anticipation. "Just get on with it, you sadistic bastard," he laughed, arching his hips up to entice Arthur.

Arthur tutted, but did John the favor of spreading the Vaseline on his fingers over John's ready hole, thrusting one, then two fingers inside of him to prepare the way. "In the future, sass like that will earn you a few smacks with a cane or a whip," he said, shaking his head. He then crawled up between John's legs until his eyes were even with John's. "But just this once, I'll let you get away with it, because I do love you so."

"And I love you," John told him in return. "Truly, I do. I've loved you from the moment we met."

Arthur kissed him, which was as good as a return declaration of love, as far as John was concerned. He knew Arthur well enough now to know that words weren't his primary way of sharing his feelings. He knew him well enough to hear him even when he didn't speak.

Arthur said volumes, everything John needed to hear, when he lined himself up and pushed possessively inside of John. It was so much easier than their first time together, but just as earth-shattering. John cried out with pleasure as his body let go of its resistance and accepted Arthur fully, along with all the pleasure he could give. And Arthur seemed intent on giving everything. He moved slowly and sensually at first, kissing John's mouth, his shoulders, and chest, managing to keep firmly inside of him.

It was fabulous and sweet, but as the pleasure mounted, they both knew they needed more. Arthur repositioned himself so that he could thrust harder and faster at an angle that stroked all the right places inside of him. Arthur hooked his arms under John's knees again and lifted his lower half with surprising strength so that he could move hard and deep. John gave himself over to it, and when they found a rhythm and position that created magic between them, they both threw their whole selves into it until nothing seemed to exist but the two of them and pleasure and love.

When Arthur let out a fierce cry and spilled himself inside of John, it was as though heaven itself had opened. And as soon as Arthur's orgasm played itself out, he let John's knees go so that he could take hold of John's cock and bring him the rest of the way into heaven with him, still holding himself inside of John. It felt so good that as his climax pounded through him, John cried out, "I love you! Oh, God, I love you, Arthur."

As fast as the whirlwind had taken them, it subsided. Arthur reached up to untie John's hands, then to rub his shoulders as John groaned in relief. They tangled into a sticky, satisfied pile together, kissing lazily and letting their hands rove all over each other's bodies.

"You know, it doesn't count if you say you love me in the middle of coming," Arthur laughed once they were snuggled together, thoroughly exhausted.

"All right, then," John grinned in return, rubbing his nose against Arthur's as though they were two, green boys. "I love you, Arthur Gleason. With my whole heart.

And I am yours and will continue to be so for as long as you'll have me, and then some."

Arthur laughed again, kissing John's lips sweetly. "That counts," he said. "And I am yours as well, and I think I might just keep you for the rest of my life."

I HOPE YOU'VE ENJOYED JOHN AND ARTHUR'S STORY. At last, they've come together, and at last Blake and Niall have Alan safe and sound where he belongs!

BUT OH NO! IS THIS THE END OF *THE BROTHERHOOD* series? Technically, yes. But don't worry! There is much more to come from the world of The Brotherhood and the men involved with it. Because I couldn't possibly leave so many fantastic characters as loose ends. At least, not for long. What about Jasper Werther and his friends at The Slippery Slope? Jasper absolutely needs to find love. So keep your eyes peeled and sign up for my newsletter so that you can stay informed about a new Victorian M/M series coming in 2022, *The Slippery Slope*.

FORTUNATELY, YOU DON'T HAVE TO WAIT THAT LONG for more M/M Historical Romance from me. Next up is an all new Regency M/M series, *After the War*. What happens when a group of naval officers whose ship has been decommissioned after the end of the Napoleonic wars spend the summer together at a remote seaside estate in Yorkshire? All sorts of things, of course. The series begins with *Between His Lover and the Deep Blue Sea...*

SAILING MASTER SEPTIMUS BOLTON HAS SPENT HIS entire life at sea...in more ways than one. Now that his ship has been decommissioned at the end of the Napoleonic Wars, he has nothing to do but accept the invitation of one of his fellow naval officers to convalesce for the summer at a remote country estate in Yorkshire. Septimus would do anything to get back to sea...

...UNTIL A PAIR OF BLUE EYES AND A MISCHIEVOUS SMILE tempt him to forget everything, including discretion.

ADAM SEYMOUR HAS HAD TO FIGHT FOR EVERYTHING he has, from the scholarship that allowed him to attend university to the right to be himself. Now, as tutor to the Duke of Malton's precocious children, he has a comfortable life in a grand country estate far away from ridicule. His goal of starting a school for underprivileged children once his noble charges outgrow his tutelage seems well within reach...

. . .

...UNTIL TEMPTATION ARRIVES AT WODEHOUSE ABBEY in the form of handsome, older, irresistible Septimus.

IT DOESN'T MATTER HOW HARD SEPTIMUS FIGHTS HIS feelings for Adam, the two men can't seem to stay away from each other. But when Septimus is offered the chance of a lifetime in the form of the ship he's always wanted to command, he will have to choose between the possibility of lifelong love and the dream that is finally within his reach.

BETWEEN HIS LOVER AND THE DEEP BLUE SEA IS available for preorder now!

IF YOU ENJOYED THIS BOOK AND WOULD LIKE TO HEAR more from me, please sign up for my newsletter! When you sign up, you'll get a free, full-length novella, *A Passionate Deception*. Victorian identity theft has never been so exciting in this story of hope, tricks, and starting over. Part of my West Meets East series, *A Passionate Deception* can be read as a stand-alone. Pick up your free copy today by signing up to receive my newsletter (which I only send out when I have a new release)!

Sign up here: http://eepurl.com/cbaVMH

. . .

ARE YOU ON SOCIAL MEDIA? I AM! COME AND JOIN the fun on Facebook: http://www. facebook.com/merryfarmerreaders

I'M ALSO A HUGE FAN OF INSTAGRAM AND POST LOTS of original content there: https://www. instagram.com/merryfarmer/

ABOUT THE AUTHOR

I hope you have enjoyed *Just a Little Rivalry*. If you'd like to be the first to learn about when new books in the series come out and more, please sign up for my newsletter here: http://eepurl.com/cbaVMH And remember, Read it, Review it, Share it! For a complete list of works by Merry Farmer with links, please visit http://wp.me/P5ttjb-14F.

Merry Farmer is an award-winning novelist who lives in suburban Philadelphia with her cats, Torpedo, her grumpy old man, and Justine, her hyperactive new baby. She has been writing since she was ten years old and realized one day that she didn't have to wait for the teacher to assign a creative writing project to write something. It was the best day of her life. She then went on to earn not one but two degrees in History so that she would always have something to write about. Her books have reached the Top 100 at Amazon, iBooks, and Barnes & Noble, and have been named finalists in the prestigious RONE and Rom Com Reader's Crown awards.

ACKNOWLEDGMENTS

I owe a huge debt of gratitude to my awesome beta-readers, Caroline Lee and Jolene Stewart, for their suggestions and advice. And double thanks to Julie Tague, for being a truly excellent editor and to Cindy Jackson for being an awesome assistant!

Click here for a complete list of other works by Merry Farmer.

Made in the USA
Coppell, TX
28 April 2022

77127292R00174